16 Middlesex Lane

A Dearth of Magic
Book 1

Matthew Wennersten

Published by

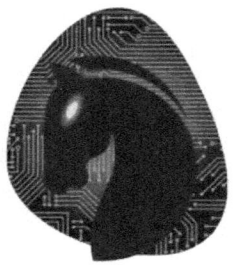

Heroes of Modern Legend

USA | India | New Zealand | Worldwide

ISBN: 978-0-9975741-0-4

Cover design by Sathya Ganapathi

For Anthony, Sofia, Sudha

and

the children of Vanavil

CONTENTS

MIDDLESEX LANE

A bakery, a carpet, a brute squad

What do you wish for, the day after you bury your father? He's not coming back – you poured earth on his grave. Wish for something better than a patternless mist soaking my denim jacket, thought Vic. She hunched her shoulders against the autumn chill. You'd think it would storm like hell, the day after an orphaning, hail sheets. At this point, she'd take sunshine, if only for incongruity's sake. Anything would be better than this early winter grey horizon, with a paint color catalog name of "Smoky Glaze" or "Carbon Trading White".

Vic tried to recheck the map on her phone. Glare made the screen unreadable from any angle. She fiddled with her too-large cap, trying to stuff her short twists under the back. Nothing helped. She should have worn her rainbow knit Rastafar, or a Kangol cap. But this was her dad's, purple corduroy with a large brim. She felt like a flower child railroad engineer. If dad was going to send her on a life-after-death wild goose chase around London, she'd wear his hat, damn him. At least it kept her hair dry. Why exactly she believed there was anything to this was a thought for another day, a day full of everything that was missing, a boyfriend, a job with prospects, a warm house, a cup of tea.

Her boot heel caught on the curb as she crossed at the sign for Middlesex Lane. The crow perched opposite on the tile roof of the modest brick terrace houses blinked at her mumbled "fuck", but didn't fly off. The crows seemed to prefer the tile roofs to the mildewed concrete of the 1950s apartments, flat facades and wide single glazed windows intruding between older buildings like toadstools. Probably a string of bombs from the Blitz. Was bad replacement architecture Hitler's final revenge? The bombardiers hadn't managed to crater a space wide enough for a tacky shopping centre, thankfully.

Some house numbers were camouflaged, some missing, others nailed in brass to investment quality wooden doors, or scrawled in blue on Malaga tile. Waves of redevelopment had ruined the sequence, A's and B's inserted on gates for the garden flats converted from the spare room and the downstairs lounge. She put the phone away, swearing softly. "Can't be that many numbers on one street. Eleven hours in, I'm bloody well committed."

She touched moss grown over markings chiseled into a granite block finial. Sixteen. Three flagstones of the same granite made a neat path to an unremarkable front door. The bell button prompted a soft chime from within. It was like Big Ben, except that Big Ben didn't abruptly stop halfway through and repeat, a tape loop with too little tape. Chinese MP3 on a chip, she thought. She rang the bell again.

Not home!" A man's voice, muffled, almost friendly. "They've gone out. If you want the bakery, 16A, around the side." She followed a grassless track along the right side of the house. Wet ground pulled with each step, moistly releasing her boots like an overfull infant at the bottle.

"Hullo?" The voice came from a wooden door a few yards into the alley, wide but child sized, a four feet high hatch for delivering something agricultural, or beer barrels. Hard up between the house and the

3

mossy brick of the neighboring wall. Vic felt the damp. The narrow alley's shade snatched what little warmth remained in the high sky, devouring it with paving stone teeth.

The odd door popped inwards with a burst of heat. Vic breathed in a cloud of freshly baked bread smell, only to choke when a head poked horizontally through the opening. One ear was up like a periscope, the other almost scraping the pavement. She bent her neck to match the baker's 90 degree tilt without thinking. He blinked at her floppy hat and soaked denim, spending a bit too much time on her jeans. "What do you want?"

The inside light gave him a sort of halo, making his expression hard to read. Vic caught a hint of broad shoulder against the stoop. He must be standing on the bottom step and leaning out, she thought, not fully pledged to street level. She walked closer to the hatch. She was not used to towering over anyone, even in boots. "Here for the bakery or for them?" he asked, jerking his chin almost vertical to indicate the house above.

Vic made a quick assessment – in his 50s or vigorous early 60s, a bit late Bond Sean Connery, although not as good looking. The beard and short grey hair on the sides contrasting with the general olive-red glow of his face, bare skin on top of his head ruddy gold. He squinted at her while she hesitated, a scout looking into the fire.

"GoldenI Bakery," she said.

"In the flesh." The head disappeared inside the hatch, muttering. "Do come in. Thought you were selling magazines door-to-door or something. Although it's come down a fair bit. Multi-level marketing moving to the cloud?" He had the air of a detective who had forgotten why he'd been called to the scene of the crime. "Give me a sec to wash up. Watch your head. And latch the door." Vic stooped her way inside.

In contrast to the cold alley, inside was cheery. Wrought iron gas lamps converted to electric sconces shone incandescent yellow onto neatly pointed brick beneath timber roof beams. She closed the hatch and took three awkward steps into a large open space. What was once a storeroom was now a bedsit and bakery. The back wall held a row of steel commercial ovens. The baker faced away at the sink, a v-shaped swimmer's back of broad planes below his bald top. He called over his shoulder, "Who are you?" Not what-do-you-want or the American how-can-I-help-

5

you. The way he said it immediately made Vic think of lyrics ("Who are you? Who-who. Who-who. I really want to know.") "I assume you've come with a reason, and it better not be trying to sell me something useless. Although you seem quite cute, so even that may be all right." A distinct emphasis on the may. "One minute."

There was no clear place to sit. The cloth-covered easy chair under the room's only window had a laptop open on the seat. No other stools or chairs, so Vic sat on the patchwork quilt thrown over a mattress in the front corner. She admired the faded maroon pattern of the threadbare oriental carpet between chair and bed while the baker fussed with a tea towel. In a group, it's easiest to say nothing, hope awkward subjects don't come up. On her own, Vic tended to vacillate between let-the-other-person-embarrass-themselves-first and bite-the-bullet. She chose the latter. "I think you knew my father."

"Your father?" The baker turned and looked at her over the white boxes stacked neatly on the butcher-block table between bed and sink. Vic said nothing, distracted by the GoldenI logo on the delivery boxes. It was a rebus, a cartoon eye with a golden iris. Cabinets, a few appliances covered in flour, an assortment of spoons and measuring cups, and a commercial refrigerator completed the side of the room. She noticed a small door leading deeper under the house beside the ovens.

"Hallooo?" he called, interrupting her survey. "Father sounds serious. Perhaps you need tea. I'd like tea. Would you like some tea?" He cleared a space on the table, oblivious to the rolling pin and flour knocked onto the floor in the process. Ignoring the pin, he stooped under the table. "And you are whom exactly? And where did I put the kettle?"

"I don't know," she said. "About the kettle that is. It's not on this side. I'm Victoria. Victoria Marrow. My friends call me Vic. And 'Yes' to tea, please." She didn't like that she sounded slightly breathless, as if holding the mic too close.

"Is that so? Hang on..." He cracked his head against the frame of the table. "Blast!" He came up a second time, holding a white electric kettle. At close range, he was strikingly tall. His head almost grazed the rafters, arms long enough to put the kettle on top of the refrigerator and plug it into a junction box attached to the rafter without shifting. A discolored patch on the wood showed that he'd steamed that beam before.

"So would that make your father, Mr. Marrow? Not sure I know any of those."

On first look, the phrase that had popped into Vic's head was 'he's got a face for radio'. On second look, his collection of bones was more rugged than ugly, handsome in the way of confident men. Grey chest hair poked out of an open v of shirt collar above the apron top. When she didn't reply, he made a half-bow. "Madam Victoria, Mallory Gregory, at your service, king of GoldenI bakery. Call me Mal. Are you sure that it's me, you and your father are after?" He ducked back under the table before she could answer.

He continued talking through the table legs. "And does this have anything to do with what is likely to become a truly spectacular black eye on your face? But before we get into that, one small favour. I normally catch the news at this time. If you don't mind, we'll put the wireless on while we have our cup of tea, and then you can tell me more about what brings you and your bruise to my little bakery, eh?"

"Where is the…" Vic hesitated, levering off the bed and scanning the room. "Radio?"

"Wireless, not radio. It's the laptop. I borrow my landlord's Wifi and listen online. Can you find the World Service, should be one of the bookmarks or favorites or whatever they call the things in this version? And quickly. We're missing the top stories."

Vic fiddled with the laptop on the chair. The operating system was unfamiliar, but she managed to open a window. The laptop screen changed from a loading animation to the spinning BBC logo. A mellow voice continued "...UN observers dispute Syrian government claims of only seven casualties. In domestic news, Stuart Wheeler, sitting Labour MP for Witney, has been tragically killed in a freak accident. While campaigning at the annual Witney Feast, Wheeler, 53, was struck by a vintage hayride tractor that veered into his election stall. Phillip Lightfoot, the Tory candidate for Oxford campaigning in the booth next to Mr. Wheeler, was first at the scene. Despite applying CPR, Lightfoot was unable to revive him. A Witney Gazette reporter quoted Mr. Lightfoot as being 'completely, utterly distraught.' While police were not prepared to make a statement, witnesses indicate that the nut securing the tractor's steering wheel is likely to have snapped. The tractor driver was seen holding the steering wheel in mid-air immediately prior to the unexpected change of course. No charges have been filed. In sport, Cambridge United has won 1-0 in the FA Cup derby over Cambridge City. More results can be found online at bbc.co.uk. And that's the news." Vic closed the laptop lid as Mallory handed her a London Olympics 2012 mug.

"I put milk in after, hope you don't mind." She nodded vaguely and took the mug. Mal sat down next to her on the bed. Vic looked around the room.

"Not much into decoration, are you?" she said. "Sorry. It's been a rough couple of days, and then more death on the radio. I'm not usually this rude." She took a long breath. "Let's start over. I'm Vic, you're Mal, thank you for the tea. I think you do know my father, I just haven't explained it very well." She took a long sip to clear her head.

When she looked up from her mug, Mal was chin forward, quite close, staring thoughtfully into her face. Thinking about it later, she remembered him looking at her the way an art restorer might look for original brushstrokes under a surface dulled by varnish and bad repairs. She held his gaze for a moment, and he leaned back. "I'll have you know I treasure my carpet," he replied, "which is most certainly decorative. And Persian. And terribly old. But a restart is a fine idea. Tell me what this is all about then. I expect your story is better than the guided missile tractor on the radio." Mal clapped his hands. "An old scamp should never ask a lady to talk about her father, but for you I'll make an exception. Who is your father, my dear?"

Before she could frame an answer, there was a heavy impact on the outside door. The thud echoed and amplified off the brick wall, too loud for the small space. A second kick burst it open, the door swinging stutteringly into the hall, latch set falling as a unit from its setting onto the tiled floor with a crack. Vic watched a screw from the mechanism roll in a small circle on the tile floor, momentarily hypnotized while the door rocked slowly back and forth, vibrating up and down against its hinge. A pale figure filled the open door frame, large Doc Martens-ish boots at their eye level on the bed. The intruder levered himself down the stairs, so thick in the body he could barely fit through the hole where the door had been.

"Goldeneye." The voice was raspy and strangely feminine. "Someone we know has been using the stuff, haven't they. You'll need to pay for that." Tea from Vic's dropped mug flowed in a puddle on the floor. Keeping his eye on the visitor, Mal picked up the carpet and threw it over the laptop, out of harm's way.

"What do you want?" said Mal. He was still sitting, quite calm, although he had somehow contrived to push Victoria slightly behind him on the bed after flinging the small rug.

"You know what I am. And I want what we always want – the terms of our agreement. You can't use our stuff and expect not to pay. Or is it your new girl that's the user?" His lips hardly moved, but his eyes followed Vic as she inched backwards on the mattress. Two more thugs squeezed down the stairs, not quite as big as the first but solidly built, dressed in army gear seconds and black t-shirts. All three were pale to the point of bloodlessness.

"I know what you are all right, just like you know who I am and what I can do. And you'll leave the girl alone." Mal reached back and grabbed Vic's arm. "Victoria, I hope, rather, I strongly suspect you have nothing to do with this. Be a good sort and go through the door by the ovens please. Don't mind these fellows, they'll let you pass in peace. I just need to clear up a few doubts." Mal stood, lifting Vic up off the bed by the arm as he rose. He made a 'step aside' motion with his free hand. The three thugs made a small hole between them. "Go, and keep going," Mal whispered in her ear, pointing her at the gap. "There's another door out to the alley. Once you clear the house, run!"

Vic tried to squeeze past the thugs without touching them, but they closed ranks slightly. Her purse strap hooked on a jacket button. She held it tightly and forced her way through. Mal snapped his fingers to get the thugs attention.

"Make yourselves comfortable, boys," he said, "And close the door. We have a lot to discuss." Vic struggled to work the door handle at the back of the kitchen. One of the smaller henchmen, the one in the wool watch cap, leaned his hip against the table. The boxes he knocked onto the floor caused her to turn. Her attention captured, he watched her scrabble at the door with the assurance of an evil house cat, 90% possession and the rest bad intentions. Still fumbling, Vic looked in disbelief as Mal put his hand out in a friendly greeting. "I'm sure we can come to an understanding on this."

"That's good, Goldeneye, that's good," said the leader. The pupils of the thug watching Vic were unusually wide, big black coat buttons framed by a sliver of white sclera. The third thug could have been a twin to the second. She watched him put the broken

13

door roughly flush back into its frame and retake his place beside the alpha.

Mal said something she didn't catch, in the tone you'd use to negotiate overdue fines in a library. She had a glimpse of chief thug extending his own hand from within its German army parka – hairless, too white, large as a ski mitt. Strange way to deal with a home invader, she thought, giving her full attention to the doorknob. The knob turned, and Mal shouted, "Go, Victoria. Now!" Something smooth and subtle happened where Mal's hand clasped the thug's, an infinitesimal shift of Mal's bodyweight changing into a full body pivot. Mal pulled the alpha thug off his feet, driving him head first into the base of the brick wall opposite the door. Vic ran through the rear door, past a neat shower stall and toilet, catching her foot on a stair riser. She got an arm up by reflex, slamming her elbow into the door atop the short flight. At least I didn't plant my face in it, she thought, shaking her stinging left arm. A wet thud behind her reminded her there was no time for self-pity. She turned and slammed the kitchen door behind her. An additional thud shook the freshly closed frame. Through the closed door came a muffled "I'm fine!" in Mal's voice, followed by "Keep going!" and several more sounds, including the crack of something snapping. She hoped it was only wood.

She bumped her elbow again in the small corridor. Cursing, she climbed the three steep stairs and slipped the bolt of the outside door. An even tinier alley connected the backs of the houses along Middlesex Lane. She ran left, trying to remember the name of a cross street. She felt for her phone in her purse. It wasn't there. It must have fallen out when her purse caught on the thug's jacket. She shouted "Help, Police, Help!" when she fetched up on the main road. Reduced to screaming like a mad woman in daylight on a London street, she thought, praying for traffic.

"The po-po? I got you, honey, you ok. Relax." A nylon track suit with a Hispanic-American accent waved at her from across the street. He was sitting on the raised stoop of a terrace house. He rose and crossed to her side of pavement, jacket open over a crisp wife-beater. He took a push-button cell phone out of his jacket pocket. "What's the number for the pigs in this town? Does 9-1-1 work here?"

"No, not correct. 9-9-9," she said, panting and swearing softly. "Dial 9-9-9, and give me the phone, thank you." Her breath puffed white in the cooling air. It's barely November, she thought. She took the phone still bent at the waist, and spoke over the operator. "Police, help, there's been an assault at 16A Middlesex Lane. Please come as fast as you can. Yes, of course I'll wait. Hurry, there were three men attacking ah....um, a baker." The tinny voice on the phone asked calmly for descriptions. "Very pale, dead white, military surplus clothing. Something about drugs." She described the street corner and handed the phone back to her less-than-stylish Samaritan. "Thank you. I don't know what I would have done if you hadn't been here."

"No problem. But honey, this one of the pendejos put that shiner on you?" Her new friend squared his shoulders, pointing his hand like a pistol into the alley. Mal limped towards them, a look of indigestion on his face. His carriage had gone from a James Bond glide to a superannuated shuffle. His voice, however, was light.

"Victoria, we're hardly introduced and already you're running off with strange men. If I wasn't old enough to be your father, I'd be quite offended. Thankfully, all has been resolved with our three friends. Let's go back to the bakery and I'll see if I can find the kettle again."

"Hey lady, what's your number?" asked her new acquaintance. "I mean, for using my phone and all? I'm barely in this town for like four weeks already and I can tell it's hard to meet the chicas. New York, man, but here?"

"Leonardo," said Mal, "she knows where you live. I'm sure when she reflects on the debt of gratitude she'll come knock on your door. I'll take it from here." Mal put his left arm around Vic's shoulders and steered her back down the alley. "A minor misunderstanding about money. They thought I owed them some and I rather forcefully assured them I did not. I'm just glad the cops weren't involved, as I'm very curious to hear your story, and a journey to the station would be quite tedious. Let's get settled down and then we can drink that cup of tea rather than use it to make patterns on the floor."

"Mal, a few things." Vic shrugged out of Mal's arm. "One, you're bleeding." She touched the cut above Mal's left ear. "Two, I did call the police. Three, what the hell just happened?"

"Not only am I bleeding, I cracked my favorite rolling pin and a rib in my right side, which is why I would appreciate it if I could put my arm back and lean on you, please." They hobbled together down the alley and turned into the cut for 16A. "Here's good." Mal grunted softly and lowered himself onto the steps down to the bakery. He rubbed his hand thoughtfully over the splintered wood where the lock was supposed to engage the doorframe. "Victoria, I need to sit for a minute. Bear with me, I'll clear up in a sec. We have some time before the law arrives."

Vic looked inside the small bakery. It was darker than before - several sconces were broken or askew. The table was shoved up hard against the ovens. A streak of red crossed the flour dust outline of the table's original position. "That's mine," said Mal, "but that's all, really. They left promptly after I shunted the table using only my bloody face. Must have been quite intimidating." A sifter, half a rolling pin, and a wooden cutting board lay on the tiles, covered in a wholesale bag's worth of wheat flour. The bed was a whirlwind of bakery boxes. The chair was turned over, exposing three wooden legs instead of the original four. A single stack of boxes remained in its original column on the shifted table, but compressed. There was a head-shaped imprint in the top box. Other than that, no sign of the three thugs.

Vic batted the boxes off the bed like balloons. Miraculously, Mal's carpet covered laptop was intact underneath. She put it to one side and helped Mal to the bed. He sat on the edge of the quilt, a striped handkerchief, conjured from god-knows-where, pressed to his ear. Vic crossed to the kitchen area, kicking the boxes into a rough pile on her way. The table was too heavy for her to shift. She was just able to reach the kettle switch atop the refrigerator on tiptoes. "Where do you keep the tea?"

"In a cabinet blocked by the table. But they've broken both my mugs, so don't worry about it." Mal held up a semi-circle in ceramic crowned by handle. "Mine was 'I love the bloody UK', but all I've got now is 'I-K'."

"I think 'IK' sums it up," said Vic. She pushed the broken front door back into its frame. It wouldn't stay. She let it swing and sat down next to Mal on the bed, where he was inspecting his handkerchief. "You want to tell me what happened here? What did they mean by Magic? After that little episode, I've half a mind to walk right out of here."

He sighed. "I will explain, in a bit. At the moment, however, this vista is too depressing to contemplate. I'd rather talk about you. What was it again that am I to do with your father?"

"You tell me. He's dead."

MY FATHER ABRAHAM

Lying fathers, faithless boyfriends, and the feminine form of an Arab king

"Dead. That's not a particularly good start. What happened?"

"My father is, was, Abraham Emir Marrow."

"Distinctive name."

"Distinctive man. People used to joke about it, but the name worked for his trade. Sound familiar?"

"Rings a bell, although I think Abraham is coming back in style. Trade? Tell me a bit more."

"Something with computer security. Do know him or not? How many Abraham Marrow's can there be?"

Mal pursed his lips. "Well, I don't think I know of any." He continued before she could object. "But I knew an Abraham Emir Ali who looked a bit like you. Would have been a long time back." Something about the way he said 'long' made Vic think 'ancient', like pantheons and pyramids.

"How long?" asked Vic. "I'm beginning to doubt I know how old my father is. Was. I thought he was young, but when I found him, his hair was completely white. I hadn't thought my father would be the kind to dye his hair." She shook her head. "And the wrinkles. His face was like a ravine. They say that you can't fold a piece of paper more than seven times, but he had so many wrinkles it was as if someone were trying to test this on skin. The last time I saw him his skin was smooth. He had a part-time pub act, 'Abraham Emir Ali, King of Deception'. I knew he wore makeup for the act, but daily? And why am I wittering on to you? What are you to him?"

"I, too, am trying to work that out. But if we're talking about Emir Ali, Ali the Great, King of Kings, then I'm an old friend. We were street magicians together. He put on a great show, sleight-of-hand, cards, cups, everything. Lost touch more than twenty years ago. That he's your father is news. In fact, I wonder if I should be suspicious of you? Before the fracas, it was you who had come looking for me, with a nice bruise." He pronounced it frak-ass, giving it an American posterior emphasis. "And then some goons show up."

"Oh, come on. Do you seriously think I had

anything to do with that? I was scared out of my wits. And they weren't talking about prestidigitation. They were talking about drugs. Magic? What is that, mushrooms, MDMA, what? Besides, my father told me to find you. He sent me a message on my phone." Vic looked in her purse. "My phone!" She put her hands on her head. "And my hat! Crap. Crap. Crap."

He touched her leg, lightly. "Your hat is on the floor just outside the lavatory. And, unlike Elvis, I think your phone has not left the building. Exactly where, I'm not sure, but I remember preventing one of our friendly miscreants from crushing it. Under the chair?"

Vic stood and tilted the easy chair, using its upside down back as a pivot. She hooked her phone with a foot and slid it out. "Here," she said after a minute's rummage with the keypad. "I-C-E-Dad."

Mal looked at the screen and then quizzically at her. "'Fnd goldenI'? From this, you came here?"

"Actually, this is the fifth place. After making about one hundred phone calls. Do you know how many people there are named Golden who have no idea who my father is and now think I'm crazy? There's also a very nice real estate developer in London who made me a decent cappuccino. The

23

detective agencies were not nearly as sympathetic. So that left you. And I was already in London."

"Did one of these detectives give you that smack on the face?"

"No, that was my boyfriend."

"Oh". The syllable hung wet in the air before disappearing, a balloon that slipped its knot, flying and farting through the air. Mal blinked. "Tell me more about your father."

"Christ, I never even took off my jacket." Vic shrugged out of her duffel coat and draped it on the upturned legs of the chair. She sat back down on the bed next to him, purse in one hand. "I'm not sure where to begin. He was my Dad. Just the two of us. He worked as a network analyst. Called himself a 'White Hat Researcher' so he could work from home. And yes, he was a magician. Strictly amateur, although one year we went to the Edinburgh Fringe. He taught me how to palm a key to a pair of handcuffs, make a coin disappear. He was constantly pulling things out of my pockets." She waved her hand and produced Mal's bloody handkerchief. "Like this."

He took back the handkerchief with an embarrassed wince. A smile transformed her face, softening the lines and putting a dimple in her left cheek. "It's alright. I think the bleeding has stopped. Fuck me, I think you ARE the right guy my father texted me to find. Where was I?"

"You were telling me about your father, the amateur magician."

"Yes, I was, wasn't I." Vic shut down the smile. "But I'm not sure I should go on. I mean, I come here and nearly get beaten up by a pack of drug dealers. You're not exactly a safe bet. Just exactly who were those guys to you? And how did you get rid of them so fast? That's a real magic trick."

Mal closed his eyes. "Magic." He inhaled through his nose. "Magic isn't real. Your father, Emir Ali, should have taught you that. And I am the right guy." He gave a shrug with his uninjured shoulder. "I'm not great at keeping in touch, but you're wearing his pearl ring. Noticed it when you came in, but didn't put it together. These old settings are out of fashion. He was my friend for a very long time..." Again, an echo of dust and ancient ruins. "What happened to him?"

Vic tapped her ring and bounced up again. "Well, you're bloody calm about it. I'm furious." She paced through the jumble of boxes, scudding them back and forth with her feet. "I'm not sure what there is to tell.

I was at work, in Bristol, when I got the text. My father never sends texts. He says that texts are a way of avoiding real conversations and decisions. I called him and he didn't pick up, which got me nervous. I told my boss I needed to check on a personal matter. Took a taxi all the way to his house. Pontprennau, Wales, near the Cardiff Spire Hospital. £67 and I didn't get there fast enough. The front door was open. I ran up the stairs and found him face down on the floor of his study, hair all white, skin like I told you, looked like he'd been killed and left to dry in a desert for a hundred years. It was horrible."

She took his handkerchief and used a clean spot to wipe her tears. "That's it. I got a text message from him. I found him. He wasn't warm. I had thought my father was middle-aged but he was old. Really old. Much older than you."

"I'm not so sure about that. We age in different parts at different rates, my dear."

She threw the handkerchief back at him. "His skin flaked off in my hand when I tried to turn his head. His bones just crumbled! Something seriously strange has happened." Vic stopped pacing. She turned and screamed at Mal. "AND I HAVE NO IDEA! NO ONE HAS ANY IDEA!" She stopped, winded. "The coroner doesn't know. The police don't know. The cause of death is 'advanced old age', which is a crock of shit because his passport says he's 59. There were a dozen computers in the house, so it wasn't a robbery, but I know that the one he liked most is missing. When I came back downstairs to meet the ambulance, the front door was closed and locked. Someone had been in the house. I called the police and sat around, shit scared. The police were perfectly useless, trying to tell me that old age catches us all." She kicked a box hard. It flew up and sideways at Mal on the bed.

He batted the box away. "And then what happened?"

"What's today, Friday? Dad died yesterday afternoon. I didn't want to spend a night alone in his house. Alone, or with who knows what. A nice policeman dropped me off at Cardiff station and I trained back to Bristol. I got home just before midnight."

"Midnight on Thursday. Almost this morning. You've been busy."

"I didn't want to be. I just wanted to curl up into a ball. But instead, I came home to a nice party."

"Party?"

"Bloody wine and Chinese. Jeremy was drunk, asleep in a chair. Two empty bottles of wine on the table, takeout cartons congealing on the sideboard. Of course, no placemat, so the wood would be all ruined. I wake him up, he sees me and, and I remember this distinctly, he asks me 'Where have you been? I've been waiting all night to celebrate!' I told him my father was dead, and he says to me 'Never mind that, I got the part.'"

"Part of what?"

"Jeremy's at the Bristol Theatre School; he's always trying to get a professional part in London. I guess I hadn't realized until that moment how shallow and useless he is. I like actors. I thought I loved AN actor. Perhaps when you spend your whole life pretending to be other people you forget what it's like to be a real human with your own family. I told him again that my father had just died and he shrugged it off, said that 'life is for the living' and that I needed to 'move on'. So I told him to get stuffed and get going. I kicked him out of the house." Her bruise filled with red blood.

"Ah. I think I see where the slapping came from."

"Yeah, I wish I had seen it coming myself. First he refused to leave, and then when I took a suitcase down from the attic and started throwing hangers full of his shirts onto it, he hit me. It's my apartment. So that was my second phone call to the police of the week." Vic gave him a long look. "Today is the third." She moved the laptop over so she could lay down, curled up to leave space for Mal. From her side she spoke again, "And my father's still dead. And my bastard boyfriend didn't care."

"Ex-boyfriend," Mal corrected, gently.

"Ex-boyfriend. So this time when the police turn up, Jeremy's still there, and he feeds them this line about how 'it's only a minor misunderstanding' and that I've 'had a bit much to drink'. He can be quite reasonable. It was a young officer, he just wanted to hold my hand, say 'there, there' and leave without having to write up a report, but when I asked him exactly how hard you have to hit a black woman to leave a mark, he got embarrassed and told Jeremy 'you better go.'" Vic made a fist in her hair and pulled her twists down over her forehead. "The policeman stayed until he had packed his things. I watched him take the gold bangles he gave me. I had a framed Breughel reproduction, 'Storm at Sea'. He took that off the wall, told the cops it was his. He knew it was my favorite but I didn't care, I just let him to get rid.

The bangles were probably only gold-plated anyway. So he finally leaves around two, and I locked up after the policeman. Alone. I hadn't cried at my dad's place but I did then, and when I woke up it was 5am and pitch black but I remembered the phone message and couldn't get back to sleep. I was in London by 7:45, on the phone Internet until 10, and here..." Vic hesitated. "What exactly happened here, anyway?"

"It's not 'What happened?', Amira. The correct question is 'Why?'"

LEGGING IT

Police arrive out of turn, our heroine serves a sardine supper, suspicions are raised. The baker plots a rendezvous

Vic let go of her hair and sat up. "Why we were attacked by that goon squad, or why my father died?"

Mal pursed his lips. "To be fair, both. Let's start with the goons, as I think I owe you some explanation for their inexplicably poor taste and timing. Although, I'm not entirely certain myself why they chose to show up now and wreck the place." Cradling his ribs, Mal stood up. "I think if we work together we can un-stick the table." He bent down to look where the butcher-block met the counter. His voice echoed off the underside. "I work with the most unreliable people in the world, Victoria. Chefs! They use drugs, they drink, they rarely pay their bills on time. And because I'm not a licensed commercial premise, they sometimes sic their erstwhile friends on me. They know I won't run to the police. This was most likely a case of deliberately mistaken identity, for which I'll have to send my deliveryman sleuthing among those of my customers who would prefer my invoices to go away. It's simple – you rip off your drug dealer, leave one of my boxes at the scene, and get two weeks credit while I'm in hospital." Vic joined Mal at the table's edge. "Grab the post on the left side, and heave when I say 'Ho'". Mal wrapped his good hand around the right corner table leg. "Ho." Mal's side lifted, pivoting the table around the corner still caught under the sink counter, half-pinning Vic to the wall.

"What 'Ho'?" she yelped. "You didn't give me a chance, Mal!"

"Well, now you have a chance to get both the table and yourself un-pinned." Mal was interrupted by the broken door swinging inward. A uniformed policeman, finger extended, stooped in the entrance.

"It was open, so I let myself in, eh? Somebody called the Bill?" The officer put one hand on the door lintel to guide himself safely down the stairs. "Ma'am, you alright? That's a nasty bruise. Bit of a rumpus here from the looks of things. Sir, please step back from the table." The police officer balanced his weight and reached for his belt.

"It's not what you think," said Mal.

"It never is, mate, it never is," replied the officer. "Now, step away."

Vic braced herself against the wall and shoved the table away from the cabinets. She dusted her hands and turned to the policeman. "Officer, I'm perfectly fine. The bruise is old, the rumpus was other people. In fact, we're trying to set things right. But I'm glad you've come. Course, if you'd come a bit faster, you might have run into three nasty men in Army surplus."

"Yes, ma'am, sorry for the delay. Seems the local MP had a heart attack and we were called out for crowd control. Reporters went a bit wild, what with two politicos going down on the same day." The officer climbed up a stair and poked his head out the door. "Roscoe, it's from here. I'm looking at the caller." Boot noises on the pavers outside - a second policeman appeared, slightly older than the first.

"Sergeant Roscoe Gardiner. Billy, take some notes." The junior officer sat with Vic on the bed while she described the sudden appearance and disappearance of the three goons. As she talked, she realized the patrolman's prompts and grunts were the police equivalent of raking leaves. How the leaves got there and what would happen to them later mattered less than getting them all into tidy piles before he left.

"Are you the resident?" asked the sergeant. Mal nodded.

"Yes. I live here."

"It looks like you do more than just live here." The sergeant picked up a ruined box. "GoldenI bakery 16A Middlesex Lane, eh? Running a business out of a residential address?" Mal, leaning his weight on the table, looked down and shook his head. Sergeant Gardiner continued, "I'll have to give you a citation unless you can show me a permit for this." Mal's head kept swinging side to side. "Right-o. Billy, take down the gent's details also. I'll go get some tape from the response car." The sergeant popped out.

Gardiner returned as Billy was finishing up. The view through the doorframe and the room's one window set black with the dusk. The two officers held a quiet conference, then Gardiner spoke to Vic. "Billy tells me that you two are more victims than anything else, but I'll have to close the business." The sergeant had become slightly more sympathetic after the walk from the car in the evening cool. "We'll run the attackers' details through the files as a matter of course. I'm sorry to say we're unlikely to get hits." Gardiner handed Mal a ticket. "It's £26 per day until you appear before the magistrate with a notice of ceasing operation or a regular license application, but you can go down tomorrow and get it sorted. Here's my card as well." The officers fixed an X of crime scene tape across the outside of the broken door. "Call us if they come back; we should be close by."

"Hey, how will we get in and out?" called Vic after them as they left. No reply.

"Never mind, Victoria, there's still the back door." Mal picked up a sifter and used it as a paperweight for the ticket and business card. With the two policemen gone, the disheveled flat felt uninhabited, as if Vic and Mal were after hours visitors at an oversized playschool, the kids having left without picking up their toys. "Hungry?" Mal seemed to be moving more easily, rummaging with both arms in the cabinets exposed by the shifted table. "Excellent." He assembled a tin of sardines and a toolbox. He walked over to the entrance stairs with a hammer.

"Mal, I'll open the sardines, that's fine." Vic picked the tin up off the step.

"Oh, yes, very good," Mal muttered distractedly. He gathered the pieces of the latch works and hammered them at a slight angle into the splintered hole in the door. "There's fresh bread in the oven on the top right, if it's not burnt by now. And a breadknife in the drawer to the right of the sink." He turned to face her, hammer in hand. "You know, Victoria, I'm completely disgusted."

"About the citation?"

"About the ticket, yes, and this mess, and most of all about your father. He must have stumbled into something that someone wanted to keep hidden."

"That's what I thought as well," said Vic, "but the cause of death was listed as 'natural causes' – systemic failure due to 'geriatric frailty.'"

"Oh, I disagree. I think there was very little natural about it. Although, passport age of 59, did you say? That would make him under 12 when he and I started performing..." He put down the hammer to accept the sardine topped sourdough slice she held out. "He was a numph.." Mal stopped to chew. "Network security researcher?"

"Yes, but I think it's his main laptop that's missing. And I just make furniture – he didn't talk much computer stuff with me."

"What about his friends?"

"I'm not sure who they are. My father mostly

worked alone, or with researchers over the Internet, people with fanciful names like 'Ciscostu' or 'RhesusPieces'. I got the impression that they never really gathered in one place. My dad's colleagues weren't the type of people who enjoyed the footie at the pub. And they don't exactly publicise their real identities, those types. I found you through phone listings, trial, error, and luck, and that only because Dad wanted you to be found."

"All the more reason we should find some of these friends. I think we would benefit from a bit more information about what is going on. And not through a personal Internet connection. My landlord will have trouble enough with the police tape on the door, without putting black flags and network snoops onto her Wifi. There's quite a nice library in Battersea, with public Internet. We can start there."

"Wait." She looked at him. "How old was my dad, really?"

"No idea, my dear. I'm not hiding his birth certificate in a breadbox. Regardless, if one day he is vital and vigorous and then suddenly he's not, something strange has happened. I don't think it was makeup. And that's worth investigating, as you are rightly doing. Although I'm a bit surprised you started looking in the physical world."

Vic stared at him. "What do you mean by that?"

"If whoever is behind this is a network researcher, their probable first thought would be 'GoldenI' is another hacker name, or perhaps a piece of software. And you can be quite sure that text messages sent from your father's phone are known to that person. I do think he meant me, which gives us a head start if whoever stole his laptop is busy searching for the cyberspace version of 'GoldenI'. But you did find me quite quickly. We'd best relocate until the library opens tomorrow morning."

"Do you think it's that serious?"

A business-like knock on the taped front door interrupted. "PC Billy Battles. We spoke before. I'd like to speak to Mr. Mallory Gregory again, please."

Mal mouthed 'I'm not home' with exaggerated enunciation, cutting his hand through the air. Vic shouted through the door, "Halloo, Constable. What about? He's not home."

"Ma'am, can I come inside?"

"I told you, he's not home."

"Ma'am, then I suggest you come outside. There may be something more to that ruckus business than he would have told you."

Mal seemed to have forgotten his injuries. He walked briskly to the back door, grabbed the long grey herringbone coat hidden on a peg behind it, and made animated gestures at Vic. She called out, "One second," and then followed Mal to where she had bashed her elbow an hour before. "What is it?" she whispered. She grabbed his forearm. "What are you not telling me?" Her face drew tight.

"Damn computerization. Everything nowadays is linked up, they get on to you before you can break wind. Battersea Library, 11am, don't forget. I'll explain then," he whispered back.

He put his free arm in the coat sleeve, then covered her hand on his other arm. "I knew your father, and he knew me. He wouldn't have sent you here as a last resort otherwise." Once again, Mal was loose and calm; the skin of his forehead seemed to tighten and smooth. "Now, when the door opens, tell the copper I've just come home so he doesn't spook." Mal unpeeled her fingers. Holding them lightly, he pushed her by the hand with the pressure of a skilled dancer leading his partner. "Don't worry about locking up." He smiled. "I'll see you."

Vic staggered back into the main hall. Mal threw the back door open with an exaggerated bang, and legged it into the night. She glimpsed the long tail of his coat flash out the door. Swallowing several troubling thoughts, she shouted, "Constable Billy? I think he's just come home. Hang on."

The snare drum double pop of tape tearing was joined by a high-hat cymbal from the latch mechanism hitting the floor a second time. The PC and Sergeant stumbled through the low opening, PC shoulder first. "Where is he?" asked the sergeant breathlessly.

"I just heard the back door. Perhaps the toilet?" In for a penny, Vic thought. She stood to one side and tried to think small, innocuous thoughts. The sergeant snapped out a tool from his belt. It extended into a wicked metal rod, which he used to poke the toilet door.

"Mr. Gregory?" Sergeant Gardiner collapsed the high-tech billy club and spat in the seat-up toilet bowl. He looked out the open back door into the night. "Billy, he's scarpered."

Billy spoke earnestly into his radio, stuttering a series of police codes followed by a description of an older gentleman. According to Billy, Mal was both menacing and harmless, the return visit of an accustomed infirmity, faded injury mixed with ill-will. They didn't mention the coat, Vic noted silently. The once sympathetic sergeant banged his hand on the table and stood close enough to give Vic a bit of saliva spray. "You may have just allowed a very dangerous man to escape. A good dozen flags on his file, arrest warrant for foul play in the disappearance of a gypsy traveler, person-of-interest in several other cases." The sergeant swept his arm in a half circle. "Plus this mess. What is this man to you?"

Vic covered her face with her hand. "I'm not sure. We just met, a short while ago. My father died yesterday. Mr. Gregory's apparently some old friend of his from childhood. We're to meet again tomorrow at Battersea Library. I guess I'll find out then."

"Right," said the sergeant. "If you go to Battersea Library and don't turn him in, I'll have to arrest you on accessory charges."

Vic dropped her hand. "Look, sergeant, don't threaten me. I haven't even agreed to meet him. I've had some trying times of my own, and this mess, as you call it, is the least of it." Vic maneuvered around the sergeant and retrieved her coat and purse from the bed. "Do you see a purple hat anywhere?"

Billy spoke up, "It's there. Looks like it's been stepped on." Billy picked it up from the lavatory

41

corridor and tossed it to her. She caught it behind her back in the motion of shrugging on her coat sleeve.

"What time did he say to meet?" asked Sergeant Gardiner. "11am," replied Vic. Coat on, she made a small fist, punched out the inside of the hat, and squared it on her head. "Billy has my contact details. Including my cell phone." She opened her purse, checking it was there. "Meet me there tomorrow if you like, it's a public place." She kicked the latch from the stairs and grabbed the edge of the open front door. "Now, if you could tape this shut, I'll make my own way, thanks." She climbed the stairs into the night.

BATTERSEA LIBRARY

A movie star, a breakthrough, an anonymous friend,
the quotidian getaway of modern fugitives

Vic reached the library before it opened at 8:45AM. Gorgeous with 19th century orange brick, the library was an industrial revolutionary on the corner of Lavender Hill Road, an overgrown house, what architects might call a real 'pile'. Carved white granite stated 'Public Library' over the entrance. A Queen Anne turret capped the corner. Vic recognized Sergeant Gardiner and PC Billy in the police patrol car half-on and half-off the paving in front of the Asda across the way, as inconspicuous as a monkey's red bottom. She walked over to Billy's open window on the pavement side.

"You're early," said Vic and Billy simultaneously.

"Jinx!" came back Billy. "Now you'll have to buy me a coffee."

"Fair enough, Billy, I'll get you. How's your sergeant this morning?"

"Un-amused," came the voice from the driver's seat. "We've been here since 7." He reached across Billy to wave vaguely back and forth. "There's cafés up and down if you're interested."

"Were you all right, last night? You said you lived in Bristol," said Billy, leaning over the sill.

"Sweet of you to ask, Billy. I spent the night in a youth hostel, with a dozen Danish backpackers. They tend to get going early. I tried to find a YWCA but I guess Morrissey's no longer true for central London. Be right back."

By the time Vic got back, two straws of sugar balanced on paper cups, the library doors were unlocked. She passed the cups through the window to Billy, crossed the street, and went in.

The main hall was grand, freestanding wooden shelves stacked double to a height halfway up the hall's twenty feet of open ceiling. A row of computers bordered a forest of carrels and magazine racks. The librarian waved a friendly hello with his fingers as Vic sat down at the first free workstation. She didn't see. He coughed into his fist, and called out "You'll need the password."

Vic swiveled her chair. "I don't have a library card."

"That's all right. Do you have a pen?" He rattled off a nonsense string of eight numbers and letters. "Just type that in at the prompt. My name's James, by the way."

Vic said, "Hi, James," absently into the screen as she opened up a web browser. She'd had all sleepless night in the hostel bunk to think about which terms to search first - she was quickly lost in the computer. As the morning aged, more people came in, but not enough to lift the library hush out of a serious, over-polite murmur. Around 10, a clean-shaven man in a watch cap sat down at the workstation next to her.

"Young lady, so serious! Looking for secrets?" Then, in a lower tone, "Keep looking at your screen. It's me. Mal."

"Mal!" Was her slight blush due to the stern look from the librarian, or a reaction to what she heard in her voice? More softly, "Mal. How did you get past the cops?"

"I've been here all night. After I left you, I cleaned up at an all-night convenience store, and let myself in around midnight. I was hiding in the lithographs section until enough people came in that I wouldn't stick out. Feels like it was my back that was stretched

45

on a wooden frame instead of the pictures. So," he puffed his lips, "What have you discovered?"

"Not much. 'GoldenI' on the net doesn't lead to anything useful, unless you're a dead pig, a wearable computer, or an award for investigative journalism. I did find my father's 'handle'. Two names in cyberspace, 'TomArrow' and 'Linkoln', he has. Had. Don't know if that helps..." Vic held back from saying 'helps us'. Was 'us' right for this fellow? Did she really want to share secrets with a wanted stranger? Not for the first time, Vic wondered who was calling the shots, her, or her father? Yesterday's threat of accessory charges knocked at the corners of her forehead. Her inner voice reminded her that she hadn't slept properly or changed her clothes in two days. Watch yourself, Vic.

"Of course it helps us." Vic wondered if he had added the 'us' on purpose. "More information is usually better," said Mal. Vic had no trouble thinking of times when it wasn't. Mal raised his hand, "James, may I have a password please?"

"Mr. Peck! I didn't see you come in. You look younger without the beard." James repeated the nonsense jumble word ritual. The librarian looked meaningfully at Vic. "Miss, you've been on the machine for over an hour. If another patron needs the Internet, I'll have to kick you off. It's pretty quiet at the moment, but. OK?" She nodded.

Mal chuckled. "We've spent twenty years devising rules to make passwords impossible to remember and easy for machines to guess. This is progress." He cracked his knuckles and faced the keyboard. "And your research is also progress. T-O-M-A-R-R-O-W, eh? As in 'Marrow'. Let's see what's out there on pwno and our other friendly hacker websites."

Vic pushed his keyboard sideways. "Look, Mal, or Mr. Peck, or whoever you actually are. This has to stop. Clearly you know some of this stuff already. And I appreciate you possibly helping me." She enunciated each word as a separate sentence, "But. I. Am. Not. Going. Any. Further." Mal raised his hands in surrender at the screen in from of him. She carried on more normally, "Without a better explanation. Or at least some story that will prevent me from getting arrested along with you."

"Victoria, we didn't have much time before." He leaned in close to the screen. "And since the clock on this computer says 10:23, and the police will surely be joining us near 11, we don't have much time now. I had nothing to do for two hours last night except

47

shave and sit in an Internet café. I also found your father on-line; he didn't make much effort to obscure his handle from his identity. But that's as far as I got." He retrieved the keyboard and flashed her a Han Solo grin. There was a small six-pointed star tattooed on the left side of his jaw. It would have been covered by the beard, she thought. "Mostly as far. I also posted some requests for help on a D-I-Y section of 4chan, addressed to some of the names that clustered around your father's posts. I put your work email as the reply-to."

"My email? What? HOW?" She stood up, furious. James-the-librarian's head popped up like a prairie dog in a BBC natural world special.

"Miss? Mr. Peck? Is everything alright?"

"It's fine, James, she was just asking for my help accessing her email from a remote computer. She gets a bit emotional this time of the month." Turning to the gaping Vic, he continued in the calm tone he'd used yesterday during his failed attempt at preventing gang violence, "You open your company's website from the browser, and there in the 'About Us' page is the list of email addresses, and a link for 'Staff Login'. I'm surprised you haven't used this before. 10:25, Vic, let's have a quick look, please." James rotated his neck in the way that men think fools women into not realizing they've just been looking down their blouse, and reseated himself at the counter near the entrance. Mal whispered, "Let's first find out if anything has come in, then you can turn me in to the police if you like, alright?"

Vic muttered, "Why didn't you use your own bloody email address?" as she followed his instructions. A list of past and present messages displayed, topped by several winning lottery entries and pharmaceutical enhancements entirely inappropriate for her gender.

Mal peered nearsightedly across at her screen. "Check for one that says 'Secrets of the Black Mona Lisa' or something similar."

"Black Mona Lisa? Very flattering, Mallory Peck." She clicked the link.

"Gregory Peck. He's very stylish. Now," he slipped into a good imitation of Leonardo from the previous night, "Cut me some slack." Their eyes locked. After a beat, they both laughed, Mal quiet, Vic attempting but failing to muffle a robust chuckle in the hush of the library. "I have an old arrest warrant that would go away if they ever investigated properly, I was beaten up last night by a trio of thugs, my home is wrecked, I haven't eaten breakfast, and I am trying to help you. That the police have lunatic ideas is not my fault. I'd rather help you then spend the day explaining my point of view to a sergeant of the London Metropolitan. Now, what's in the email?"

"It's a list of the top 6 search terms originating from TOR node 62.236.1.108."

"I expect that's your father's router. Go on. I can't read from here."

"It says 'electronic voting machines', 'private polling firm intrusion detection' whatever that is, 'English constituency boundaries', 'poll data manipulation'." She closed her eyes briefly and sighed, "'Victoria Yohannes', 'UK election market research firm'. That's the whole mail, no other text. And the sender is apparently my email address as well."

"Well, assuming your middle name is Yohannes, you made the top 5. Although why Yohannes and not Marrow?"

"Too many Marrows. I was beaten to the Internet by a primary school student in Wiltshire.

vmarrow@yahoo, vicmarrow, vic dot marrow. Not so many vyohannes." Vic rubbed her eyes.

"I don't think it's rocket science. My father was

looking into something about the upcoming general election."

"And intrusion detection is to catch someone trying to break in electronically," said Mal. "I think the fix might be in. Or at least an attempt to mislead which candidate is likely to win each seat."

"So what do we do now? And how do you know this stuff anyway? IT is supposed to be my generation's game."

"Constant learning, Vic. It keeps me young." He leaned forward again. "10:27, time to scoot."

"The cops are just out front. How are you going to get away?"

"I'm not. I plan to check back into 'Hotel Battersea Lithograph', and make my way out this evening the same way I got in. The police don't have the budget for a two-day stakeout on an old arrest warrant. We can meet up again tomorrow, if you're amenable, although I'd suggest you stay somewhere other than at home tonight. I'd also suggest you tell a reporter about what we've discovered. Know any friendly ones? Do give me your number."

"Just don't pass it to Leonardo." He wrote her digits in blue biro on his left forearm. Vic saw another small tattoo, an Asian letter near his left elbow.

"What kind of danger do you think I'm in?"

"Very little. Only a bold fool would suddenly decease both father and daughter and expect the police to look the other way. But I don't know any other type of fool, so you should take some elementary precautions."

"Such as?" Vic had always envied people who could raise only one eyebrow.

"Basically, go shopping. Get some new clothes, change your hair, withdraw a large amount of cash, throw away your debit card, remove the battery from your phone for a few days so you can't be tracked."

"How will you reach me if my phone's switched off?"

"I'll leave a message. Call your voicemail from a payphone. There are still a few left in London. Bloody expensive, mind you, but hard to trace."

"10:30, Mal. You'll call me?"

"Well, Gregory Peck certainly will. He was never one to leave a damsel in distress."

"I'm still not certain about all this. I do know a journalist, but it feels a bit thin to print. My next move is what? Ring up polling firms and ask them if they've had a break-in? From a payphone?"

"That's not a bad idea. Don't worry, my dear, if it

doesn't feel like a happy ending, that just means the movie's not yet over." Mal rose and then sat right back down. A uniform was standing by James' desk.

Keeping his head below the computer carrel, Mal called out to the librarian, "James, these numbers on the spines of the book? Could you use them to put every book in the library back in its correct place?"

James turned away from the police officer. "Of course, Mr. Peck. It's Dewey Decimal 22. But could you come up? I think there is someone here to see you."

Mal pushed his chair back and stood up. The cap and beardless face flummoxed Sergeant Gardiner for only a moment. He sprinted his bulk towards the computer desks, slaloming through magazine racks like a whale on skis. Mal reached past the still seated Vic and gave a hard shove to the top corner of the row of standing bookshelves. They toppled like dominos. Books catapulted off the shelves into Gardiner in a cloud of flapping covers and sheaves. The end bookshelf crimped a wire magazine rack. Mal darted across the hall and heaved down the opposite shelves as well. His face glowed red with exertion, eyes glinting yellow under the fluorescent library lights.

The sergeant sprawled under a teepee made by

two collapsed shelves and the crumpled wire frame. His face was hidden by magazine covers. Vic stared dumbly at the vibram soles of his boots. "Decision time, Vic, no waffling," Mal said urgently. "Stay to explain or come with me now."

Mal tugged her upright by the lapels of her coat. He jigged through the piles of dumped books, grabbed a stunned James by both upper arms and gave him a wet kiss on the cheek. "Sorry, James. I'd stay to help out if I could." Vic noticed that in kissing James, he'd maneuvered the librarian aside from the entrance. Mal glanced back at Vic. "Follow me out." Mal was bouncing with an almost convulsive energy, showing no signs of yesterday's discomfort. Apparently a night on a library floor was as good as a night in hospital. Fewer sick people perhaps. But if this is manic, Vic thought, I'd hate to see depressive. Under the shelves, Gardiner made moaning progress towards extricating himself. Vic was convinced that a few of the bookshelves had come down by themselves, as if they had been only waiting for the right moment to bring the word to the good sergeant. Vic skipped lightly over the book piles, made a helpless shrug at James, and ran out the door.

Mal was in the street, unmindful of traffic, grey

coat and watch cap moving purposely towards the patrol car on the opposite walk. Vic watched from the pavement as he banged heavily on the driver side window. Billy started from the reclined seat on the opposite side. Mal stepped up so that only his coat was visible from within the car. "There's been a bust-up in the library. Some sergeant's in trouble. If he's with you, you better get in there."

"Crap!" Billy fumbled for the seat belt and the door release at the same time, catching his utility belt on the retracting seat belt strap. Mal knelt below the driver's door while Billy bundled out of the passenger side. The constable pulled off a surprisingly good imitation of a '70's TV cop, sliding on his hip across the bonnet to the library side. Billy ran across the road, hands out to stop traffic, and through the arched doorway. Vic held the door open for him. Mal closed the door of the patrol car and took up watch in the adjacent bus shelter. Ignoring the gobsmacked look of the stopped dry cleaning van's driver to her right, she joined Mal in the bus shelter. A carriage was approaching. Digging in her shapeless leather purse, their faces were obscured by the driver's cubicle as the cops burst out of the library and surveyed the street. The bus carried two low-speed fugitives away from the empty patrol car in a sweet cloud of natural gas exhaust.

The sergeant put a staying hand on his partner's shoulder. "It's not worth it, Billy. The station's around the corner. We'll put the word into the CCTV people and a flag on the girl's file as well. They'll turn up on the electrons somewhere soon." The two officers drove back to the station. In front of the library, the steady hum of rubber-on-tarmac resumed, the distant call of a jackhammer from a hidden jobsite breaking the relative quiet after the departure of the #77 bus. An Asda shopper tapped on the plastic route map fixed to the bus shelter wall, tracing a finger along Heathfield road to a Roman bank icon - Wandsworth Prison.

SHOPPING THE SURVEILLANCE STATE

Our heroes change in meaningful ways, racing slowly against time. Victoria receives a cryptic message

"I'm starving," said Mal, one lanky arm wrapped around a pole and the other steadying Vic. She didn't like the feel of the vinyl straphangers and the overhead pole was too high. "My last meal was a Quickie-mart cup-noodle."

Vic cocked the corner of her eye at him. "Careful, you don't want that as your epitaph."

"Oh, there's life left in this old carcass yet."

Vic had close up view of a the tufts of white hair he had missed along his jaw, under the ear. "Actually, I've been meaning to ask you about that."

"About my emaciated condition? Very kind. I fancy a fry up."

"No, about your rejuvenated condition. You're

pretty spry this morning for someone who slept rough with a cracked rib. Last night you needed my help to walk down the alley, this morning you're Samson. I saw you topple a full bookshelf with one hand."

"Well, Victoria, I've always been a fast healer. Perhaps yesterday I just wanted to put my arm around a pretty girl, and you were the nearest available."

"Convincing act. You looked pretty battered to me. And that doesn't explain this morning."

"Think of your father. He and I were young magicians. Prestidigitators. Conjurors! We made a living forty years ago on parlour tricks and cheap props. There are three things you need for success with sleight-of-hand: hand speed, balance, and a gift for getting things to change direction. I'm flattered that it looked natural, but I was throwing everything at the far corner of that shelf. Once you get one to tilt, well, over they go. I will admit I'm stronger and faster than your typical pensioner. Lifetime of manual labour and all that." Vic felt a wiry bicep flex through the wool coat.

"Rude health and worse manners. Why must all men make jokes about menstruation?"

"Must have been the low blood sugar. Hang on." He released her to press the red 'Stop Requested' button. "I smell an ATM." He rubbed his hands. "And breakfast." Vic knocked against him as the bus braked to the Penwith Road stop. He bounced off the soft cushion of her shoulder and out of the bus, "and shopping. It's in our future."

Mal led her into Earlsfield station. "There's a cash machine by the grocers," she said.

"There's also Computer World and a funeral home, but nothing that would put people off the scent of your money. A train station ATM implies a train journey, which makes us that much harder to find."

Vic punched at the station cashpoint. "How far are we likely to get on 300 pounds? That's the most I can take out. And who exactly are we hiding from?"

"I've been pondering on that myself. Fortunately, I think the police are on the scene by chance, more bad timing than anything else."

"You're a bit casual about being wanted by the police. It's not a pleasant or usual feeling for me."

"You will get used to it," Mal said, straightening her hat. He yawned and leaned against the side of the ATM. He was constantly propping his frame on something. Beautiful day to be on the run, she thought, so much better than yesterday, one of those crisp November days where the clouds down tools, leaving a blue sky and sunshine that warms so well you feel the chill doubly the moment you pass into shade. Everyone seemed to be catching the noon train, brunch dates, pensioners, and a surprising number of business suits for a Saturday. Vic used to wonder how everyone else was able to so casually slope off in the middle of the day. The disconnect from normal life hit with renewed force. She had Sunday. After that she'd have to make an appearance at work. She realized Mal had been talking.

"...so my people have survived on their wits for hundreds of years. Carnies, Roma, Gypsies, Travelers. I'm constantly accused of being a persecuted minority. I've got a UK passport. The Heathrow immigration officers always ask me if I'm Jewish, though they're not supposed to. Of course, I haven't travelled by passport in a long while. I might be Jewish. Something Egyptian or Syrian or Semitic in the genes, not really sure." Mal's eyes were closed in the sunlight. He brandished his head in profile. "Exhibit A – the nose. And my skin of course."

"I thought it was the deep set eyes." She tucked pound notes into her wallet. It was soft blue Italian leather, the colour you paint the crèche for a baby boy, an extravagant birthday gift from her father. She put thoughts of her father aside with the money. "When you've had proper sleep they might even be charming. Let's get something to eat."

"Not here. As you said, we're not sure who's involved. Frankly, I'm concerned about the political angle. If it's the ruling party, and even if it isn't, they'll find ways to tap into our lives. The establishment definitely should have an interest, and they're a pack of snoops. Let's avoid the law for the moment as well. They're slightly more savoury than the politicians, but not much. Speaking of savoury, I remember a fancy gastro-pub just up the road, 'Jolly something'. You strike me as the jolly gastro-pub kind."

Before Vic could muse out what 'gastro-pub kind' meant, Mal stole her hat, hiding it and his watch cap in the pockets of his herringbone coat. "Hey!" Ignoring her, he took off the coat and folded it over one forearm.

"'A tall man in a grey coat and watch cap walked into the station with a darkie in a purple hat.' Makes a better punch line if two different people walk out," he said. Sunlight gleamed off his shaven head. "Like the Patrick Stewart look?"

"Who? Darkie what?" she asked.

"Never mind." Without the coat, Mal was in the plaid work shirt and tan cords from last night, complete with flour dust and bloodstains. She gave him an up-and-down. "I know," he said, "Not exactly 'Action Man'. But sometimes distinctive and remarkably bad can be an advantage. Like when we change out of it." He unbuttoned the work shirt and put it in a platform dustbin, revealing a bright Free Tibet t-shirt. He made for Garratt Lane with long steps, coat held like a matador. Vic hurried to keep pace. Mal said, "I'm beginning to think that the characters who busted up the bakery last night might be related to your father's death."

That doesn't make sense, thought Vic. "How are you mixed up in a voting machine scandal? Or are you suggesting my father was involved in drugs?"

"No to both. But your father may have involved me through you. Don't you find the timing curious? They showed up so closely on your heels? Perhaps it wasn't me they were after."

"Mal, they called you by name."

"Which they could have read off a text message, or a bakery box."

"I know my father. He got scared when he found out I had marijuana in the house."

"And you know he was 59, and didn't dye his hair as well."

Vic stopped. Mal's stride carried him several yards further down the walk. She was still shaking when he turned around.

"Piss off, Mal, I've had quite enough of this! Not only that I'm involved in something criminal. You haven't explained anything. You insult me, my father. To hell with you. I can still find a reasonable policeman like Billy and sort myself out. I'm not sure I want to learn any more about this. And I certainly don't want to take any more crap from you." She gave him two fingers and bustled back towards the train station.

Mal caught up to her before she reached the platform. He tugged on her purse strap when she didn't turn her head. "First, let me give you back your hat. It's obviously your father's. Then you can go," he said. "Look, I'm also worried about you. I know your father is not the Tony Montana of South Wales. We should consider the possibility that whatever danger he was in might splash on you..."

"Shut up," she said. He was infuriating, thoughtlessly thoughtful. They stood on the pathway to Earlsfield station like lovers reluctant to fight in public. "Shut up. I'm hungry and curious. Probably stupidly so. I'll eat. Just don't insult me. Convince me with your penetrating insight, you son-of-a-bitch."

Mal looked around and led her back up Garratt Lane. "Good. Keep an open mind. I didn't know those fellows who barged in on our first meeting, but I do know the type. It might not be drugs they were after. The last thing we should do is draw attention. Let's clear out of here quickly and quietly, get comfortably anonymous and full-bellied, and I'll tell you everything I think I know."

The Jolly Gardeners proved to have an eye-wateringly expensive and truly delicious lunch. At the lunch table, Mal laid out his theory of the inconspicuous bikini. "It's getting harder and harder to go incognito. Used to be you could parade down high street in a string bathing suit. You would start some gossip, but in the main, people would have forgotten it by tomorrow's breakfast. Now we live in a surveillance state Orwell would have marveled at. CC TV is everywhere. Your little bikini parade is on Youtube in moments, from three angles. Did you know that the local councils have been using CC TV footage to make sure you're not smoking where you shouldn't, or that the off-license doesn't sell to under-ages?"

"I don't smoke," she said.

Mal popped an ambitiously heaped fork of salmon into his mouth. "Mmph. You should. Only a few, though. Too many spoil the taste when you kiss. And what exactly did you do with the marijuana you hid in your poor father's house?"

"Fine. Occasionally," she said, "I smoke. Rarely."

"Right," he continued, "It used to be that all the cameras on the main roads, the underground, shopping centres, schools, some person had to be watching. Or if they weren't watching, they had to check up in a few days or else the videotape was re-recorded and over-written. These days multiple cameras stream into a server. They store this stuff for years. Multiple backups. What's worse," The older couple dressed like Oxfam shop models at the next table looked up. He quietened, "worse is that they've tied into the same kind of image recognition software that puts names to photos on Facebook. Any government security officer thinking about a girl in a bikini can plug a search term into the recorded feeds of a thousand cameras. If you didn't make the news the first time 'round, you'll be tits up on an upcoming broadcast, if you'll pardon the term. And then the news in Estonia, or Malaysia. Those kinds of pictures make the rounds." Mal meditated for a moment, "perhaps not Malaysia, I believe Islamic Republics aren't prepared for buttocks on screen." Mal held up a finger.

"And you had to purchase this bikini somewhere, which is the main difficulty. The bank databases are all linked to the government." Mal made single-quotes with his index fingers, "Depending on who is a 'Person of Interest'. A single swipe can bring the law down on you. Of the card that is." Vic mentally cursed again her inability to raise one eyebrow. She settled for staring impassively as Mal mopped his plate with focaccia. "Decent bread, actually," he said.

"OK, I accept the need to keep a low profile," she said. "After this spread, we've got two hundred odd of my pounds and whatever you have in your wallet to buy a change of clothes and continue our investigation at some other Internet café. But unless something big pops up, I'm going to the police tomorrow."

"And buy some false IDs, change our looks, stay off the radar, obfuscate our trail across London, make sure we're not being followed. And I have to make a few calls. My customers will be wondering why there have been no Saturday deliveries."

"Why the false IDs? I said 'tomorrow'. How long do you think we'll be on the lam?" she asked.

"At last, a smile!" he said. "I think you're finally getting into the spirit of the thing. We can fight Big

Brother together."

Vic sat back in the booth and stretched out the ache in her shoulders. "Actually, I was thinking of a song. Blue Oyster Cult. Not important. One of my father's favorite bands. 'I ain't no sheep'. Speaking of Oyster," Vic grappled with her purse and pulled out her wallet. "I don't suppose you have an Oyster card? It was a pound more expensive to pay our bus fares in cash." She opened the coin purse section, wondering if desire alone could conjure up more change.

"Don't believe in them," he said. Of course you don't, thought Vic. "My freedom is worth the extra pound. In fact, we need to get rid of your Oyster card, and your ATM card. Did you take the battery out of your phone like I suggested?" His face softened. "I'll buy you another Oyster card with my own money later, and the bank will reissue your card for free. But trust me on the phone battery, it won't hurt it."

Vic explored her purse and found the phone. She removed the back case, reversed the battery, and replaced it. "Good thing I can't afford a fancy smartphone with a fixed battery. But don't mistake my doing what you say with agreement." She counted out the contents of the folio the server left on the table. "My wad is £264 pounds plus shrapnel. Let's go. But I'll warn you, I'm pretty useless at shopping. I'm better at not buying. Especially bikinis."

They headed away from the station, up Garratt Lane. Mal's strides consumed the pavement the way he ate lunch, voracious and inattentive. A Bristol girl is used to walking, but Vic was relieved when, after a brisk two kilometers, Mal stopped in front of a restrained sign for "Southside". It was either a warehouse disguised as a temple, or the other way around. Vic wondered why all the new developments had names like "Northpark" or "Westlane". Were they coded directions, engineers describing how to orient the refueling lines of crash-landed spaceships disguised as shopping centres?

"This should play." Mal scanned the list of shops on the hoarding. "T-K Maxx, H&M. Affordable style, Vic, that's us. We'll need two outfits each, something radical and something drab, and most definitely warm enough to sleep in."

"Mal, I've already had two awful night's sleep," she said. "You'll have to find something better than a doorway to flop in if you want me to stick around."

What followed was the unusual adventure of a man shopping attentively with a woman. Mal focused on the cheapest generic-world clothing stores, styles for a happy English suburb imported from Vietnam. "I'm not sure I'm allowed do normal things with you," said Vic. "And I never thought a crowd of shoppers would be more relaxing than being alone." Vic was reminded of the time a police car put the flashing lights on behind her on the motorway, only to swerve around and chase someone else. This was the first time she felt a mild euphoria while shopping, if you didn't count the time she spent thirty minutes in front of the peanut butter display at Tescos in 6th form, coming down off her first joint. She wondered if Mal was genuinely sweet and patient, or just trying to make up for throwing her onto his own police warrant. Never mind I'm a potential fugitive in company of a wanted man, she thought, as she took six pairs of jeans into the trial room. When would be the next time she'd be with someone who could speak frankly about what flattered her arse?

Mal made a face at the men's undergarments. They seemed to have time warped back to the Victorian era. His options were either striped three button drawers or an unholy marriage of a speedo and long johns. Vic surreptitiously put a pack of men's bikini briefs in their basket.

The ended up buying, in cash, an assortment of undergarments, snakeskin printed bright red jeans for her, mustard yellow flares for Mal, another pair of black jeans each, four screen-printed t-shirts, two thick reversible hoodies and a 'young adult' size yellow raincoat that crumpled into a convenient blue waterproof cinch sac. The raincoat fit Vic beautifully and would keep her warm under the sweatshirt if pressed. Which it might need to sooner than one hoped, she thought, as she looked at the two lonely £50 notes in her wallet.

After changing, they sat in a post-consumerist haze, comparing t-shirt slogans in one of the shopping centre's mass-market baristas. Mal's had an innocuous cartoon rodent in crosshairs over the words 'Beaver Hunter'. Vic's had 'Crestfallen' superimposed on crossed guitars. Their old outfits were in the new shopping bags. Their hooded sweatshirts were tied around their waists. Mal had touched up his shave with a razor from the centre's chemist. Vic pulled an eyeliner from the menagerie in her purse. Mal closed his eyes and let her tug a bold line of black from the edge of each eyelid toward the centre. Was he smiling because it tickled as she smeared it upwards with a moistened thumb, or was he the kind of guy who liked makeup? She smacked his forehead to open his eyes, and admired her 'guy-liner'. The bald, glam look rewound his appearance to late thirties or early forties max. "Still a bit bony, but you'll do," she said. "I'd say, 'approachably rough'." Mal didn't have to fake being self-assured enough to wear makeup outside of the club. He reached towards her head.

"Always," she groaned, ducking away. "What is it with you people? I know a white guy for five minutes and he wants to touch the hair."

The red bandanna he was going to pull from her ear was half-caught inside his sleeve. "Here, take it," he said, shaking his wrist so that it puffed up and down. "And I'm offended by that characterization. I would prefer to call myself," he paused, "Mesopotamian. That would be Asia, not Caucasia."

"Sorry, Mal. Although you understand I'm a bit twitchy." She took the bandana and tied it neatly over her twists. It matched the jeans, but wasn't half as tight. "I don't remember paying for this," she said. "Have you suddenly discovered money?"

"Pure hand speed. But I'll pay for the coffees. I need to save cash because, unlike you, I can't go back to my day job at the moment. Besides, Jews don't buy retail."

"Retail," she repeated. "Jesus, Mal, shoplifting? You seemed happy enough to spend my cash," she said. "Let's get out of here. I think it's time we found an Internet café and got back in touch with your hacker friends. You owe me some more info."

"Phone shop, not Internet café. And I've been meaning to tell you about those hackers. I think whatever you got in the email was all we'll get. They aren't my friends, and I reckon whatever favors they felt like doing your dad, they've done them. But we should check again anyway."

"I'm a prisoner of hope, Mal." Vic was again reminded why her dominant emotion with men was exasperation. This one in particular was, in fact, homeless, jobless, and mildly charming, but surveys of her female friends had been pretty consistent – it wasn't just the Indian husbands that were caring but useless.

They left the café and found a mobile phone store. Mal immediately started arguing with one of the shop assistants over 4G speeds on different phones. What an age we live in now, thought Vic. It used to be the size of your motor engine, not download speed. Either way, insulting a man's gadget is a personal attack that can't go un-rebutted. The phone salesman borrowed his mates' iPhone and smugly passed it, along with his own Samsung, to Mal and Vic. "Go ahead, open any page you like on the browser. They're both on Vodafone."

"How about your email, Victoria?" She and Mal typed in the URL on the small keyboards as Vic called it out. "The home page loaded faster on the iPhone," said Mal. He was gleeful.

"That's because you're using a faster browser," said the salesman. "If you put Opera on the Samsung, it'll be equally fast if not faster. Try downloading something." They swapped phones so Vic could key in her password on both.

"Any new messages? Something with an attachment?" asked Mal, taking back the iPhone.

"Two. Looks like one from colleagues of Billy and Gardiner, inviting us in for a chat. And another message from myself I don't remember sending."

"I see it," said Mal. "Ready to race? Open on 3, 2, 1!"

The email subject was 'Top 20 Health Foods'. The salesman made farting noises when Mal's phone displayed the infographic JPG first. He snatched the borrowed iPhone from Mal's hand. Vic read out the captions as it loaded on the Samsung. "Yogurt, olives, uemboshi plums, radishes, eggplant, mustard, almonds, incaberries, lemongrass, cashews, okra, malt vinegar, peanuts...' and so on." She closed the phone browser and gave the phone back to the salesman. "I'm not convinced about 4G, but the message did come through," she said.

Mal sniffed. "Don't let him sell you a slow phone. Dealing with these men, it's like dealing with large children."

"I know," said Vic, "I got the message." She turned to the salesman. "I think my husband and I need more time to decide," she said, tugging Mal towards the door. He stooped to collect their shopping bags and kept mum until they were outside the store.

"Message?"

"No one I know calls aubergines eggplant. And ooo-em-boshi? It was an acrostic. 'Your email compromised', spelled out in vegetables. Time to go, Mal. Whoever is watching will soon figure out the phone numbers or IP addresses or whatever 4G uses to access email at that store."

"Right-o. Fancy another bus ride?" He hefted the bags. "We need to stash all this before we get to the rest of our errands." He leaned the bags inside the bus shelter opposite the shopping centre, their squared sides neat columns of brightly uniformed soldiers made tactically obsolete by modern firearms.

Vic watched the hands tick on a reproduction antique clock mounted on the column of the small park opposite. She wondered again if she would be better off alone, or away, out of England, someplace where pulling a kerchief out of a sleeve was something you did to impress children rather than disguise yourself from 'Big Brother'. The seconds dripped past. Wasn't a bus stop just another type of government waiting room? Perhaps the day would soon come when the surveillance state could put time itself on remand, the algorithms controlling bus schedules delaying them just long enough for a trace to go through and for patrol cars to arrive. A late bus was only a temporary irritation. People would hardly notice. It would be like Mal's bikini theory, but in reverse. Shoppers would note the arrest, probably remark on it to their partners or friends, but it wouldn't make the news. All thought of two disappeared gypsies would be gone by Sunday breakfast.

BECOMING A PRINCESS

Two meat lockers, a public transport adventure,
a Musselman, and disturbing news

"Deliverance, thy name is 44!" thundered Mal, startling Vic out of her reverie and carrying her onto the bus on a microwave of positive energy. Mal seemed genuinely to be in good cheer. Maybe because he's not the one paying, thought Vic, holding a large note helplessly at the driver. Mal boomed again, "Saturday night, Victoria! What are we going..." He blinked twice, like an owl, "To dooooo?" She took her change without answering and sat down on the wide bench running lengthwise behind the driver. As Mal plopped next to her, Vic saw with dismay that the black line labeled N44 on the route map traveled along Battersea Park, directly past the scene of this morning's contretemps.

Mal carried on, "Victoria Station, Victoria! A hub of power, near the heart of government, jumping off point for the whole of the South. We are but two small spiders riding the web of transport, two tiny jewels in London's crown, intoxicated by the damp air of winter! We might even be in time for a beer."

"Shut it, Mal. Not in the mood." They passed Battersea Library, her lips turned down and his up, without incident. He gave her periodic glances out of the corner of his eye, but kept quiet.

They got down at the Victoria terminus. Mal asked an agent at the ticket counter, "Can I buy two tickets to Gatwick from that machine?" He made a big production of cocking his thumb at the electronic kiosk opposite. The ticket agent gave a distracted nod and kept on counting his change. Mal had an American-tourist-talking-to-someone-who-doesn't-speak-English grin. "Do you know how much it will be, pal, Gatwick?" The agent took in the eyeliner, the 'Beaver Hunt' t-shirt, and the horrified black girlfriend in a red bandanna.

"Eighteen pounds each one way, two-for-one if you buy return. The machine makes change from twenties." Mal winked and thanked the agent. He dragged Vic over to the bank of machines opposite.

"Are we flying somewhere?" asked Vic.

"Definitely not. We still have an investigation to

prosecute." Mal's accent warped on certain words. It was English-ish, but with a trace of something more ancient thrown in. Latin? Norse? It made prosecute sound like persecute. Mal lingered at the machine, pushing random buttons, until a businessman queued behind them. Mal pushed up the plastic coin guard and fished in the tray for nothing, then grabbed the bags and hustled Vic onto an escalator. The top of the escalator deposited them into a shopping mall that, apart from quirks of its layout, could have been a carbon copy of the centre they had only recently left. "I believe this one has a Sainsbury's. Fine store, Sainsbury's."

Vic again found herself hustling to keep up, even with him carrying the bags. Mal pirouetted neatly around the knot of people clustered at the store guide, lifting an H&M bag at the last moment to keep from braining an owlish fellow in a cardigan who straightened unexpectedly from the centre map. I guess he found his destination, thought Vic. Mal wasn't completely successful. The arms of the hoodie tied at his waist flicked cardigan-man on the backside as he spun past. His momentum carried him to the end of the corridor before anyone made a fuss. Sainsbury's glowed orange-ly, its entrance a maze of slots and mini-conveyor belts. Vic made her way through the modern shoppers' cattle chute in the only slightly intensified chaos of Mal's wake. She saw him duck behind the meat counter and barge through the hanging plastic slats that divided retail from the employee section. By the time she fought the meander of shoppers and reached the back of the store, the banging of the slats was a soft tabla. A white jacketed deli staffer greeted her with a disposable oversized clear plastic glove.

"May I help you?"

"Um." She considered her options. "Any specials?" Vic's embarrassment vanished as Mal burst back through the slats in a dozen rim-shots of plastic clatter. He threw his arms wide and began to sing.

"I'm special! So special! I gotta have some of your," Mal snapped his fingers, "attention. Give it to me..."

The deli woman pointed at the customer side of the counter. "Employees only. Make a fuss and I'll get you thrown out of the store."

Victoria was already shushing him. "I thought we were trying to be incognito."

"Well, yes," said Mal, drawing her down a tall aisle. "But if they think I'm a crazy person, they won't investigate that I've left bags in the false ceiling of the employee's toilet. And even if they do, they'll think we've going to Gatwick on the next train. This place is open early 'til late, better than a left luggage locker. Job one done."

Bags-free Mal was even harder to keep pace with, but by now Vic was used to his marauding walking style. They reached the Victoria underground station entrance in under a minute, and spent another ten minutes navigating the crush of passengers going in and out. "Where are we going?" asked Vic, as Mal dragged her onto a random platform.

"Trust me," he said, "I have a plan." He didn't say another word during a two-hour tour-by-Tube of the most congested stations in London, from Victoria to Euston, Waterloo, Oxford Circus, Bank & Monument, to Kings Cross, changing lines each time. They finally exited at Paddington. As they walked down Edgware Road towards Marble Arch, Vic cribbed, "You know, we could have walked directly here from Victoria. It would have been a lot more pleasant then sharing an afternoon with half of London while you played dumb-and-stupid. We can just as easily lose someone in Hyde Park as we might have by switching trains."

"That's true. But we wouldn't have laid as much smoke. If they ever go to search the tube camera footage, they'll see us at various times on various lines, without any idea of our final destination. They'll need staff to check every minute of a ton of footage, which will put the politicos in conflict with the bean-counters. If we're lucky, they'll economize, miss one or two sightings and assume we picked another train. Besides, when I visit Salim, I always take an odd route. It's a courtesy for him. He'd rather not advertise which people made a path to his door either." They ducked into a Lebanese café. Mal gave a half-wave to the Arab looking man behind the counter and picked a table midway in. The counterman smiled in recognition and immediately brought over two thick black coffees.

"Salaam aleikum."

"Aleikum salaam." Mal and the man had a quick dialogue in a soft desert language. Persian? Kurdish? The Arabic syllables seemed to transform his face, skin becoming more Middle Eastern with each syllable. If she covered her ears, she saw a goth version of the older Italian James Bond she had first met. If she took her hands away and listened, she saw every terrorist stereotype short of the funny beard. I know very well that looks, religion, and family background aren't destiny, so keep a straight face, she thought, but she couldn't help but wonder what would happen if her second thoughts ever changed into thirds. Almost a whole day of running around and the only new insight was that whoever was behind this was slick enough to hack her email. Still, the café booth was comfortable enough. Falafel felt more likely than a firefight. But then again, she mused, who really knows what goes onto the shwarma spike? She felt her shoulders ease at least an inch when Mal finally slipped back into English.

"Victoria, my dear, this is Salim. He needs to know what name you want on your driver's license."

"I don't have a driver's license, Mal."

"You will soon. What's your mother's name?"

"Lilith. My mom's name was Lilith Mayron. She died giving birth to me."

Mal gave a dismissive shake of his head. "Too complicated. Have you ever seen an Asian person try to say 'Lilith'? All tongue cramps and saliva. We'll make you Amira. Salim will appreciate that. Princess Amira Myron."

"And you?"

"Gregory Myron. Your uxorious husband."

"You wish. How much is this going to cost, Mal? Is it really necessary? I'm leaning towards being back at work on Monday."

"I need you to spend the money. Going black is more important than what this will cost."

"Damn it, Mal, I'm black as can be already. When are you ever going to tell me what's really going on? I feel like I'm running around with the Lebanese Biggie Smalls and his ten crack commandments, or hashish commandments, or whatever, so long as you never let me know how much dough you hold. This is my last..." She fumbled out her wallet. "Eighty odd pounds. And I do want to take a shower this evening."

Salim broke in, "Madam, I am sure my brother here will make you whole. Come to the back, we must take some photographs." He led them behind the counter and through a false-wood paneled door, past a row of deep fryers. They came to a solid metal door with a circular handle, like the hatch of a submarine, hinged on one side. Salim pulled the handle and gave the door a firm tug. It opened with a loud un-suctioning sound, like a new jam jar giving up the factory seal.

The compartment was harshly lit, white and icy.

There was a stool in front of a taut blue sheet hung in a small open space. Behind the sheet, Vic glimpsed a row of bloody piñatas – skinned goats, suspended by fist-sized hooks through their necks. Salim motioned her to sit while he busied himself over an expensive looking digital camera he had retrieved from an Eskimo box in the corner. He set the camera on the tripod pre-positioned over a taped X on the floor. Vic was grateful that the whole process went quickly – she and then Mal taking turns on the stool in their t-shirts, trying not to shiver. Was it the cold or the biriyani-in-the-raw, nothing but a thin sheet of plastic between a carcass and the back of her neck?

The kitchen, though darker, was warm and human. Mal took Salim in a full hug. Vic's brown skin hid her flush when she overheard Mal whisper to Salim, "It's too easy to be mistaken for jihadis these days, when all a man wants to do is get a little anonymity. We'll be back in a few hours to pick things up." She saw Mal dip his hand into Salim's front pocket, and then slap Salim on the back. It was so smooth and quick, she wasn't sure whether Mal had put something in or taken something out.

"Inshallah," Salim replied, escorting them to the front of the restaurant. Another Arab-looking man had taken Salim's place at the counter, but they weren't introduced. Mal and Salim exchanged a few more words in the language they had spoken previously while she waited on the pavement. Mal joined her in the street, two regular urban citizens.

"Now what?"

"Now, my princess, we wander and wait. It takes a few hours to make up the papers. With new IDs, we can investigate properly without fear that 'the man' will trip over us. In the meantime, I need to make a few calls. Can I borrow some change? Be right back."

Mal left Victoria at a row of televisions installed as the storefront display of a high street electronics chain. She idly watched the flickering wall, tuned to the early evening news. A speaker mounted in the eave carried the soundtrack on low volume. She moved to stand beneath it. If it bleeds, it leads, she thought – dominating the headlines was the death of a prominent opposition MP from Glasgow's north. He'd apparently fallen into the river at the bottom of the stairs by Kelvingrove Park and drowned. Alcohol was suspected. There was a breathless Scot re-enacting the supposed scene for the camera, "...had been reported missing by his wife Wednesday, however, as per policy the local constables did not make details available to other UK police forces until 48 hours had elapsed. His body was found by a Friends of the Kelvingrove Park volunteer while removing invasive species from the river bank this Saturday morning. When I spoke to her, she described feeling his hair in the muck as 'the strangest weed she'd ever pulled', before bursting into tears." The station cut to an equally bereft wife being consoled by members of the constituency office. A Scottish newsreader continued in voiceover, "The Shadow Finance minister was scheduled to campaign today in support of his party's bid to win the upcoming general election and Scottish Assembly. With three weeks before the election, it is unclear if the Labour party will be able to register a new candidate on the ballot." In the newsreader's accent, unclear became 'un-clair'. Mal returned just before the Scottish football scores, preventing her from finding out if death and sport sounded equally jolly in Scots.

"Funny thing, that," said Mal, taking her hand as they walked away.

"What?"

"You hardly ever see an excited Scot."

"No, Mal, but you're right, it is funny. Third

politician to pop off this week, which is a bit strange. Finished calling your girlfriends?"

"If you must know, I was calling my customers to tell them the bakery is closed."

Vic stopped with a stamped foot, her hand pulling away from his. "Isn't that terribly unsafe? We just spent several hours trying to lose any tails. What if they tapped your customers' phones?"

"I'm not that important. Well, my customers certainly aren't. The police might figure out to whom I sell eventually, but not quickly. They didn't even know I had a business until you came along." Mal winked. "Don't fret. The number one enemy of every police force is paperwork. If they want to follow your credit cards or your phone, thankfully they must first still file a warrant. Saturday evening, quite unlikely. How about a pint?"

"On me," he said apologetically, before Vic could retort. He'd put on his hoodie at some point between phone calls. She should have done the same. She still had a chill from the freezer, a chill that was only deepening in the quickening dark. Maybe just to keep herself warm, or maybe because of the 'Not Me' shrug and brotherly laugh Mal gave Salim in the café when, as they were leaving, Salim pointed at the spot on his

face corresponding to the fading bruise on her cheek
– Vic realized she wanted to pick a fight.

"Hey, Mal, don't you find it odd that a possibly
Jewish person like yourself is buying false documents
from a Muslim?"

"No. Should I?"

"You tell me. With Israel-Palestine going on, do
you think it's fair to deceive a nice Muslim boy like
Salim into breaking the law for a Jew?"

"A Jew and an Ethiopian. Or at least half-
Ethiopian."

"But if he knew what you really were, would he
still do it?"

"My dear, I'm not sure if anyone knows what I
really am, including myself. Will you stop going on
about this? Salim is a friend."

"And in your world, a world of criminals and
thugs, that's good enough, is it?"

Vic had seen but not felt Mal's sinewy strength
first hand. Until now. He clamped on to her left arm
just below the armpit and turned her bodily with the
roll of his wrist. He pinched her right ear with his free
hand, finding an inch of flesh between her four
piercings. It was an unusual spot to be touched, and

she froze, staring up at him. "Let me make one thing clear, that you of all people should know by your gender and the colour of your skin. Any person, any regime, any caste that demonizes one group as somehow being less dignified, less righteous, less worthy, less human on account of their religion or affiliation or anything having to do with who they are rather than what they do..." He released her, punctuating "I. Will. Not. Stand. For," with a poking finger to her sternum. "What is most surprising about the aspersions you cast is not that they persist but how long they have lasted in the presence of thinking people. As for Israel-Palestine, or any other of these asinine conflicts where one group seeks to paint the other as less than human, both sides are equally bad, and I'm confident such ignorance cannot endure. I'm for people, and I hope to see two states in my lifetime. Are you satisfied?" Mal was hot, a red blotch forming under both cheeks and lighting up his forehead like a miner's beacon.

"Yes. You've been pissing me off all day. About time you felt what it was like." She walked away. He joined her in silent search of a pub.

LIKE MERITOCRACY

A drink and a kiss are more trouble than they're worth - Mal resorts to drastic measures

Vic and Mal's particular stretch of Edgware Road was apparently halal, not a place for alcohol in sight. They walked a few blocks, their silence imperceptibly more peaceful with each step. Mal suddenly spun on his heel. "Let's try a side street."

Vic was nonplussed. "Didn't we pass a nice pub near Paddington? Let's just backtrack."

"Too twee. Come, down here." He turned off Edgware Road into an unprepossessing lane of flat-sided, three story brick terrace houses. The repetitive facades made a wall off to the vanishing point. A clump of bare branches hid the vague horizon. Small stone bridges covered trenches of basement apartment window boxes, all guarded by cheap copies of Georgian iron railing, the black London version of picket fences. It was the kind of street where neighbours don't tell each other about the bedbugs.

"Well, there's nothing much down here," said Vic.

"It's not what's there but what it leads to, madam. Victory is always just around the next bend." Mal's good humour seemed restored, but with an undertone of agitation.

"Stair Street Video," she read aloud from the lone hoarding. The road was as flat as the taste of dust. "Not exactly an up-and-down road." She was falling behind, more from lack of enthusiasm than shorter stride length.

She heard a triumphant, "Ah, the Rob Roy!" from around the corner ahead of her. He reappeared. "Let's save that for another day, shall we?", he said, reaching her patch of pavement so fast they collided.

"Mal, what the hell?" He steadied her, tugged her hood up over her head, and pocketed the bandana in her hair in a single movement. She'd also been turned 90 degrees, allowing him to guide her down a side road marked 'Sale Place' with an urgent and unexpected push on her spine. He must have untied the bandana knot with one hand, she realized. They proceeded quickly, hoods up, past a boarded-up shop and some other nondescript doors. Mal ducked under a painted steel beam that served as a private gate, pulling her with him into a cobbled mews. Yellow lines painted over the paving stones gave the impression that a public city street continued under the beam and through the depth of the entrance arch, but the stables and carriage houses beyond were clearly private, and upmarket, digs.

Mal didn't give Vic much time for property hunting. "Run."

"Mal, you idiot," she whispered, already moving towards the far end, "You've led us into a courtyard." Which is more likely to be abandoned, the posh street or the slum? Perhaps it's only poor folks who have the time and numbers to populate a sidewalk. The cobbles were deserted. No lights in the windows. Worse, the rounded curve of pavement at the end led only into new bricks, an addition closing off what would likely have been an 18th century exit. They ran anyway, along the row of ornamental trees in planters, under another wide steel beam spanning the close some yards before the new brick wall. The yellow street lines made a semi-circle at the end and met beneath their feet as they gathered themselves. A pair of potted palms flanked them at the back of the mews like the pulled curtains of a stage.

Vic dashed left, barely managing to avoid garroting herself on the thin chain of a child's swing hidden in the twilight. It would have been pitch dark but for London's permanent skyglow, refracted neon from the commercial streets and apartment block CFLs. The glow didn't help with escape routes – it revealed only bricks, barred windows, and locked doors. "What are we running from, anyway?"

"That." Mal dashed right, a leaping step taking him halfway up the right hand wall. He left a smudge at eye level where he pushed off, turning in the air to make a parkour landing. He faced back the way they had come, legs shoulder width apart, chin pointing towards the entrance. Despite age and a lanky frame, his steps were soundless. He bounced lightly as a wisp. If ears were to detect them, she'd be done in a wooden clatter of suede boots, and he'd glide on by. Didn't matter though. Sight was about to give them up. She followed his gaze to the dark window of the mews arch. Her feet hurt a bit. Seemed likely something else was going to hurt worse in a minute.

"I saw the first one on Edgware Road itself, then his friend outside that pub, the Rob Roy." There were four, and familiar. Night made the army-style wool coats black instead of green, but the shoulders were the same broad stones, topped by pale faces shiny as moons.

"How did they find us?" She was still whispering, even though it was obvious they'd been seen.

"Good question, Victoria, and worth asking," he whispered back. He stepped forward, and in a voice that echoed off the canyon walls of the courtyard asked, "How did you find us?"

"You screwed up," replied the lead figure conversationally, walking closer, but cautiously. "We have a friend at the phone company. Gave us a list of all the numbers called from your bakery phone. When three of them were rung from the same payphone in Edgware, we came here."

Vic edged behind Mal and spoke softly into the back of his hoody, "I'm not happy about this."

Mal kept his attention on the leader. "What did you promise this friend, eternal life?"

"Our version of it," said the thug, softly. Peeking around Mal, Vic couldn't make out much detail. The voice was the same guy who had smashed in Mal's door less than twenty four hours previous. He spoke with that same odd combination of mince and menace. The thug held up a white palm in the gloom, reminiscent of shading his eyes from the sun. It gleamed, a photo-negative in the scattered illumination of a reflected city.

"I kept the covenant!" shouted Mal. "I haven't used in forty years, same as Emir Ali. And in return you were to leave us alone, and subsist elsewhere." Vic gave up trying to follow the conversation. She turned and started kicking the low wooden door set into the wall behind. Yet some portion of her brain kept listening.

"That may be true, but we're dying. Soon we'll be gone. Someone is killing us faster, taking that which was left to keep us alive, and we think you know who, Goldeneye." All four were through the arch, standing abreast. No one was answering the door for Vic, and she wasn't making much progress on breaking it down. Apart from her, Mal, and the four off-brand-soldier goons, there didn't seem to be anyone alive within earshot. She went to cross over and try a door on the other side of the swing, but the gang of four adjusted ranks to keep her in. She didn't exactly see their movement, rather, she sensed it in the way shadows cut the faint light into a new pattern.

"I'm trying to find out just like you are," said Mal, moving to keep himself between them and Vic. "You can let the girl go, she's got no part in this."

"She's mixed up now." The quiet tone emphasized that the four thugs were now only a few yards from where Vic half-crouched behind Mal. "You asked for a day's time. That was yesterday. What have you found?"

"It's not what I've found," said Mal, "but what I've lost. Starting with my patience for this. If the covenant is broken, then all bets are off." Mal walked backwards, pinching Vic towards the back wall, and keeping his eyes on the gang of four. The figures in black jackets were absent spaces in a deepening night, eight feet away, less. Mal quickly turned and tucked her beside the door, between a fold in the wall and the drainpipe, her thick sweatshirt cushioning the rough surface. His touch was, for the first time, timid, as if he were sure it was going to hurt. She was used to being prodded and led around by him; this was strangely tentative. "Forgive me for this," he said quickly, and kissed her. It was a long, full kiss, his lips pressing her more generous mouth. Passion, and something else, or perhaps less, a taking away, the sensation of longing, an almost physical tugging as if her spirit was being drawn forth from her body by the flesh of his lips. Some other time, she thought, she might enjoy the sensation, his mouth soft and almost as wide as her own, yet a feeling of bleakness suffused her. Something had been lost. When he broke the kiss, she coughed, slumping into his arms, her whole body weak. I didn't think I was that kind of girl, she thought, as he let her down gently onto the stones. She sat, helplessly, knees together, legs splayed to one side, her head and shoulders wedged against the wall, spinelessly flopped like a corkscrew yoga pose gone bad. He had set her so that she had a good view of whatever was about to unfold in the alley. Without the wall, she knew she would fall over. Her arms were dead. She couldn't move at all. I should be scared, she thought, but mostly she just felt exhausted, facing the confrontation like a stuffed animal tied to the stadium rail, a lucky charm nailed to the ring at a bullfight.

Mal straightened to face the gang again, his height somehow more fearsome than before. A wet tear on his cheek was momentarily picked out by and made golden by some reflected ray, perhaps the moonlight, or an incandescent street lamp bounced across rooftops from a distant lane. Mal wiped at his face and the teardrop became a small trail of liquid on his hand. It remained lit, illuminated like yellow mercury. He made a fist and held it up. It glowed, as if the golden water on the palm inside had transmigrated through his skin, burned through his pores, transformed into some unholy sweat which scattered as his hand swept up and around in an interrupted circle. Fat golden droplets sketched an arc upon the ground in front of them, hundreds, far more water than the small smear he had drawn from his eye. More droplets fell from his fist. They formed a curved line, first thickening, then smoking and spitting until suddenly flames leapt up to waist height along a boundary arc, separating their cobblestones from the assailants. "Come to me now," Mal hissed. "I have some answers."

Vic tried to blink. She was hallucinating, or maybe had hit her head on the wall as she fell from his kiss. Flames but no heat, she thought. The thugs looked startled, but they only paused instead of retreating. Inside the half circle, the usual noise of the city had ceased. Noticeable by its absence, the low rumble of traffic, the snatches of conversation no longer borne by the wind, made Vic realize what great comfort she took from the city, of not being alone. This new version of Mal was force, certainly, but no companion.

There was a gap, though, on the edge of the arc. Some drops had landed inside the pot of the palm tree instead of the ground. The far right thug jumped through the gap and inside their burning circumference, his white hands and expressionless face weird in the gold light of the burning ring. Mal turned on him with the unearthly speed she'd observed before, taking the intruder's throat between finger and thumb before the thug could get any closer to Vic's observation post. Her unblinking eye read the open pores on the thug's nose, made plain by the light of Mal's still glowing hand. And then there was nothing to read.

The powerful form had been soundlessly exchanged for a fine silt of grey ash. An empty jacket fell onto a limp pile of dark clothes and dust, muscled interior gone, its superstructure like a replica suit of armour, wires and string revealed now the visor lid was raised. Mal made his strangler's hand into a cup and caught some dust in his open palm. There was still no sound but the kick of blood in her ears. Mal took a breath and blew – powder, maybe a fragment of a tooth, scudded across the fiery barrier and settled on the remaining three like mist.

"Time," said Mal, "a day, a year, a luxury and an indulgence. You live on sufferance! You scavenge what people now don't even realize is gone. Go now. Tell all of your kind not to molest us." The timbre of Mal's voice had changed, compressed and metallic, as if, though very close by, he were speaking through far away copper wires, laid under the sea in the first vintage of the Industrial era. Her lips couldn't twitch but she thought to herself, Vincent Price lives.

"We were not the first to break the agreement," rasped the leader, standing stiffly behind the flames. He looked ready to step forward, despite the flames and the fate of his henchman. The flames were dying down, guttering, perhaps only knee high.

"How do you know the agreement has even been broken?" asked Mal.

"True. It was only between us and a few of you, not all. But the rest are dead, or dreams. Only you and her father remained. He too claimed innocence, to the end. Which makes you the guilty one, and you must pay the penalty." The leader paced along the arc, stopping near where the other had leaped across. He looked down at the flickering yellow flames. "This cage of fire won't last long, magician." From his mouth the word magician was full of contempt, a bouquet of dead blossoms. He took a black folding knife from his coat and extended the blade until it locked.

"I have kept my side until today," Mal replied flatly.

"YOU BURN WITH IT MAGICIAN! GIVE IT TO ME WHAT YOU HOARD!" roared the pale figure, shattering the terra cotta pot of the tree with a stamp of his heel. He leapt high in the air, leaving a bootprint in the pot's dislodged earth. The spray of damp soil had made the gap larger. Though the flames reared up, doubling in height as Mal raised his arms, the thug lunged up, over, and through, planting one hand on Mal's shoulder and leapfrogging himself, Mal his pole vault staff. Off-balance, Mal was knocked to the ground. A somersault carried the thug over Mal's supine form. He landed nimbly in front of Vic. Instead of attacking her, he back-heeled Mal in the ribs. Knife held blade-down in his fist, the thug pivoted over Mal, coughing and prone.

"This is not the way," wheezed Mal. Mal's hand fumbled at the gang leader's leg, scratching at the sock above the top of a Doc Marten boot. "It is not yours to take." Vic watched the thug's head tilt down. Then Mal's hand touched white flesh, and the clothes repeated their emptying trick. A dry pile of soot hung a deeper black outline in the night air before falling in a rough cone. The knife fell into the cushion of his empty jacket. Mal heaved himself to his feet. The semi-circular flames went out completely. He looked at the remaining two. "If I am the last, then it does you no profit to seek me out. I have pledged not to use up our shared store. If you believe me, you should leave me alone. If not, know that I keep enough to destroy you still."

"Aye," said the thug on the left. "We'll leave you be. I will spread the word. He was rash, and old and full of need."

"Come, I'll show you faith." Mal beckoned the new leader across the blackened line that marked where flames had burnt. Mal laid his hand along the side of the other's neck. The thug shuddered. A look of spectral ecstasy transformed his too-white face, drawing back his cheeks and showing his canines. For a heartbeat, pale white was replaced with pale gold, a flicker, and then the thug jerked his neck away from Mal's glowing hand.

"That will do, magician." The 2-man gang turned away, brushing the chains of the swing as they left.

They filled the narrow archway entrance of the lane for a moment, then vanished.

Vic's head slumped to one side and banged against a brick. The sound of the world had come back. She sat numbly and counted four bass blasts of a bus horn before Mal stumbled over to her. He kneeled down and asked her, "Can you walk?" He looked suddenly old, a haggard caricature of the man who had walked her into Salim's.

"You absolute bastard." The small effort of speaking made her too weak to do anything but slump helplessly, a sensation of pins-and-needles coursing through her arms and legs. "You said magic wasn't real."

The forced movement of air through her throat seemed to give her strength. "My father told me magic wasn't real. He said magic was misdirection and deceit. But it is real, isn't it?" She lifted her head experimentally, accidentally clouting his nose with the crown of her head as he crouched over her.

"Ow." Mal sat down heavily, holding his proboscis. The quiet grace was gone.

She flexed her toes inside her boots, and limply flipped her arms over, as if to show off a suicide attempt. My wrists are clean, she thought. What about yours? She ached all over. "What were those things?"

Mal was still holding his nose. He looked awful. Vic wondered how she had convinced herself that he was attractive. Thick ridges of veins stood out on the backs of his hands, a highway map connecting villages and towns made of liver spots and moles. His ears stood out against his shaved head. His skin was so thin that, in the pale twilight of the city's electric glow, she could see a red capillary twitch. More thin blood flowed freely from a dislodged scab on the side of his head, staining his face, meltwater from a hot corpse in snow. He made a sound like 'whites'.

"Whites?" She managed to straighten her legs. "You think I didn't catch that? Not very illuminating. Bloody half of London is white, and this crowd didn't look like skinheads. I can handle myself with them."

"W-I-G-H-T," repeated Mal, coughing. "Wights. Not people. Dead things."

"They looked alive enough for me."

"They're as alive as me, or your father."

"What are you talking about? I'm sick of your rubbish." She tried to stand up, couldn't. "Help me up."

"Your father was old," said Mal, shuffling to her

side. "The EMTs said he died of natural causes because he did. It was unnatural causes that were keeping him alive. I've known your father for hundreds of years. He was one of the oldest. From Ethiopia, like your mother, but with pale skin and hair that could 'pass'." Mal put a papery hand under her armpit. "It was magic keeping him alive, like it keeps me alive, like it keeps those wights half-alive. They're just like me and your dad, only not as good at it."

"Magic is more than just scarves and coin tricks, isn't it?" She raised her arms from the shoulder, her wrists still uncooperatively limp. "What the hell haven't you been telling me?"

"Let's get to that pub. It's a long story, and I could use a drink." Despite his withered appearance, some sinewy strength remained. He hauled her up and slung her arm around his shoulders.

"Get off of me!" She flung her arm down, staggered, but managed to lean upright against the wall. "I'll walk on my own."

"Suit yourself." He wiped his face with his soiled handkerchief and threw the bloody mess into the low metal bin by the wall. He stepped carefully around the swaying child's swing. Even iron chains were disturbed by the gang's arrival and departure. With each new step, his stride lengthened. He would not be mistaken for youth, but he straightened and his gait unfurled. Within a few paces, he was ten yards away.

"Mal." A resigned whisper, more curse than prayer. Louder, "Mal! I can't walk."

"I know." He stopped but didn't come back for her. He spoke loud enough for her to hear clearly across the distance. "They live on magic, but magic is dead."

"What?"

"The wights. Magic used to be. It was real. Your father didn't deceive you. Real magic is now just a dream. Like meritocracy, an ideal that perhaps existed once but no longer on this earth. Those stories, of djinns and vampires, sleeping spells and floating castles? All real, once upon a time. Dimly remembered for thousands of years, long buried, everlasting in fantasy and fairy tale. Your father and I were born in a time of magic, and we used it up.

"Towards the end, we made an agreement with the wights, and all the other magical beasts that still clung on. We ceded all right to magic to them, let them scavenge among the scraps and wisps of magic that remained, and so keep themselves, if not alive, then at least not dead. They agreed to leave us alone, and we agreed to never use any more magic, beyond self-preservation, on pain of being hunted down and killed. We had a covenant, and someone has broken it. They killed him for it."

"What?" Vic repeated. Could she take a step without falling?

"As I said to you before, my dear, it's not what, but why. I'll help you now, if you'll let me." She nodded sulkily. He helped her to the pub. "And not only why. Now, most especially, who?"

EVERY JOURNEY STARTS WITH A PRAYER

Vic makes a new friend, spends the wrong money, mocks the credulity of human nature, and changes the rules of the game

"Christ," she grunted, banging a balky knee on the side of a stool in the dark. Someone at the bar called out a late warning. Mal helped her to a seat.

"Bartender, what beer and whiskey can't cure?" asked Mal.

"There's no cure for," replied the bartender, looking up from two fat glasses under gleaming taps. "Two whiskeys? Every drink's a double." The interior of the bar was dim but warm, bar-front, stools, and banquets in the heavy oak that cued memories of a traditional pub, except for the clean floor and new sheen.

"Got any of the glens?" Mal had a hopeful look. Vic tried to stay upright on the tall stool without gripping the brass bar rail.

"Glenfiddich and Glenmorangie. But try the Oban."

"Indeed. Four Oban, doubles."

Vic chuckled despite herself, "Reminds me of a joke about blowjobs."

"Oh?" Mal looked at her, a laugh pre-loaded in his eyes.

"I'll tell you later." Vic eyed the four glass tumblers half-full with amber liquid.

"To health." They each drank the first glass in one go. The smooth alcohol left a smoky honey flavour in Vic's throat. Perhaps it was Mal's suggestion of cure, but as the whiskey tingle reached her stomach, the lingering pins-and-needles in her feet and hands vanished.

"You can taste the peat and the salt air. It's a natural tonic." Ruddy colour had also returned to Mal's cheeks. His skin seemed to thicken. The shine from the mosaic glass lamp behind the bartender caught Mal's earring but she couldn't see veins through the flap of his ear like in the alley before.

"There's magic still in certain spots, Vic." He had put his mouth close up against her ear to avoid being overheard. His breath tickled. "Stonehenge is used up, of course. My God, that was a powerful spot! What an orgy of consumption took place there. Hundred years of sorcery before the well ran dry. Now it's peat bogs, a few old caves, the South Pole, places where people aren't, that's where you'll find the last remnants. And sea foam!" Vic felt his eyes sparkle. "The sea is the last reservoir left. It's why we feel refreshed by a trip to the seaside, and why the oldies like to take a cruise." Vic didn't have the energy to point out the oddity of Mal referring to others as 'the oldies'. He continued in a rush, "The ancient mages didn't spend much time on salt water. Ships were poor and the depths too trackless. Will you be all right here for a mo'? And can you give me sixty pounds?"

It took a minute for the questions, hidden in the run of undifferentiated words, to sink in. Mal was waiting for an answer. "Sixty pounds," she spluttered.

"For the papers. Salim. I have to go get them." Mal used the patient tone of a nurse in the pediatric ward.

"Just take...whatever is left in there," she said, moving her chin microscopically to indicate the purse strap on her shoulder. She kept her eyes forward, staring at the shelved bottles. Mal's furtive fingers flashed in and out of the purse, notes hidden in a quickly folded square and covered by the shield of his palm. No one in the bar would have seen the pickpocketing. The bartender bellowed, "Oy, I thought you were going to pay," after Mal as he slipped out. Vic made a desultory head bob to indicate the bill should come to her. She sat at the bar and sang softly to herself, sipping on the second whisky. "In the presence of another world, a dreadful knowledge comes."

The pub was about half-full, customers milling between upholstered booths and bar stools. She sat for a while unmolested, but Vic's hope that four glasses would be a deterrent failed eventually. A slightly overstuffed patron made tsking noises at her black eye and sat in Mal's vacated seat.

"Did you hear about the MP for Cardiff?"

"Is this a joke?" Vic turned gingerly to face him. He looked to be in his mid-thirties, a gelled cowlick topping a kind face. Average shouldered with a strong hint of beer belly filling the front of a lilac poplin stripe shirt. It was the kind of smart casual thing you would wear out on a Saturday night if you weren't dancing or watching the football, and then wear it again to the office the following week. Clearly an extrovert, but he'd struggle to match a tie.

"Not a joke. She popped off this morning. Bit of a micro-light enthusiast. Went for a flight and got tangled in a high-tension line."

"That's awful."

"Seems it's the fourth one this week. Plaid Cymru." The speaker must have been a bit Welsh as he pronounced it 'plied come-ree'. His overture was interrupted by a loud halloo.

"My darling, I've returned!" Mal slipped neatly between the two stools of Vic and her new friend. He slapped a red bank-cheque delivery envelope down on the bar. His back was full in the face of Vic's temporary companion. The rough cotton of Mal's sweatshirt hood swept dangerously close to the other man's face, heights evened by the tall stool. "He gave me a bit of a hard time for stinking of whisky, but he's a good fellow." Mal shrugged off the hand placed on his shoulder without looking around. "Your face seems to have gotten a bit worse." He centred her gaze on his with a hand on her chin. "Has this gentleman been troubling you? I can help with that."

The stool emptied behind Mal on the magic word 'help'. Mal confirmed that their threesome was back to two with a sly glance. He leaned into Vic conspiratorially, "I meant about your face, not the fellow." Mal dipped his thumb in the last full whiskey and rubbed at the bruise on her cheek. "Was he friendly?" Vic felt a tingling feeling through her skin. "There, it's done."

"What do you mean, was he friendly? His pickup line was deadly." The bartender had rung up the bill on seeing Mal return. He tore off a thermal printed receipt and put the curl of paper on the bar next to the bank envelope with a meaningful look. Vic glanced at the black and white slip. She gave a low whistle. "Thirty two pounds. This will have to be you."

"A necessary indulgence, my dear. After a whiskey ministration, your cheek looks as soft and radiant as a cherub. A black cherub, mind you, with excellent skin. I have a confession to make." Vic had an intuition the confession would be financial, which Mal confirmed. "I left the house completely skint and nothing since has changed the situation. It's a cash business and what money I have is in the freezer at home, where I dare not go."

"Well, between the tube fares, your phone calls, and the sixty pounds for whatever you've gotten, I've only fourteen pounds left. Even if we wanted to use my ATM card, we maxed that out in the morning."

Mal reclaimed his stool and assumed a thoughtful pose, contemplating the light as it filtered through the whiskey in his glass. "I don't fancy doing dishes. What we need is a friend who can break into my bakery and liberate some funds. I fear, though, that might take more time than our bartender has patience." He drained the tumbler in a sweeping motion, the smooth movement quite opposite from the trembling ancient who had helped her from the alley and into the pub. "But there's good news: We've been found by one group chasing us and dealt with them. We've got new IDs with which to brazen out a fresh encounter with the law. I should think we can risk using a credit card." His face became a picture of innocence, "Do you have one?"

"Of course. Jeremy convinced me to get a VISA in 'his and her' names after a long stint of him being 'between work'. He wanted a bit of credit to take him through until his next gig." She looked wistfully into her purse, "I guess I need to cancel his."

Mal passed her credit card to the bartender and opened the red envelope. "Here, put this in your wallet, and hand me all of your old cards." An illicit thrill as Vic saw her own face on the UK driver's license of Amira Myron. Someone had done some photo-retouching – she was slimmer and darker, to hide the bruise. There was a Lloyds bank card in the same name. "No money on it today. Salim will get someone to open an account on Monday, then we can reprogram the magnetic strip to match, but it backs up your ID. Nothing fools the Man better than the lies they tell themselves. They might doubt the driver's license, but they when they see the bank card in the same name, they doubt their doubts." Mal dismounted with a jaunty "I'm just going for a slash, back in a sec." He walked towards the toilet at the other end of the saloon.

The bartender was taking a long time with the credit card machine. "Miss, I'm afraid your credit card is declined. Do you have another you'd like me to try?"

"Bastard," shot out of Vic's lips. "Not you, my ex-boyfriend," noting the bartender's narrowed eyes. "He must have gone on a shopping spree after I kicked him out." She groped around in her purse. Her hand encountered another card, tucked in what most people used as the cell-phone pocket. "Here, use this one. It's the emergency card my dad gave me for if I ever got into trouble."

Mal returned just as the bartender came back with

the receipt in a neat plastic clipboard. Mal looked at the card tucked under the spring at the top. "That's not the same card you gave him."

"No, it's my dad's card. Jeremy buggered up our joint one." She signed the receipt and did the customer vs. merchant copy minuet, re-pocketing her emergency card.

Mal turned to the bartender. "Have you ever come across a foolish girl?"

A charming, natural smile at last from the bartender. "Daily."

"This particular foolish girl has been consorting with some rough trade. You'll recall she came in with a bit of a bruise? She asked me, her uncle, to come down to London to try and extract her. She's pretty enough for a number of games. Looks like they've also done a bit of credit card fraud, you know, 'honest face, can walk into a bank'? You'll get your money, don't worry, but I think the cops might have some questions about who just swiped that last card. Worse than the cops, there's some bent characters who will sell her name if she does get picked up. I wouldn't want her being bailed out by the wrong blokes, if you know what I mean." Mal touched the bartender's arm at the elbow, half-confident, half-pleading. "Is there a way we can get out of the pub without being seen?"

"There's the beer cellar." Vic thought she heard a faint siren, like an echo of a distant call to prayer. The bartender lifted the counter flap and motioned them through. Below the taps was a grille the bartender swung up and out of the way, thick beer-wet fingers a claw. Vic saw a stubby metal ladder bolted to the side of a brick shaft. "Go down there, look for the ramp. There's a delivery trapdoor outside." The grille clanged shut above them. Rectangular shafts of light shone a grid through the grill onto the concrete floor. To one side, a row of stubby metal kegs sucked at the hoses dangling from the taps above. More kegs lay opposite, stacked in a rough pyramid four kegs high, five-wide at the base. The light through the grill sparkled off their silvery sides. A narrow passage ran between the tapped kegs and the reserve stack into darkness. The siren outside drew louder and steadied, whirling decibels speaking the universal language of pursuit.

"Shhhh," admonished Mal, leading her deeper into the cellar, out of the crosshairs of the grille. Vic noticed that though her heart was pumping furiously, her legs were steady. The light through the grill shifted and greyed as the barkeep stepped across it upstairs. They heard the bartender's side of an official-seeming conversation.

"No sir, they paid and left." Some murmurs. "A man and a woman. He said he was her uncle." An indistinct groan. "Four whiskeys, like it says on the bill." More murmurs, more strident. "I've no idea where they would go, they're not regulars." The creak of the counter flap lifting. "You're welcome to search the place. They've buggered off." A muffled bang as the flap fell back into place. Angry footsteps on the wooden floorboards in the main saloon.

"I can't believe he fell for that weak story," whispered Vic. "Uncle, my arse."

"Any story that plays to human nature is a strong one. He's chivalrous, believes the attractive damsel is in a spot of bother. He has to choose between authority or a bit of a lark. My only trick was to make him the hero. We all want to be the hero of the story."

She swore. "I think you used some kind of magic on him. Why wouldn't he give us up to the police? You flat out told him we cheated his VISA machine."

"You have no idea of the nature of magic. Besides, I'm all out. That year I stole from you is used up. It was pure, what's that phrase used these days, 'social engineering'. He gets to feel like he's put one over on the man, like he's part of the counter-culture, and we get to escape. You don't hide out for a couple of hundred years without learning some basic appeals."

"Well I think it's bullshit, and maybe even this story about you being older than Methuselah is pile of crap as well." She paused. "What did you steal from me?"

"You mean besides your heart, and your good nature?" She felt his warm hand on hers in the dark. "A year of your life."

Vic squeezed his hand as hard as she could, trying to roll his knuckles. Her whisper was venom, "No wonder I feel like you drained my juice box. You complete fuck. Tell me now why I don't just climb up this ladder, tell the police you're a crazy man who ought to be arrested, bury my father and go back to my reasonably decent job in Bristol on Monday. All you've done is spend my money, talk shite, and drag me further into shite."

"Bullshit, crap, fuck, and two shites?" Mal let her keep squeezing. "Keep quiet, and I'll tell you. We know who killed your father and we know why they killed him, but they got it wrong. Someone is out there, using what little magic there is left on an industrial scale. And I expect it's related to voting machines and poll results, or whatever your dad was investigating before he died. He was always much smarter than me. He probably got a scent of what was going on the same as the wights. And if you doubt that it's serious, think how long it took our loyal guardians in the Metropolitan police to arrive after you swiped that card? People are murdered every day. Somehow I don't think they all get the electronic watchdog that's on your father's portfolio." Though his voice was hushed, Vic could hear the anger. It reminded her of the time her father had told her off, while on the phone with their over-curious neighbours, handset pressed into his chest for moments of quiet spitting menace, interspersed with 'oh, really?' and 'is that so?' in normal tones when he held the receiver to his ear. But there wasn't a receiver. And perhaps there wasn't a normal, either. "Now you can go up there and spill your guts, take your warning like a good citizen, go back to upholstering sofas or whatever it is that you do and hope that what is likely to happen this election doesn't happen, or doesn't matter, or, you can stay with me. I believe elections do matter. The choice is yours." Vic's hard squeeze had lost its grip. The siren outside had gone off during their whispered conference. Not the dopplered decrescendo of a departure, but the truncated squelch of a dashboard switch. The police were still outside, or in the pub.

Vic gave him a level look. "If I'm to stay with you, you're going to have to help me understand a bit more of what has happened. Or else I will get you arrested. It's not your father who got killed. As for politicians, I could not give a toss. You're going to follow my lead. For your first trick, get us outside without getting nabbed."

THE NATURE OF MAGIC

Mal, fooled twice by Muhammad's daughter, sleeps away a death-defying journey and destroys a table to win a heart

"You know, in your mouth, 'citizen' sounds like a swear word." Vic managed to squeeze her head next to Mal's by standing higher up the slope of the keg ramp.

"Depends on the context. For example, this citizen," Mal said, jerking his eyes at the wedge of bike tyre pressed against the opening of the blocked keg trapdoor, "could be an arsehole, or, he could have thoughtfully considered that deliveries are done for the evening and since he'll have moved his bike after a quiet drink, the trapdoor is a sympathetic choice to lock his bike out of the way of fellow revelers on the pavement. Did he have to be so thorough with his cable, and use such a strong lock, though? That, that is the question."

The metal lid of the trapdoor was stuck at about

ten degrees, giving them a shallow periscope from the pavement out into the street. It was hard to tell whether the hubcaps opposite were a police car or not. No telltale flashing lights, or boots and cigarette butts, for that matter. "Well, my princess, what should your faithful servant do now?"

"Damn right you'll call me Amira from now on. I guess you'll have to get us back out through the bar."

"Done. And I'll repay you the year I took as well."

They waited in the well of light between the kegs. Mal put his legs out and propped his back against the exposed wall opposite the ramp. Vic sat between his legs, resting her back against his chest. He put his arms around her. They sat in silence, listening to the clink and murmur of the pub above them.

Minutes went by before the bartender's feet eclipsed the grill. The rhythm of his boots seemed harmless, slow shuffles when his hands were full of glasses, quick turns for the next order, a busy Saturday night restored. They stood. Mal climbed the ladder, stopping halfway to shoot a helpless look over his shoulder at Vic behind him.

"Gary," whispered Vic, "I read his nametag while waiting for you."

"Gary," said Mal, "sorry to trouble you. Seems the

keg ramp is blocked. Is the coast clear?"

Gary lifted the ramp and laughed at the two of them. "Some hero you are. I can see why the girl needs protecting, with a family like this." Mal laughed along with him, a brotherly admission of defeat. Gary and Mal together helped Vic up the last rung. As they went through the counter flap, Vic saw that Mal had somehow contrived to palm the wallet out of her purse.

"Gary, you've been a great help. You've prevented a great injustice. In fact, you've helped my niece out more than money can express. This is her last ten pounds. Please take it, with our thanks."

Gary pocketed the tenner but stood for a moment with palms flat on the bar. "You two are too odd of a pair to be criminals. I've been keeping bar for fifteen years, I can tell. And the squaddies left shortly after they came, so you can't be too important. Come back anytime. Rob Roy was an outlaw as well, he'd be happy to help."

Mal was making for the door. "Actually," inquired Vic, "can I borrow your phone?"

Watching Mal try to get comfortable on the trestle tables outside the pub was itself painful. It reminded

Vic of chimpanzees trying to eat out of a jar whose neck was wide enough for their open hand but too narrow for a fist full of nuts. They were alone on the street, the November night cold enough to drive even English drinkers indoors. Mal and Vic had their hoods up and their hands in pockets. Every few minutes, Mal would stand up, stamp his feet, do a little march around the tables chained to bolts along the edge of the pub. He was mid-lap when a late 90's Vauxhall hatchback pulled up to the double yellow line at the curb corner. The car subsided after a few seconds of dieseling. It was a mongrel, one side panel green against a more generally scratched and oxygen faded blue. The windscreen had a long scar etched as if someone had run a windscreen wiper without the blade. Both side windows were down in disdain of the cool night air.

Despite the shapeless coat and scarf, Mal could tell that the driver was young, female, and slim. He watched the tassel on her woolly bobble hat bounce for a brief moment as, head down, she moved a large pile of jetsam from the passenger seat to the rear bench, and then with an awkward shovel, over the seatback and into the hatch well. The back of the car shook with the tender fillip of exhausted springs.

Harmless, thought Mal, dismissing the driver and resuming his cold bench parade.

"Mal, you rude git. It's her!" called Vic. Vic stiffly unfolded herself from the bench and wrapped her arms in a fierce hug around the now animated driver. "Fats. Thank god you've come."

Mal marched over to the pair. "This is Fats? Some sort of an ironic nickname?"

The petite newcomer struggled free of the hug and pulled the Dr. Who scarf off of her face. "Short for Fatima." She was a bit breathless, from cold and the enthusiastic pressing. "My father. Was very taken. With Fatima Whitbread. Until he decided she must be a man. By then it was too late," she gasped. "And then I met Fatima, Whitbread that is, the real one, when I was covering a regional track meet. She's a lovely woman, has a sweet boy, all a bit of mystery really what the fuss was about, she's very nice." Mal endured the fire hose of words in bemused silence. Fatima carried on, syllables like cans off a conveyor belt, oxygen somehow miraculously absorbed mid-phrase, "So that's why I'm called Fats, and you must be the dickhead?"

Mal gave a small bow, "A gracious dickhead. Thank you for coming, Fatima. Please call me Mal."

"Call him Greg. And I'm Amira," said Vic, opening the front passenger door and pulling the seat forward.

"Not among friends, my dear. Fats seems quite harmless."

"Yeah, well, looks can be deceiving. Getting into this car is taking your life in your own hands."

They piled into the car. Fatima resumed her machine gun delivery, "Sorry about the cold, my brother told me that I've got a hole in the exhaust pipe, a rusted out spot under the cabin, so I've got to keep the windows down when I drive to keep from being poisoned by carbon monoxide, and can you fit in the back seat Mal, so I'm deadly curious, you sounded so hush-hush mysterious on the phone, I'll take you back to my place, but you can start telling me all about it on the drive, is this a one-way street, you'll never guess that I only made one wrong turning on the way here, don't even have to pay the Congestion Zone charges if I detour down this Sussex Gardens, that way we have a straight shot to West Ealing from Bayswater Road..." Mal had folded himself sideways on the narrow back-bench, instantly asleep.

When he woke, they were parked in the forecourt

of a semi-detached Victorian row-house. Victim of a generous layout, it had been converted from its single family better days into a mini-apartment building. The street was quiet, irregular hedges, large houses, enough street lights to pick out stray details but too few to give comfort. Fatima and Vic rolled up the windows while Mal extracted himself from the back. Fats wrestled a steering lock almost half her size onto the wheel. They went quietly up the stairs, Fatima making urgent hand gestures about sleeping neighbours. Even with boozy traffic, it had been a short journey, 9:45pm on a Saturday night. Fatima explained the need for silence at the entrance to her third floor walkup, "Mr. Krishnan in the ground floor flat is up at four thirty and asleep by eight. He gets quite stroppy if people make noise coming in after eight thirty. Have you ever been cursed at in Tamil? I'm sure it means something quite hideous, sounds quite ferocious, vata-kaynay-akka-olli-khussum-kala-nala-such-and-such."

The inside of the flat was diagonal ceilings and white paint, comfortable throws and blankets of mixed description on every surface. An alcove formed by the wide front bay window held a round pine table. Mal sat to avoid cracking his head. "A perfect place for a diminutive person," he observed.

"I prefer short. It's simpler." Fatima took a lap of the main room of the flat, turning on floor lamps and unpeeling her scarf. She draped it on the battered wooden side table pressed up against the laminated edge of the kitchen enclosure to the left of the stairs. After the tundra of the car, the rising heat of the top floor apartment was a cheerful relief. "And I like the flat, not far from the tube, can park my car out front and still be in London. But tell me, what's really going on? Sounds juicy."

"I expect Vic told you the good bits in the car. Are you some kind of reporter?"

"Strictly free-lance, which is to say, broke. But this is about friends, not a story. Victoria and I go back to grade school. When she said that she was lost and homeless in London, and didn't trust a soul other than me to turn to, well, here we are. It's all a bit flattering really, 'Super-Fatima, saving the day!'" With the thick scarf and sweater off, her pixie form radiated happy honesty like an infra-red bulb, "Tell Superfats what really happened." Vic came out of the washroom and joined the two of them at the table.

Mal bridged his fingers. "What really happened is about a secret agreement that held good for forty years. I'm not sure we should be all bla-bla-bla around the dinner table about it. No doubt Victoria mentioned the political aspect, and with MPs dropping off like flies, it's quite clear that a certain amount of danger is involved."

"Danger," Fatima sneered, "danger is reporting on woman's rights in Kabul. Danger is piloting my embarrassment of an automobile into London traffic. Danger is walking while female in shorts in Quetta. A little bit of talk won't kill me."

Mal rubbed his hands slowly down his nose and cheeks, pulling ruddy skin downwards into an exaggerated grimace. He looked out the window and spoke, "Victoria. Be very sure of your friend. Once Pandora's box is opened, there will be more questions, and answers that would be unwise to make public. How much do you trust this girl?"

Vic stood from the table and slammed her head into a roof joist. She stumbled, bent double, onto the circular rug in the middle of the room, hands covering her head. "Ouch, shit, ouch. God damn it, Mal, just tell her. Fatima came and picked us up from some faux-Scottish pub in the middle of London on one phone call. I've known her for years. She's tough, tougher than my freaking skull. She's ok." Vic staggered to the worn loveseat on the sidewall, and curled up on it, one hand cradling the crown of her head like a cap.

"Very well." Mal sat up and inched his chair nearer to Fatima's at the round table. "Fatima, everything you know about magic is wrong."

"What do you mean, magic? Harry Houdini or Harry Potter? Because Vic's dad was a demon at the Houdini stuff, one time he went to kiss my hand and my ring was missing and then he asked me to check my back pocket and in it was my earring and then I touched my ears and hanging from the other earring was my finger ring, it was so exciting, he just..."

"Not that kind of magic," Mal interrupted, "Harry Potter magic."

"Right. And I'm the queen."

"It's real, Fats," Vic said, from the sofa.

"Really real? Harry Potter?" asked Fatima.

"It's real. Just not very available," said Mal.

Fatima clapped her hands and rocked forward in excitement. "I knew it, I knew it, you know Mr. Marrow was so so mysterious and handsome and cool, and, there was something magical about him, he had a shine, and you're one as well, I can tell, you're just like him..."

Mal enveloped her small hands in his own and held her forward over the table. "Fatima." She quietened, transfixed by Mal's serious look, plaster death mask brought to temporary life by urgent purpose. "Listen to me. Victoria's father was killed because of this. Allow me to explain, but, first, are you sure you want to know?" Fatima nodded slowly, her lips pressed together, eyes alternating between curiousity and joy.

Mal drew breath and sighed, "Magic is a fossil fuel. It accumulated thousands of years ago, perhaps millions, deposited unevenly over the Earth like oil. Some places were rich with it, Central America, England, Ireland. Some places were barren, like Mongolia and Siberia, wide expanses of arid land. We have tales of magic from pre-history because we encountered it long ago, in the same era our species discovered salt licks and tar pits. Humans then were like children, and like children can hear sounds beyond the normal range, there were a few of us who could sense it. Of those few, there were even fewer who could work with it, in the way that we can all smell gas off the marsh but most of us know nothing of how to use it for any purpose. I remember telling my childhood friends about certain hills that would have an unusual shine at dusk, certain caves that would echo with more than just the sound thrown at them. Along some shores, the moon-tide would ache with gentle phosphorescence. But they saw nothing, and heard nothing, and I didn't know what it was that I detected. In those days, the store of magic was overflowing, wells yearning to bubble up to the surface in an exuberant cascade. I wandered over the hills, with a flock of goats, and in every direction there was at least one spot that held greater significance. When I stood in those places, I was full of life. My arteries fizzed! But there was nothing I could do besides linger there, and eventually, when I had to move on, it was a small loss, forgettable, like stepping out of a sunbeam, a memory of a minor pleasure, no more.

"All this changed when the traveler Lan Tsai came to our village. To me, he glowed like the sun, a ferocious golden orb that I couldn't bear to look at directly. My friends, my family, all the people of the village observed him easily, in fact, they gave him close attention. A traveler with such unusual eyes and yellow skin had never before come to our small corner. I could not. I had to turn my face away. I tore a strip from the hem of my tunic to cover my eyes.

Seeing my behaviour, of course the traveler sought me out. When I tried to run, he performed a miracle, and impressed my fellow villagers to catch and hold me. As he drew closer I remember writhing in their grip, desperately trying to look away from his burning radiance, and then suddenly he went dark, as if a shield of smoked glass had interposed itself between me and his unholy bonfire. He explained to me that I could see ku, his term for magic, and he took me away to be his apprentice, and learn its ways, settling some gold on my parents as the price of making their child a magician's slave.

"Lan Tsai taught me the truth of magic, that it was fickle, ephemeral, quickly used up. Unless you continue to channel magic into a creation, it reverts to its mundane state. The coins he gave my parents I'm sure were dust before Lan and I had travelled a hundred miles. And in a way, magic is like opium. Once you get the taste, you have to keep using it, and yet the more you use the less rush you get, lost in a fantasy world of dreams until your supply runs out."

"At that time, Lan was almost two hundred years old, a wanderer for at least a century. When you could see him clearly, which was rare, as he loved to cover himself in glamours and charms, he looked like a young man, sometimes a young woman, perhaps twenty at most. He had left ancient China after waves of flying dragons and other miracles had burned off the scant magic in that resource poor place. He had first gone to India, which he told me was the biggest tragedy of all, a place over-rich with magic, plundered and strip mined by a few adepts who gave themselves blue skin and many arms, and set themselves up as gods. He taught me that magic had been so rich in India that even the peasants could see it like a standing wave upon the rice paddies, and that someone with the least talent could make themselves a giant or a demon. A single generation of magicians exhausted the stuff so quickly that the geology collapsed. In the north an entire river, warped and made 'holy' by great magics, drained into the soil and vanished, leaving a desert where people had once lived in numbers. He left that place in a hurry. By this time his own addiction was so great that he needed regular and large doses, far more than what was left in the sands of Gujarat.

"Fortunately for us both, he discovered that I had a singular talent. The magic secreted in different nooks to me had different scents. I became a finder and connoisseur of hidden pockets. I had perhaps one hundredth of his skill at manipulation, but I could search for magic, differentiate it in a way that was hidden from him, or her, depending on its mood. For Lan, magic was power. His only measure was 'how much?' For me, each deposit held a unique flavour. I lingered over each pool, savouring the small sips I could extract, trying to find ways to store little reservoirs from each source, returning to the tiniest of streams to taste their variations. Lan would stand by a waterfall and drink it down in a single gulp. In this way he was insatiable. He enjoyed the use of magic so much that, though preaching restraint to me, any sultan or sheik could convince him to raise a palace or magic a sword. Despite the lessons from his journey across Asia, he quickly hoovered up what magic remained in our crescent of the Middle East, making and then devouring manticores, burning what could have been a thousand years of sustenance in the creation of scores of fantastic genies, genies that carved whole towns out of the desert cliffs with hands as strong as a hundred men. He was in love with the sensation of magic coursing through him, and also the adulation of those not able to sense the play of magic in the folds of the earth. I was his scout, taking him deeper into the wastelands, not in search of water but of something else. We swallowed it all.

"By this time, other mages had discovered their talent, its fuel, and the trajectory of loss. A tremendous competition arose for what remained. Terrible battles were fought for the right to draw from certain reservoirs, which mostly ended in their full power being drawn out and expended in a foolish race to outduel the other. And so Lan, who thought himself immortal, died, not from an enemy's blow but by lingering too long in an area completely drained of power. Having exhausted everything he had, and without ready access to more, he reverted to what he truly was, a very old woman, feeble, thin skin peeling off his bones in the grit of a sandy wind. There was nothing of him left, in the end, his clothes, his jewels, his mounts and carriage all creations of magic, fading away to nothingness in the desert. I had lost track of years, but would have been just past my prime, perhaps as old as fifty. Of course, in those days, most humans didn't live so long. My family would have been long dead, if they even remembered me. There in the desert, in front of his crumbled bones, I looked very similar to how I do now. Fortunately, then, I didn't need magic to survive. So I became a harmless old man, and taught myself how to blend in, and make friends without charms or ensorcellments, and learned a few trades. And I used what little magic I could find to keep myself alive, in secret, moving from town to town when people questioned why I didn't seem to age as quickly as the rest, and always one eye out for the next golden traveler, bleeding power and consuming the meager store I needed to survive in a second's inconsiderate fury. I left Egypt when Moses depleted the remnants of an ancient, rich vein in eleven days of plagues and exodus. I landed in what is now Greece, an inhospitable place, a country whose elders had discovered magic early, raising giants and hurling thunderbolts in man's prehistory, until all that remained was a few decrepit sages in pockets of unusual sanctity and peace. I found one in a cave by a particularly beautiful bay. He told me a tale of Atlantis, a dead zone in the Mediterranean that even fish avoided, brought down in a decade by the hubris of sustaining false hectares, floating islands of palaces and temples. Atlantis was raised on a font of magic that welled up from a volcano beneath the sea. It turned off like a spigot when the magma hardened. My cave dweller had survived the inevitable dissolution and swam ashore here, finding a refuge in his cave with its small supply, enough to sustain his life, no more, and not enough to share. I moved on.

"Everywhere I went, I found a similar story, fantasies and legends of powerful magics told by people living in soulless patches, a dry sea of no-magic across Europe, rich in fairy tales, now dead to magic. I had refined my sensitivity to the point where even in this relative desert, I could find pockets. I spent a long time in the far north, in places the mages of simpler times had not explored, magic to them as abundant as the warmth of the sun on the Aegean. Occasionally I would find magicians, or magical creatures, like those wights, creations of magic, but of course they were jealous of what scraps were left and would take pains to make me leave. Until I met Victoria's father."

Vic sat up from where she had been listening on the small couch, "Where? When was this? Is that how my father died? He ran out of magic?"

Fatima had listened patiently at the round table, mouth open but silent. Her small, even, non-English teeth glistened with a wet flood of words held back. She pushed her chair away from the table. It screeched on the unpolished floorboards. The levee broke. "Vic, look, I can play a credulous fool, but I can't believe you're responding seriously to this crap. Magic, really? Greg or Mal or whatever his real name might be is obviously a con-artist and a huckster. I've seen a few. What is he, three hundred pounds into you, and now, Atlantis? Rubbish! I bet you told him your father died in an unusual way, so he spins some romantic fable. His story might be as old as human nature but for your own sake I think we need to throw him out. Now." Turning back to Mal, rapid-fire, flat and acrid, she said, "Magic is real, my arse. I've been lied to by idiots and arseholes from here to Kazakhstan. I gave you a hint and off to the races you went. And you can bloody well leave now." She pointed at the door. "You've gotten my friend into enough trouble. And you've surely spent enough of her money." Fatima's solemn face stood out against her colourful clothes and the cozy, chaotic flat.

Vic crossed to her friend, who was standing, shaking, by her chair. Vic gave her a one-armed hug, using the press of her hip and ribs to disarm Fatima's door-pointing finger. "It's ok, Fats. He can be full of crap. Scratch that, he is full of crap, but I think in this case, the magic bit is real. Despite all of my dad's protests to the contrary. Mal, show her something."

"I can't. Everything I took from you, I used up."

"How convenient," sneered Fatima, cheeks pale.

Mal snapped his fingers. "I can recharge. Do you have any whiskey? Or any fancy spirits, other than vodka? Not much magic in potatoes."

"I don't drink. Not even cooking brandy. And you're not helping your case by asking me for free booze."

"Then get me anything old. As old as possible. Something which might have caught some scraps over time. But preferably not something you'll miss."

"I can still throw you out, you know. Vic, speed dial 2 is police." Fatima stomped the short distance to the kitchen, her short form upright under the low beams that made the edge of the dormer window. Her stamping weight was too slight to make the floorboards do more than creak. Mal hid his smile in his long fingers, a light band of skin showing where he must have worn a fat ring.

Fatima tried and failed to keep a mean edge as she came out of the kitchen with half of a wooden spoon. She held it like a scepter, its bowl shallow and darkened by a thousand meals, the shaft an inch or two of truncated stump, with a jagged edge. "Try this." She skittered it across the pine table to where

Mal was seated. Mal touched the spoon. It revolved loopily on the table, as if he'd managed with one tap to find its centre-of-gravity. "My great-grandmother's cooking spoon. I broke it a month back trying to unstuck the blender but can't bear to part with it."

Mal regarded the spoon the way a communist would the Pope, part humility, part suspicion. He balanced it on his upraised palm and examined it closely, running his nose along its length. Fatima readied a sarcastic comment as he sat motionless, eyes closed, head bowed, a man holding a communion wafer up to a waiting sinner. Before she could speak, he opened his eyes. They were yellow, not yellowish around the edges but a deep rich gold iris. And then they blinked, and Mal's eyes were a normal dark brown, ordinary, the colour of a billion other eyes. During that blink, his hands had blurred and thrust the spoon through the table. A fraction of the bowl projected out of the centre of the table like the head of a wooden fish, or a miniature concert shell. The jagged handle was concealed inside the central shaft of the table's post. There was no break between the spoon and the table, the spoon's darkened wood a natural vein in one carving from a single block, slotted finer than any join visible to the eye.

Fatima leaned over the table and hooked her fingers around the projecting bill of the spoon. She tried to wiggle it back and forth. It was stuck fast. More ferocious tugs shifted the table slightly on its carpet, rucking the edge. Vic grabbed the table and settled the carpet with her foot. "Leave it, Fats. You've got a new centerpiece."

Mal put his head down on the table. Sweat dripped from his forehead. He was out cold. A small drop spilt from the white stubble on his cheek onto the smooth pine. They left him slumped at the table and sat down together on the couch. "What do you think?" Vic asked.

"I think it's fantastic. Fantastic as in unbelievable. Like Uri Geller spoon-bending unbelievable. But that's my spoon, in my table. I'm not sure what to think. And who cares what I think? No one would believe me anyway, I'm too activist for the mainstream news. But I will take the exclusive on anything real we discover."

"This is real. Really real. I need to hear the rest of his story. It's like my father is my father and a secret second person, completely hidden from who I think he is. Was."

"Look, I'm a reporter, I've seen all kinds of things. I don't trust this guy, Vics. But I'm open to hearing him out, when he wakes up. If he wakes up. He looks about a hundred years old."

"One hundred years old and hungry." Mal stretched and yawned at the table, "If you'll feed an old, tired conman, that is." He rubbed his eyes with the tips of two fingers. "And then we need to get to work. The cops we can deal with, the wights we've dealt with, but we still don't know who stirred up this mess in the first place. Fatima, I'll need you to run a few errands, perhaps rescue our clothes from Sainsbury's, take some money from me for a change, but do you by chance have anything to eat in the house? Furniture modification takes a lot out of me."

"We can call in for something. I'll get the takeout menus." Fatima was halfway to the kitchen when Vic's purse began to ring.

A CALL FROM CURIOUS GEORGE

*A monkey clarifies the political landscape, Mal
attends to some 'urgent business'*

Vic's purse made an antique telephone noise, the
rat-a-tat clang of a mechanical arm striking a double
bell. Fabric muffling only made it more incongruous.
She easily beat Mal in the footrace to her bag,
dropped on the floor when they had come in.

"What the hell is that, Vic?" shouted Mal. He was
as hot as when she had teased him about Israel. "I
watched you disable your phone. Are you daft?"

"It's my dad's phone," she said, scrabbling in the
bag. "I completely forgot I had taken it. Must have
got lost in there." She pulled a battered plastic phone
out of her bag, amplifying the ring. "Hello?"

A suspicious male voice, a bit high pitched.
"Linkoln? Who's this?"

Mal watched her stand straight and hold the
phone formally, an actor trying out for a bit part as a

receptionist. "This is Victoria Marrow. You've reached my father's phone, Abraham Marrow. Who is calling, please?"

"Is he there? Your dad?"

"I'm afraid he's not available. May I take a message?" Vic shook her free hand at Fatima, who ran into the kitchen and started pulling drawers, looking for a pen and paper.

"I need to speak to him urgently. His ears only."

"He's dead."

Up until this tidbit, George was in a happy place – the freshly painted third floor suite of a mostly-built office building in Birmingham, surrounded by plastic drop cloths and boxes of false ceiling tiles. The allen wrench for the modular desk he'd just assembled sat by his laptop. Its power supply balanced on a wooden spool of CAT5 cable, connected to a power strip hanging from the metal rails in the open ceiling. He'd spliced a new terminator onto one of the medusa's head of wires above his borrowed new desk. A disposable black cable ran from the ceiling cable tray into the side of his computer. An audio wire ran from the laptop to the thin headset wrapped around his head.

"Are you still there?" Vic's voice cut through the

flat silence of an IP phone connection.

"Yeah, I'm here. Dead, huh?"

"Yeah, dead. It sucks for me too. What was so urgent?" Fatima was trying to bring Vic pen and paper, but she couldn't get past a wildly gesticulating Mal. He was making throat-slitting gestures, pointing at the phone, and shaking his head. "Hey, is this line ok?" asked Vic, "Can someone trace this call?"

"Don't worry about it. I can erase your dad's cell phone log, and I'm calling you from a place that doesn't yet exist. Hang on." The line went dead in Vic's hand. She kept the phone clamped to one ear and swatted at Mal with the other. She pointed him at the table and walked into the kitchen where Fatima had found a pad.

The line came back. "We're fine. I've told British Telecom your phone is paired with a base station off the A355 in Windsor, and I'm standing in a new office building that just had its central trunk turned on for testing. It's free anonymous Internet via cable straight to the mother ship. Don't believe in Wifi, mate."

"Who are you?"

"Your dad called me Curious George. Call me George."

Vic wrote 'hacker friend' on Fatima's pad, "Ok, George, what have you got?"

"Hang on. Who are you, again?"

"Victoria. His daughter. The only living relative."

"And why should I trust you? Hang on again."

The same curious deadness, no sound at all, not even phone hiss. George came back faster this time.

"How's your credit?"

"Terrible. Thanks to a certain Jeremy Arsehole Gray."

"Right. That's you. Ok, look, none of this is official, you didn't hear it from me, alright? But Linkoln, I mean, your dad, right, he sent me this link, kind of a W-T-F-this guy, rootkit access to some terminal where..."

"George. You're not making sense to me. Rootkit?"

"Hacker shorthand. W-T-F, well, it's a request for me to check out what some guy is doing. So when I click the link I get remote access to a computer somewhere and I can watch what that guy types in. So I ran a video capture with a timestamp on my computer. When I checked the logs later he or she or it was doing some crazy stuff."

"What do you mean, crazy stuff, George?"

"This guy, whatever, they've got their own rootkit on Ipsos Mori's corporate network, they're logging into the election tracker poll database." Vic wrote 'ipsos mori' under the first line on the pad, Fatima standing on tiptoes to see over her shoulder. "So, ok, that makes sense, they want to know who's in the lead ahead of everyone else. By the way, I did a trace on the IP of their computer and they're logging in from a Westminster network, probably a PC in one of the offices within the government. Fine. Then I actually watched the database searches, and the guy doesn't care about who's actually ahead in any constituency, he's looking at all the seats where the Tories would come in close second. You know, if they took the vote today and they totaled up all the first and second preference votes, who would have been the first loser, which is strange, because it's supposed to be one of those first-past-the-post, winner-take-all things. So I rewound and took a look again, and the polling firms do a tricky thing where they ask people in the survey if they had to vote for someone other than their preferred candidate, who would it be, right?" Vic made go on noises into the phone. "So, if the winning person is Labour, you'd expect that the second preference would be somebody even further left, right, like the pinks or the raving monsters, but sometimes, they might like the Labour candidate as a person but still want to vote Conservative, or something like that. So the searches showed all the places where, if the winning guy wasn't there, the Tories would win a seat. You with me? Hang on, I need to reset the phone log, one sec." The line went dead again.

Fatima grabbed the pen and started writing questions on the pad. Before she could finish, George clicked back. "OK, so now your phone, I mean, your dad's phone, is on the A4 in Maidenhead. At least," he gave a snort, "that's what the base station records say. Where was I?"

"You were looking at the polling predictions."

"Yeah, spooky, right, so all these districts that were safe seats for somebody other than the Tories, but where the," his voice went higher, "second leading candidate was a Tory, I mean, you've already guessed it, right?"

"Spell it out for me, George."

"That's where all those MPs, you know, like your dad." The line went quieter. "Dead."

"Yeah, I thought that was where you were going."

"OK, so you've got Stuart Wheeler, Witney, Nasim

Khan, Tooting, Willie Brown, Glasgow, and then the gal in Cardiff last night, Andrea Wilmott." Vic could see him in her mind's eye counting them off on four fingers. "Those were the top four hits on the database search. But you know, all four of them, the death is strictly natural accident, right? I even hacked the hospital records, no signs of foul play for any of them except the guy in Glasgow – he had a blood alcohol level of 0.18 but apparently that wasn't too unusual for him. I even went into the Cardiff MP's bank records."

"George, what were you doing?"

"Look, I can't tell you and you didn't hear it from me. But anyway I've heard the winds around Cardiff are rough as guts so you'd have to be barmy to go up in a micro-light, but no, she's got debits going back a few years at the airstrip every couple of weeks or so. Girl was nuts to be flying, right, so none of this will stand up in court, yet natural or not, they're all dead. And just recently."

"It's not a coincidence. But do you know who's doing it?"

"Um." Several seconds of silence. "OK, so here's the thing, your dad was the one who got into this computer, spear-phishing, social-eng, I don't know how. I'm just following-along like. I don't know whose it is other than that it's on a network in Westminster. And once you hit the router it's impossible to say which office it is, and I'm standing here in a half-built office suite in paper suit and booties, you know, not like I'm about to start walking the halls of power going 'Anyone want to confess to a bit of scary mur-der, could have got clean away but instead you'll reveal yourself to me, eh?' I did a search on the hard drive but these things are all remote wiped at the end of the day, no local files, and a user name of office008 means it's probably a shared terminal. Hey, look, I've got to shut down, I've already been using this tester connection too long, some workman can come in here any minute now."

"George, who's next on the list?"

"Don't worry, I've already sent them an email to take a long vacation. 'Course I used a disposable account with a spoofed address. What I want to know is how did whoever is behind this do it? I mean, because apart from the deadness, it's bloody cool, cause some accident on command."

"I know George. It's like magic."

"Exactly. Except magic is what I do. All you need is a computer. In real life, it's not so easy. Look, this conversation didn't happen, I don't exist, and throw this telephone away. If you need me again, post a message to the twitter tag HonestAbe saying that you want to reach CuriousGeorge. I'll find you."

The phone clicked off before Vic could reply. She put it down on the counter. Mal immediately swooped with a pincer hand, smashed the plastic back plate on the counter edge, and scratched the SIM card and battery out of the case.

"Fatima, where's the nearest wheelie bin?"

"There's one in every forecourt."

"Thanks, be right back." Mal collected the bits of phone and took off running, pounding down the stairs.

"Mr. Krishnan!" yelled Fatima, but too late. Some muffled shouting, followed by the bang of the apartment house front door.

Victoria turned to her friend and filled her in on her tête-à-tête with George. "What do we do?"

"I'm not sure there's much we can do. It's not clear if it's the Tory party, one particular candidate, some crazy party worker, or even the PM himself. If we try and tell someone about it, they'll say we're barking." Fatima scratched the tip of her nose, "and I'd agree. I still think this whole thing is crazy."

"Yeah, well there's a spoon sticking out of your dining room table."

"I know. But even seeing it doesn't make me believe it. OK, look. I think we have to make a decision before your boyfriend gets back."

"He's not my boyfriend."

"And I don't believe in magic, so we're even. I say we ask our scarecrow magician why he didn't use his magic sniffer nose to track down the new magician like the others had tracked him down."

"What about the other MPs? I think we should try and alert them. I'm not exactly confident that an email from Curious George is giving them a fair chance."

Mal had left the apartment door open. His hands on their shoulders made both women jump. "Who said anything about being fair? And do you have twenty pounds? I found a payphone and ordered pizza. They must have had one in the oven. Seems he's here already."

HALLEY'S COMET

A religious conversion, a saucy time with a Spanish
wench, and a series of revelations

"Mal, you bastard." Vic put her hand to her chest, thankful it was only him and not a policeman.

"That's the second time you've called me that. I can assure you, my parents were most likely married at the time of my birth."

"Shut. Up!" The pen rolled off the counter and clattered in the gap, a mini-burst of applause for Fatima's interjection. "Sit. Down." She enunciated like Barbara Woodhouse talking to a pup. Mal and Vic sat side by side on the loveseat, schoolboys on a bench. "In a minute, I'm going downstairs, quietly, to meet the delivery boy, and when I get back, I think you," she pointed at Mal, "need to do a bit more explaining, or storytelling, or lying, or whatever it is you've started here tonight. I know my friend Vic's in two minds but she and I have to make a decision about trying to alert some other MPs, we've no idea who, or how, and all we think we know is that someone is using nefarious means to pop off these poor sods. If you and all the other magic users have been around so long, you should know who they are and how to find them. So, Mr. Magic person, before I go, this journalist wants to know – who are the usual suspects?"

Mal pulled a throw from the sofa arm over his legs, its tartan pattern giving the strong suggestion of a kilt. He spread his hands in defeat. "I'm as stumped as you are. Apart from Vic's father, well..." He shrugged, "I thought we were the last two. Your father was killed, which means there must be someone new. I thought that was impossible."

Fatima paced back and forth in the small living room, "Don't you talk to me about impossible."

"Fair enough. But can you take care of that downstairs business? It's much nicer warm." Fatima pressed her lips into a thin white line, shook her head once, and snuck off down the stairs. Her forty-five kilos made no impression on the thin risers.

They sat on the floor to eat, the table feeling off-limits with its spoon addition. Mal picked up where he left off. "Perhaps a better question than 'who?' might be, 'why aren't there more magicians?' You have to admit it is very strange. Only me and your father left? No one else was born with talent? There's reasons for that. It's not just that magic has run lean in the world, rather, it's especially because magic has run lean in the world that I don't see how anyone new could have learned to pick it up. There's not enough around for young people with talent to get a whiff of it, and there isn't enough to keep the old addicts going. I survived mainly because I was never really a heavy user. I wasn't good enough to build castles out of sand or raise the dead. So I never got the big hunger for it. From the beginning the only thing I had was an unusual sensitivity. Another interesting question you should be asking is how I and your father were able to stay alive, when everyone else couldn't.

"Abraham was one of the most powerful mages I encountered, and one of the oldest. Unlike Lan Tsai, he understood the lesson of those early, unrepentant days of loose magic. We used to tease him and call him the miser. My talent was finding magic. His talent was in hiding magic and storing it. He also used to practice needing less and less of it. He was fascinated by efficiency in the same way that hackers yearn for elegant code. When he saw rivals sucking dry the potency of a thousand year well simply to rain meteors down on each other, he went to ground. Weaned himself off of it. He used to make these little devices. He could catch magic in a bottle, or store it in a ring. I used up my last one of those when the wights showed up at the bakery, burned it clean off of my hand. Vic actually has one on right now, one of the largest reservoirs. Abraham's pearl ring."

"This is one of the things I don't understand, it's been troubling me. In fact, I think I may have it wrong who killed him. He, out of all of us, kept a private stash, magic saved over a thousand years in various tokens and trinkets, lockets and little bottles. No wight would have caught him without magic. No other magician could have caught him off guard, with more juice. And there aren't any other magicians I know of on this earth."

Vic had pulled one leg up underneath her, and was staring at the floor with a soft expression. Quietly, she asked him, "Tell me about meeting my father."

"Have you heard of 'peak oil'? 'Peak magic' must have been around 1000 AD. Of course, we didn't know it at the time. There were never that many of us, and we lived dangerous lives. The real collapse didn't happen until the Renaissance, somewhere in the 1500's or so. All those guys trying to turn lead into gold? They knew it had been done, but didn't have the puff. This was a desperate time for those of us who didn't age naturally. The Church was burning us all at the stake, and we'd exhausted the best part of what we needed to defend ourselves. There were some of us, from all over, a Roman, an Indian, a Celt, a gorgeous Negress like you, a Hebrew from Chelm. We had contrived secret means to stay in touch, post a bill on the door of this inn, hush-hush stuff. By necessity we had to stay both hidden and far away from each other. It was like a nuclear deterrence pact. If any one of us got too close for too long, we'd suck an area dry twice as fast. Worse, we'd be tempted to kill each other, strip the corpse, and hightail it before the authorities figured out what had happened. We didn't meet. Then a notice came out in a Paris paper that used some of the words of our various codes, and promising sanctuary and reward if we would agree just once to gather. We of course hated each other, players in our extreme form of beggar-thy-neighbor. We met under a dark star in Notre Dame Cathedral. A temporary peace, all of us suspicious and angry and ready to explode in flight or combat or escape. From out of a side vault came your father. That's how we met.

"He looked very similar to how you must remember him. Of course the clothes were different. Slight figure, physically unintimidating, but an air of calm authority, a certain credence that made us all give him a hearing. The first thing he did was give us each a token, a small medallion containing 'essence' as our reward for coming together. That's what he called it, not magic, but 'the essence'. He said that our time had passed, but if we agreed to work with him, we could make way for the new era in safety. It was he who first came up with the idea of the covenant, that if we would give up all but the most essential of magics, just enough to stay alive, he would help us conserve and extend what resources were left. He told us he had found a technique for storing magic, and the medallions were convincing proof. It was like giving a baggie to a junkie just as he's about to 'jones'. We could feel the heat inside them. I learned then that he had been keeping tabs on us all. Besides our gathering of seven, there were perhaps four or five others. How your father was able to track us, I'm still not sure, perhaps it was part of his devices. I never learned. But he told me that the Greek I had met in the cave many years earlier, his time had run out. Emir was probably the oldest of us left. There was a powerful mage dying slowly in a distant continent that we now call Australia, a few in the New World, living on the scraps left over from the Mayans, and the few like me in Europe, on the run from humanity, the Church, our own kind, and everything and everyone else. Not even a dozen. Those few normal fellows unlucky enough to 'discover' magic in that time were punished for their sins, or, their source ran dry so fast they never mastered it, and died of old age like everyone else. But of course instead of signing a covenant, we fought, we disagreed, we disbanded. He and I agreed to meet back in Notre Dame the next time the comet came again in the sky, if it ever would. The others took their medallions and fled. Or so I thought.

In 1682, Halley's comet came again. I was a long way from Paris, but I took the trek anyway, from what is now Nepal. And they were waiting for me, he and the Negress. They had formed a team. He had become Emir Ali, the fantastic fakir from Africa, an entertainer, a crowd pleaser. He cut a strange figure in front of the cathedral, waiting for me. His act must have been on for months. The Church was displeased, but as he wore a gold cross at his throat and tithed half of what he earned from the crowds each day, they let him be. What better way for a true magician to hide than as a charlatan and mountebank? He'd perform some tricks with sleight of hand, and then he would show the Cardinal the method later, in his chambers, to convince him it was dexterity, not witchcraft. That Cardinal became quite handy at coin tricks. When he died, they found unusual pockets in his vestments, and they say his corpse kept flicking the pennies off its own eyes. Your father taught me a thing or too as well. And the witch..." He stopped, half-apologetic. "Ladies, what should I call her?" he asked. "These days we're full of new terms, like chairperson or postal service staff."

"Just go on, I'm listening," said Fatima. She cleared the pizza boxes and joined Vic on the couch.

"So she, the witch, was his magic act assistant, juggling the cups, finding unusual tokens in the pockets of members of the crowd, passing the hat. Always smiling, always seething. Imagine a proud and capable woman, so black she was almost blue, dressed in motley and barefoot so that the crowd could laugh at the pale soles of her feet when she turned somersaults. She literally hissed when she saw me. At the time, I was dressed as a priest. I had to do some fancy maneuvering to keep the crowd from lynching the devil's assistant, a woman who tried to curse a man of god. But we got inside and found a place to speak more civilly."

"It was just us three. Emir Ali told me the Hebrew had seen a bad time coming and had hidden himself away in some kind of safe or crypt or clay coffin. The Roman had also contacted Ali. That fellow, Gaius, had discovered the trick I used on you, Vic, for extracting magic from living creatures. And it had come back to bite him. Gaius was being hunted, not by religious fanatics but by undead, creatures of magic that tracked him by his smell and hungered to consume him body and soul.

"In addition to fossil magic, there has always been some spark in every living soul. Apparently, Gaius fell in love with a woman and couldn't bear to see her age. Yet he knew that another magician in the world would only make his own time run out sooner. He desperately sought a new source of power. At first, he gathered up all the relics he could find, to harness the energy of objects so powerful, even brutes could feel it in them. He collected the shroud, the tooth, the holy fibula. But there wasn't enough. Most relics were fakes, anyway. So he set up experiments, and he perfected a new form of magic. Necromancy.

"This was a shameful period. He killed a very large number of people, setting off grim rumours and a wave of suspicion that drove me and the rest of the last of us even further underground. Have you ever wondered why vampire tales have lasted the longest, and seem to have the most recent history? It wasn't blood they were after. In his experiments, he accidentally created things, almost dead things, re-animated with life magic. In the process of being drained, a few clever people, perhaps ones with latent talent, could see and feel the process and turn it back on their attacker. Gaius panicked, and cast them out, but then they had already learned this one art. They began to prey on others.

"Ali swore me to secrecy, which was a fine joke. I had already discovered these things first hand! You see, for creatures who live on magic, Ali and I were great bonfires, beings of immense power, beacons almost too hot to see directly, the way old Lan Tsai had been to my childhood self. I had encountered one, a deliciously attractive Spanish girl. She was young, and had no obvious magic, at least, none she knew how to manipulate. She was able to manipulate me into her bedroom. And when we kissed, what a shock! But of course, she had never before encountered someone with my talent. I felt my life force draining away, but I could follow the trail and put it to work. I learned the trick and applied it back at her. She tried to draw out my spark even faster. It was a terrible race to see who could drain the other dry first. But I had been an apprentice to Lan Tsai, who could drink the ocean with a single sip. She exploded into dust, clogging my nostrils, covering my hair with a fine powder, half-blinding me. But that which had given her life, only sapped my strength. There was something peculiar about killing these creatures that left me also diminished. I wasn't able to taste or smell for a week."

"In a way, the Roman's discovery of the blackest magic should have ignited a new magical era, a death-fueled age of wonders, but his castoffs were untrained, mostly dead, with no one to teach them, and they also struggled for their own safety. Any town they frequented soon became crazed with fear. We who could teach them were literally deathly afraid of them. After the Spanish incident, I was on high alert. I refined the trick whenever I encountered

167

one. As long as I could touch their flesh, connect with exposed skin, I could rob them of their entire spirit. Over time, they too developed some sort of cabal or underground communication. Eventually they seemed to leave me alone, or at least, I encountered fewer of them. Gaius had asked Ali if he was willing to help him track them down and remove them from the world. This, Ali relayed to me in Paris. I'm not sure what your father decided. I felt it was all a bad business, and was selfishly pleased at our next meeting when Ali told me that Gaius had been killed by his own creations. This was in the late 1700's. The last true sorcerers of the world met anew at the cathedral. Again, Ali asked me to agree on a binding covenant, not to use magic, to conserve what little was left in the world, but I refused. By then magic had grown terribly weak, but we were very few, the only four or five who walked the earth, and I was proud and curious and perhaps more addicted than I cared to admit. The Celt had become like the Hebrew, self-entombed, having turned his back on the world. Ali said the Celt would join us again in the next cycle, in the hope that Ali's research into collecting magic would have improved. The Hindoo and I chose to wander. This was the Age of Exploration, and the

Earth was newly vast. I went off on a long voyage by ship, to the New World, and the Indian told us he was going to explore some temples in the south."

"In 1835, we met as five: Ali, his companion, myself, the Hindoo, and Martin the Celt. I had kept my wandering monk disguise, Ali and his companion, motley. But the other two were wild and disheveled, full of tales of constant combat, of being tracked for weeks by young vampires. I shared some of my defenses, but of course the real reason for our meet was Ali. He had made some progress. We conferenced for a week, sustained by vials Ali had prepared. But we argued constantly. Again he proposed that we, the last stewards of an ancient art, if we used the last drops, all knowledge would also die with us, that we had a duty to somehow turn away from magic, conserve not only our spirits but our knowledge. His plan had become more ambitious, for us to record the ways of magic in written form, to bury ourselves away with his devices in suspended animation, until such time as the world would be again ready for our new old art. He convinced Martin, but the sadhu and I would not. The world we lived in now was changing at a blinding pace, and also shrinking, with railroads and steamships reducing journeys of months to mere days. Fierce weapons and new constructions, engines of immense destruction, cannon balls that could throw down the walls of Jericho faster than any Joshua. I had been restored by my long sea voyages, and swore that no cave or tomb could be made safe enough to preserve us. So we went our separate ways."

"In 1910, we met beneath the Eiffel Tower, a final quartet of me, the Hindoo, Ali, and the witch. The Emir informed us that the crypts of both Martin and the Hebrew had been discovered and despoiled, their bodies reduced to ashes. All the other authors of power he had tracked or traced or heard of in the known world, which by now was the whole world, had vanished or been killed. Meanwhile, the Hindoo had reinvented himself. He was an ordinary looking man with a bushy mustache, in conventional clothes, crackling with life and youthful vitality. He had made it his mission to stamp out the children of Gaius, and gone on the offensive. He had found some way to feed on them before they fed on him, living on the second hand blood of the undead, scouring the world. He had largely succeeded in wiping them out. Tales of Dracula were only novels written to scare children, after-images of a vanished tribe. He told us that a stubborn few survived, and in fact had grown older, wiser. They were learning, but that by the next time we met, the Hindoo predicted they would all be gone. What he would do then to keep his youth we dared not speculate. Ali's wife argued that we should forget this foolishness and escape with her. She had discovered a rich source of magic. But it came with a catch – leaving this world behind. She had found a doorway to the kingdom of dreams, where anything is real, or nothing, and, as even small babies know, dreams are full of magic. Again, we quarreled and split up. The Hindoo had his quest. I, though scared of the mundane evil that seemed to lurk in every corner of this fast unrecognizable world, was too fond of my ways to depart from them. I left with a promise to meet again in 1986.

"I thought the two World Wars would kill us all, yet I got word around 1950 that Ali, his wife, the Hindoo, we had all made it through. The Hindoo had the easiest time. He had been stranded in Ceylon, and despite a dearth of magic had made it through without much conflict, blending into the population by making himself a village elder. Ali and his wife retired to the hideaway they had prepared for us in the 1800s. They took lonely decades in turn, standing guard in the far reaches of Norway, beyond Trondheim. I had been in the Americas, which would have been quite safe but for my own foolishness. I had grown fond of sea voyages, and sailed to Hawaii, one of the few places I had not yet been, just before the war in the Pacific. Still, the weather was nice.

"The Hindoo resumed his quest after the war. It seems that the chaos and conflict had given good cover to beasts, and their strength had soared in the '40s. What victims would be missed in the vast charnel house of a global war? I continued my wandering, becoming better and better at needing less and less, to the point where I could almost live on air and shoe leather. Somehow Ali tracked me down, from Argentina of all places. It was a good thing too, as I had settled in, enjoying a remote place with virgin supply of magic, a vein probably thousands of years old. He called me back with urgent news, saved me from the Falklands War. We met in London, the only place with convenient transport from the Malvinas at that time.

"This was 1974, forty years back. Truly, I don't think any period in history has had more hideous clothes. Ali had disturbing news. The Hindoo, one of the most powerful individuals the world had ever seen, was dead. Killed by the wights he hunted, who had grown fat on decades of conflict and death. He suggested we meet with the wights who killed him, and declare a truce, take up the covenant he'd been planning for generations, renounce our claims on the world. At last I agreed. We were prepared to give up all rights to using magic, in exchange for our being left alone, and for the wights to rein in their bloodlust. They should take a portion of magic only, not kill people, and therefore create more of themselves. His logic was plain. Natural magic was almost completely used up. We would only get weaker, while the wights, drawing from the spirit of an ever larger number of living things, would get stronger. Now was the time to strike a bargain, while we still retained some power, not for conservation, just survival. The world had become a too dangerous place. He also told me that he and his wife wanted to have children. During their years of tomb-side vigil, and then the wars, they had realized they longed for a different form of immortality."

Vic gave an involuntary shake here, but let him continue.

"I cursed them both, called them fools. I told them that if they had children, they'd be too tempted to

173

teach them magic, that they wouldn't bear to see their children age and die, and any bargain with the beasts would be broken. This was how the wights had come to be in the first place, when that idiot Gaius couldn't let his mistress go. We left on bad terms personally, but not before meeting the leader of the wights. We signed a deal in blood, that in exchange for peace Ali and I would never use magic beyond what we needed to stay alive. That was the covenant, me, your father, and the beasts."

"And the witch?" asked Fatima.

"At the last minute, she left – she refused! My angry prophecy had struck home. She said that she had no need of peace, and would instead defend herself against any that moved against her, and if she should choose to teach her children magic, let them be apart from the covenant. I knew this was the beginning of the end of their relationship – how can one partner make an agreement the other declines, and hope to remain together?

"I decided to stay on in England, to observe what happened. But years are long, even for someone like me, and I was never good at keeping touch. Life in the 80s became much more complicated, registrations and rules, laws and amendments, indexes and rosters that made my existence in the regular population harder to explain. Where had I gone to school? What happened to my birth certificate? I became a fugitive in the country whose passport I carried, as the birth dates in my official documents slowly became ridiculous. I do know that she and your father lasted ten more years. I got a letter from Ali that they had had a daughter.

"He said that children had destroyed them, and that he would raise you according to the agreement he had made. Lilith had left him, vanished into the realm of dreams. We didn't meet in 1986. What would have been the point? Paris was a ferry trip, a jaunt, not particularly exotic. He had you to look after. I was happy enough alone. And then you stumbled into my bakery, full of hurt and confusion."

AN APOLOGY, A SEDUCTION

Ages don't match the documents. Confessions lead to an apology, and a bit more

Victoria had listened to Mal's chronicle in silence. Once he finished, he noticed that she had pulled her knees into her chest and had been rocking back and forth with her hands tucked under her armpits, face wet, for some time. She could have been a stock photo for the hashtag '#upset'. They waited for Vic to speak.

"My mom."

"Yes?" His voice cracked.

"She's alive."

"Fatima, can you fetch us a tissue?" Mal asked. He bobbed and rotated like a Jewish Stevie Wonder. "Not sure, my dear. Perhaps?"

Fatima wordlessly held out a pizza company paper serviette. Vic didn't look up. "You knew her," she said.

Mal took a long breath and blew it out through puffed cheeks. "Look, I had an inkling of who you were the moment you came into the bakery, talking about your father and wearing his ring. I didn't want to use up the last one, but it has power inside it, locked up tight somehow. I could get juiced just holding your hand, although whether for that or for another reason I'm not sure." He held up a hand, forestalling her angry look.

"But I had a terrible choice as soon as you told me your mother had died in childbirth, not quite Sophie's Choice, but a Scylla and Charybdis nonetheless. I could tell you I recognized you, that I knew your mom and she obviously doesn't want anything to do with you because she ran off and left your father over a fight over something that doesn't exist and I certainly can't talk about without you thinking I'm crazy. Worse, this-woman-your-mother clearly hasn't made any effort to contact you for any of your thirty years. That was option one. So I took option two, to leave you in relatively happy ignorance and let it be."

Victoria held his gaze, and said "Twenty nine."

"I'm sorry?"

"I'm twenty nine."

"Oh." Mal looked to Fatima for help, but none came. "Salim made you thirty on the license."

"I know. For another week, it's ok."

"I don't follow."

"I turn thirty next Sunday. My father and I were going to get together. We had an idea to come to London, see 'A Chorus Line', perhaps watch Jeremy in rehearsals if he got the part. My dad never wanted to see Shakespeare," she trailed off.

Fatima sat down next to Vic on the floor, arms around her. The two women made a tribe, Fatima holding a rough paper tissue to the other's face.

"Victoria, I'm sorry." Mal's voice was mild. "I'm sorry for not telling you, I'm sorry you've gotten into this, I'm sorry you've had to find out your family history this way, you deserve better. I'm sorry I haven't been more grateful to you and your friend for also helping me out of a jam, I'm sorry your friend doesn't like me but I hope she's still going to put us up tonight. I'm not good at this stuff. I've spent a very very long time alone. You watch scores of people you love grow old and die and you lose the part of yourself that is allowed to care so much. I'm sorry I'm not particularly close to my best right now, when you obviously need better. These last two days have been a tad disruptive and I haven't been behaving with my usual…"

Fatima looked up. "Arseholeness?"

"I was going to say panache. In part because I'm completely knackered. I expect Vic told you about the events of last night. So, whether you accept my apology or not, I'm going to clean up a bit and make myself comfortable on the couch, thank you very much Ms. Fatima, and pass out."

Fatima stood up, "Look, that last comment was a cheap shot, of course you can stay, at least until Vic throws you out, and there is no way I'm going to allow you to squeeze your six foot plus onto my tiny couch, not while I'm an undefeated five and oh, that is, five foot zero to your six three, it's a love seat, take the bed for god's sake, the sheets are mostly clean. There are spare toothbrushes in the medicine cabinet, towels in the wicker hamper, give me a minute to get Vic cleaned up a bit. If you could break down the pizza boxes and take them out to the blue bin on the corner I'd appreciate it, just, be a little discreet, I have to live here and the other lodgers don't like to listen to the stairs taking a pounding." Mal got a little breathless just listening.

He had to knock to get back in. Mal had left the front door of the building on the latch but, learning, Fatima had bolted the apartment door. After letting him cool his heels for a moment, Fatima opened the door. She was wearing pink pajamas printed with flying pigs. "I know, they're from the kid section, but that's what fits the best, what can I say?" Fatima used a new blue toothbrush in its retail plastic and cardboard bubble box to point him to the apartment's only bedroom. "I gave her an old t-shirt, just go on in." He took the proffered toothbrush and obeyed, noticing happily that Fatima had fixed herself a pillow and a fresh series of blankets on the couch.

Fatima's apartment was a simple rectangle with a cut-out for the stairs. The building had too few floors to qualify the roof as a penthouse. Instead, her front door simply topped the last half flight, opening directly into a living-dining. If you entered and made a hard left turn, you found a reasonable kitchen that might have been called a galley if it actually led somewhere besides the free standing oven under the eave. Across from the front door was another door that led to the loo and bedroom 'nook', a fancy way of saying that there was no door between the toilet and the bedroom. Thankfully, partitions blocked the view from the toilet to the bed and vice versa. There was no closet. The sharp angle of the roof meant that unless you were Fatima's height, you were mostly lying down. Mal made for the bathroom, Should he call it a beeline, he thought, if it was really a pee line?

Mal heard Vic opening drawers and padding around the bedroom. He looked up from washing his face to check his look in the mirror. Some food and rest and the grey hair was back to black. He called out to her, "Darling, what did Fatima mean by 'mostly clean'?"

"It's a friend's way of saying she won't mind."

Mal tried to contemplate this, but his full mental energies were required to maneuver around the shower cubicle, washbasin, and toilet without banging his head on the roof. He turned the corner. It took several seconds to process that Vic wasn't wearing Fatima's old t-shirt. "Your panties have bananas in pyjamas on them."

"What were you expecting, a light socket?" She stepped out of her panties and lay naked on the bed, her arm behind her head. He'd later claim the thing he noticed next was that she had painted her toenails a dark chocolate, but they both know he lied. Skin smooth with youth, nicely covered, neither fat nor athletically muscular, a slight spread to the belly the way that honey bells off a spoon, tight curls of hair and the deeper brown shades that matched her smiling lips.

He didn't move. She sat up on the edge of her bed and held out her arms, palms down, hands offered to be taken. "I don't bite. Much."

"I'm too old. And a bastard, remember?"

"Even so. You've improved a little. My boyfriend hit me, my father died, we've been attacked by god knows what, my mother apparently hates me." Her arms fell limp. "I could use a bit of affection. Come to bed."

"Your friend Fatima is just outside the door."

"She and I have enough history, it's all right." Still he held back. "What? So many sweet young things throw themselves at you? Am I not desirable?"

"No, I mean, yes, you're a lovely, attractive, very desirable, extremely naked, very, very desirable woman." Mal pulled off his shirt and threw it behind him. The tattoo on his left pec was a Chinese dragon. It curled down his collarbone under salt-and-pepper hair. There was a hint of another tattoo peeking over the top of his black jeans.

She put on a sexy smile, "Tell me again."

Mal stopped unbuttoning his jeans. "Hmmm. Desirable..." He grabbed her by the wrists and pushed her back into the bed. "Let me get a good look at your twenty nine year old self." Her feet were on the floor, knees bent over the end of the mattress.

"I think your secret is your knees. Very smooth knees, not particularly lumpy." She blinked, twice, and he ran his hand from her knee to the inside of her pelvis. "Goodly long legs, considering your height. And gorgeous skin. Very smooth." He traced an eight in her curly hair and up her stomach. "A womanly figure, with the most delicious belly, slightly rounded. Luscious." He parted her knees with his hips and moved between them, the dragon on his chest seeming to breathe as his muscles shifted. She noticed that hair ran from his wiry chest to the triangle of pale olive skin exposed by the open waistband. If anything, she thought, he was an older, skinnier Roger Federer, minus the nice suits. Wide shoulders and trim solid flesh. He took his weight with one hand on the mattress and cupped her breast with the other. "I think you know how delightful these are." She was smiling properly now. "You have the most adorable face when you smile."

"What's that supposed to mean?"

"It means I want to see you smile more often." He pushed off the bed to tug down his jeans.

She laughed. "Is that what I bought you?"

The red low-rise briefs were flare bright. Mal mumbled a terse 'yes'. The tight fabric confirmed his high opinion of her. "I've got to take these off. And my socks."

When he stood up again he was as naked as her, the tattoo on his hip revealed as an ankh stretching halfway down his thigh. He looked 'older', not old, wrinkles from a life outdoors rather than age. His muscles were clear beneath the skin, all strength and tendons.

"You can touch the hair now," she said.

"I have been curious."

Afterwards they lay together with the light on, on top of the duvet, she inside his arm, head on his shoulder. Her breasts puddled against his ribs. She made idle circles on his chest with a relaxed finger, twirling loops in his soft chest hair. She asked him, sleepily, "How many problems get solved late at night, by naked people?"

"How many more get created?"

She slapped his chest lightly. "What are we going

to do?"

"I was thinking of waiting a few minutes, and then doing that again."

"No, I mean about politicians, this mess, our lives." She ran her hand across his stomach.

"Big questions are hard to think about when you've got your hand on my penis."

"I am trying to help you concentrate. Don't all men keep their brains down there?"

"That may well be true." Mal shifted his hips. "But I'm not all men. And while this probably isn't the time to bring it up, I think our next move is to go see your mother."

She stopped her hand. "What the hell, Mal?"

"Your friend Fatima asked me to round up the usual suspects. Well, there's still one left besides me. In fact, your mother is the only one with any real power left."

Vic raised herself awkwardly in bed. "An hour ago I didn't know she existed. You thought it best not to tell me about her. Now you want to go see her?" She stared into his face. He stared back. "OK, fine, I suppose I can accept that. Care to tell me how we're going to pull this off?"

"Well, that part is simple. I'll need to borrow a bit

of juice from your pearl ring. And then we go to sleep. She is, or at least was, the Queen of Dreams."

THE NIGHT TRAIN

One's not keen to meet a lover's mother, curious things happen in the nighttime, and enquiries on the small matter of abandonment

Vic rolled over on top of Mal. She pressed the weight of her body into him, enjoying the feeling of control. "So explain to me how exactly we're going to do this, again?"

"Well first you're going to have to be less distracting. I can feel every inch of you, including some invitingly soft inches."

She stole a lingering kiss and rolled off him. "I didn't exactly beg to get you naked."

"Right. I'd put those briefs on again, but they are ridiculous. Just lie there and listen for a minute."

"Every man's dream."

"Impertinence. OK, um, where to begin." Vic was still making eyes at him. "Stop that. Listen. Ah, around the turn of the last century, your mother

Lilith discovered something important. If magic is the very essence of unreal, then dreams might be the essence of magic. Anything is possible in dreams, as you very well know. It was Lilith who put these ideas together, and found a way in. But like all things magical, it's not straightforward. To leave this world, you have to enter through someone else's dreams. And that of course, takes a lot of magic. Apparently, getting back takes even more, but in the realm of dreams, magic is not exactly rationed."

"OK, so I'm the dreamer and you're the magician. Where's the problem?"

"I've never actually done it."

"Oh." Vic abandoned flirting. She searched along the side of the bed for some clothes. "I thought you were Mister 'Been everywhere, done everything'. And everyone, for that matter."

"You weren't complaining about my experience a few moments ago."

"True. But you didn't have cold feet then."

"Look, it's..." He trailed off. "Your mother. She and I. She's not a fan of me. More of a hatred, really. So I've stayed off her turf."

"You do tend to inspire some strong feelings. Any reason for this particular harsh opinion?"

"The usual. She looks like you. Or, rather, you resemble her, which stands to reason."

"That, and all black women look alike to you folk."

"No, it's true. She is definitely your mother." He quickly added, "Not that I've seen her this closely."

"So you made a pass."

"One or two. Which were not well received. And while it was real disagreement and not just because I'd got the cold shoulder, I argued against her plans and ideas. All of them. Which was unlucky. Or poor coincidence."

"I could see a woman not trusting that." She laughed, wet tongue flickering. "How did my dad take it, you being on the pull for his wife?"

"Well, one of Emir Ali's charms was that he always saw me as a whole person. Not that either one of us is Italian, but he understood that I couldn't be around a beautiful woman for more than five minutes without trying one on. And he was completely and correctly confident. I mean, compared to him, I was a harmless buffoon. He later told me he figured she could handle herself. And I agreed – it was always Lilith I worried about, or rather, I worried I'd get it in the neck from her. Add to this that I'm fornicating with her daughter. Nor does it help that I'm the one to explain our story to you, and not in the most flattering light for her."

"Yes." Vic put on his t-shirt. The point of her collarbone poked out through the collar, and the crosshairs of the beaver hunter were sighted over her right breast. "So I shouldn't be surprised if she's not thrilled to see you."

"That, and let's keep certain, how would one say, 'facts of life', to ourselves, shall we? One other thing. What happens in dreams isn't true, of course, which means that you can't trust anything you see, or hear. While there may be some truth in it, or it might feel like the revealed truth, it's only a dream. At least, that's what your father told me. So if something awful happens, it may or may not be. Just try and be patient and relaxed and let events unfold."

"Anything else?"

"I need to wear your ring. And where is the light switch?"

"On the crate, the bed side table. The ring, not the switch. It's a floor lamp, no wall switch. And I'm not getting up to turn it off." He got out of bed, kissed her chastely on the forehead, palmed the ring, and turned off the light. Vic felt the bed compress with his weight in the dark. She wondered if she would have trouble falling asleep, and, for a brief moment, whether shifting from Jeremy to Mallory was an upgrade or not. As she compiled a relative mental checklist of their attributes – paleness, attentiveness, kindness, rudeness, she missed the moment when she was already asleep.

"You're rude and kind. It doesn't make sense. People should be one or the other, but not both." Vic was shouting at him from her seat opposite. The cabin shuddered and swayed from side to side to the beat of iron rails below them, vibrating through the rattan-covered benches. It was an old-fashioned sleeping car train, a couchette. Bright, vague light pumped through drawn window shades. Vic looked down to see that she was wearing a Mary Poppins outfit, fitted travelling coat, long skirt, white lace, and high buttoned boots. Mal wore a rough wool suit, three-piece, but not formal, business-like, with a high waist and a careless burgundy cravat. He was mouthing something back at her but she couldn't hear over the noise of the bogies. He tapped the knee of the man sitting next to her, dressed in a similar style, and swapped benches to sit beside her.

"At last you're awake."

"Where are we?" she asked. Before he could answer there was a knock on the wood cabin door. Through its wavy glass window, they saw a hazed image of a peaked cap. The metal latch on their side of the door moved by itself. Vic grabbed Mal's knee, relaxing when she saw that the latch was joined by a cylinder to an identical latch on the outside of the door. A man in uniform filled the narrow doorway, mustache, brass buttons and epaulets gleaming.

"Ticket Collector, TC, tickets and travel documents, please."

"What tickets?" she hissed at Mal.

"It's a dream," said Mal, "I can take care of it." He reached inside his suit coat and flourished two paperback-book-sized folios in red leather, yellow cardboard tickets peeking out the tops. In the cut out window of the first cover, she saw her name written neatly in a graceful schoolgirl cursive and wondered if she knew how to write like that. The two other passengers in the compartment stared at Mal's passports. Their travel documents were green. But the TC collected all four without complaint, and held them in a thick stack under his wooden ledger board. A sheaf of onion skin paper was tied to the board with yarn run through two punched holes in the wood. The TC ran his finger down the list until he found the compartment number. He opened the stitched passports one at a time, turning the stiff pasteboard pages carefully, a monk reading from a newly discovered illuminated manuscript. The whole process lasted about two minutes, the TC flipping thin pages and consulting a small manual from his back pocket as the glare of what must have been a late afternoon sun faded from the drawn windows, leaving only blackness. It was almost unbearable.

She remembered when she'd taken an HIV test at university. You knew there was nothing wrong, the results would be negative, but from the moment the procedure started it was somehow, 'what if?' A hundred imagined deaths went strangely unrelieved when the results came back, safe. It had taken days for the emotional response to leak out of her bloodstream. She had that same spiky feeling now. The TC passed their co-passengers' documents back, but lingered on theirs.

He handed Vic's folio directly to her, keeping Mal's under his board. There were round spectacles without earpieces balanced on his nose, a cord fastened between the frame and a button on his chest. The flat lenses turned opaque as he changed angle, looking down at Mal with curdled lips. "I'm afraid, sir, your tickets are properly paid but in the wrong names. Says here on the list, one Ms. Victoria Yohannes and lover. In cross-checking currently registered lovers for Ms. Yohannes, there's a Jeremy Gray with an A, G-R-A-Y, no fixed abode, and definitely not Mallory Golden. Sir, you'll have to exit the train."

"Wait!" Vic snatched at the ledger board. Her grasp fell short, the board high above her head. The TC had grown gigantically large, more than twenty feet tall. The shins of his trousers were level with her head. There was a loud whistling noise and she looked up to see that the roof of the compartment had vanished. Black sky and stars surrounded the TC's gargantuan hat, snatched away by a raging wind. A patch of ginger comb-over flapped atop his head like the loose hatch of a cargo ship. The giant ticket collector smiled, a row of even tombstone teeth. It reached one monstrous hand down into the compartment and plucked Mal up by the neck of his suit coat. In a micro-second strobe picture, Mal was gone, flicked out into the night. The TC continued to grow, the swelling tops of his black polished shoes lifting the benches up and pinning Vic and her two remaining companions into the wall. The huge hand came down again, dipping into the open carriage box the way a child might rummage for the last candy in the bag. Vic felt her head enveloped by flesh, and then she was outside, free-falling in night.

Below her was a train track suspended in space, no countryside, no landscape, just an iron coil hardly visible amid blackness and pinpricks of light, not stars but a crude parody, poked holes in a sheet of black velvet that obscured any landmark. She felt nauseous with the sensation of falling quickly, yet the train descended even faster away from her, no engine, only passenger cars, the space where the front compartment of the second car should be topped by the torso of the nightmare TC. He rode the car down to blackness, red hair whipping in the howling wind. The track plunged ever deeper into void, taking the train further away from Vic. She spiraled through a few faint wisps of clouds, or mist. Buffeted by wind, she spun away from the train. Mal was gone.

All she could feel was the wind. No bearings, no directions, no up or down, lost in a deafening hurricane, the sensation of furious motion within an invisible tempest. A few dots of light in the distance spun crazily, so confusing as to make her stop seeing. She tried to speak but, unable to hear her voice above the rushing air, just moved her lips, making the shapes of the words 'it's-only-a-dream', 'it's-only-a-dream'. Her hair was itching. She put her hand to her forehead and crushed a spider. She was covered in spiders. Thousands of tiny spiders. She grabbed a handful and threw them into space. They sailed off, trailing gossamer threads, abseilers attached to her hair, her skin, her frantic fingers, spiders pulling themselves back along their threads or being whipsawed by the wind and wrapping around her more securely than they could have woven. They streamed down from her hair, covering her face in silk, threads enclosing her mouth and nose, her ears. And then it was quiet, the white threads blotting out all light and sound. Her limbs were trapped in place, insubstantial fibres assembling a legion of concrete.

Inside the cocoon, the sensation of motion stopped, her inner ears unreliable. How long had she been falling from the train? Cursing herself, she began to cry.

Where her tears touched the spider silk, it dissolved. A scene emerged from the edges of her eyes. She was no longer falling, no longer in space. In fact, she was lying on an elaborate carpet, in a brightly lit room, a palace. It could have been a throne room, with rich embroideries on the floor and walls, but instead of courtiers there were giant spiders with the torsos and heads of men like eight-legged centaurs, surrounding a giant African woman. The queen was large and naked, ebony breasts hanging low over a wide round stomach. Vic was still immobile but not scared. Is this what I'll look like after forty kilos and too much time in the sun, she wondered. The queen and I could model for a fertility statue catalogue. Vic found herself humming, one of her father's tunes, seasons don't fear the reaper, nor do the wind, the sun, or the rain, and she had no fear.

And then Mal walked in, from somewhere to her left. With her new calm, the tears had stopped flowing, leaving the rest of her silk cage intact. She couldn't turn her head to spot from where he made his entrance. He was still in the suit from the train, grander and finer somehow, more piping and a black satin band added to the lapels. He gleamed with energy, fit and solid. And young! Lustrous black hair, a handsome man in full command. He walked forward confidently, knelt in front of the naked queen, and greeted her formally. "Lilith, my queen, my rival is dead. I have come to claim my place beside you. Raise me up as your king."

"At last," the queen replied. Vic was startled. Her mother's voice was just like her own. Shouldn't be too surprised, she thought. Lilith stood and lifted Mal up by his chin, holding him in space with an arm both fat and strong. She pulled him into a long kiss. A feeling of emptiness embraced Vic. I should be angry, she thought. Perhaps being stuck in a cocoon muted feelings of shock and betrayal. Her mother and Mal parted after an age. Set down, Mal licked his lips and described to Lilith his struggle to find Emir Ali, who he called the rightful king. Mal told how he had stirred up trouble in England to create conditions where Ali could be surprised, and killed. Vic stopped listening. Something was sliding along the inside of the cocoon. A slithery sensation traveled up to her neck, dry and cool and slightly rough.

She felt the tongue of a snake flick out and touch the butterfly back of the her earring. The snake's voice was papery, "Took me ages to find you again." It was familiar, the snake's voice, like Mal's, but more sibilant. "Remember, nothing is real."

"I know. Mal told me. After kissing me. Before kissing my mother."

"That's not me."

"How do you mean?"

"I'm Mal. That's some dumb show she's putting on for you."

"Why would she do that?"

"She hates me, remember? Wants me to be the bad guy."

"Why should I believe you're you and not that guy? Or believe you but not my own mother?"

"Who else but me would come back to you as a trouser snake?"

Vic had to smile, "That does sounds like the Mal I know. So now what?"

"Sit tight. I'll think of something."

"I can do nothing but," she said. Suited Mal walked over to where Vic lay on the floor. "Hide, he's coming," she whispered.

She felt a thin loop of the snake's body trickle down her side, then the snake voice again, "I've got a better idea. If I can get rid of the fake me, use the opportunity to talk to your mother in private.

Something you've been wanting to do for years, no?"

The duplicate Mal nudged the cocoon with his shoe, then bent over to look in the eyeholes. "My queen, she's awake," it said. Vic felt a burning on her neck. A mottled grey snake with golden eyes shot past her cheek, through the melted opening in the cocoon. The snake sank hooked teeth into the duplicate's neck, above the vest collar. She saw a small rattle on the tip of its tail swing past her fixed vantage point, Mal as snake hanging against the chest of Mal the suit. Then the knees of the suit were kneeling next to her head. She felt the duplicate collapse over her, covering her view. She heard a light rattle. The body on top of her bucked a few times, then went still.

"Drag those things away. Who let that snake in here? And stand up the girl."

With a skittle of chitinous legs, Vic was upright, held on either side by two of the queen's spider men. A third spat on the cocoon over her face. The silk smoked and steamed until it too melted away. She was still a prisoner, her head in an oval frame of white thread, but she felt better for being upright, with her face clear. Lilith stepped closer.

"What have you done with Mallory?" Vic demanded.

"Your first question to the mother you've never seen is about that man? I had higher hopes for you, Victoria," Lilith replied.

"So you know who I am?" Vic marveled at how calm her voice sounded.

"Of course. I gave you life. I see myself in you. And your father."

"So where have you been? Why didn't either of you tell me the truth? I love," Vic corrected herself, "I loved my father, but I wanted, I deserved a mother. Where were you?"

"I was here."

"But why didn't you come see me? Why did you let him tell me you were dead?"

"Because I was dead, to your world. I entered this realm shortly after you were born. And your sainted father forbid me to return."

"What do you mean?"

"Your father, Abraham Emir Ali, the most powerful magician the world has ever known, punished me. On pain of death, I was never to visit the real world again."

"Why?"

"Because I disobeyed him."

"How?"

"I would not agree to give up my magic."

"So instead you gave me up."

"Yes. I did. I gave up my only daughter so that I would not have to give up magic. I gave you up because I knew I could not bear to see you age and die in eighty years while I stayed eternally young. I gave you up because I would not trade my ten thousand years for a few decades on Earth. I gave you up because he forced me to. If you think me weak, so be it. I knew I was too weak to be with you for long and leave you again, so I too forbade myself to return. I gave you up to him, to myself, every minute I am alive I give you up again. And I was right to do it."

"He's dead. Come home with me."

"Emir Ali has been dead to me for almost thirty years. My home is here."

"And me? I'm here now. I need your help. There is another magician, someone new, I don't know who, killing British politicians. I need to know who they are so I can stop them."

"I can't help you."

"Can't? Or won't?"

"Does it matter?"

"Of course it matters. I matter. Your daughter matters! Weak or strong or selfish I just don't care, you've seen me now. I'm a grown woman. Don't you want to know who I am?"

"What difference will it make? In a moment, you will wake up, and this will be just a dream. You have no arts. Without Golden Eye, you will never find me again." Lilith turned away. "You cannot possibly understand. Your father forced me to make an impossible choice, between life or his desires, between the father of my children and the child he gave me. I have learned to harden myself against the temptation to see you, over and over again. I will go on."

"So that's it. You'll just blink twice and let the daughter you never knew go out of your life again. What am I to you, a disease?"

"You are what you are. A regret. A child of my younger self, the one who loved your father for more than six hundred years. A reminder of what I had to give up. A reproach. An independent woman who does not need me."

"How can you know that?"

"He told me."

"What?"

"Your father and I spoke every night. He came to me, and I to him, in my world, the world of dreams.

He was a handsome man. Didn't you find it curious that he never took another woman?"

"You try not to think about your father having sex. But I don't believe you."

"I'm your mother. Why would I lie to you?"

Vic woke up.

She reached in the dark for Mal, but she was alone in the bed. Why am I not surprised, she thought, as she fumbled for the lamp. "Fats," she yelled, "Fats! Wake up!" Vic stumbled into the living room. She could see by the faint light of the moon and streetlights through the bay window that the front door was locked but not bolted. The house key was lying on the floor before the door, exactly where it would be if someone had borrowed it, locked up from outside, and slid it underneath while she and Fatima slept. "He's gone, Fats."

Fatima was disoriented with sleep. "What? What happened?" She stirred on the couch, and rolled over, mumbling, "Go back to bed, it's too early."

"Wake up, Fats. The bastard left me. Scarpered. It's like a trend at the moment."

Fatima opened her eyes. "Not surprised." Her voice was fuzzy but stronger now. She was tuning into consciousness on an analog dial. "I knew he was a waste, didn't trust him. So what happened in there?" She nodded her head towards the bedroom door.

"About what you'd expect, except that I met my mother."

"Sounds kinky. I only heard two voices."

"Pretend you didn't listen. But seriously, I think I met my mother, or at least I dreamed I did, and she didn't want to help me either. I was hoping at least that bastard Mal wouldn't let me down. Now what?"

Fatima propped herself up on one elbow. "Well, Vixen, if we let men discourage us we'd commit suicide on a daily basis. Three weeks to the election, and like it or not we're the only people left who seem to think anything unusual is happening, or at least care about it. Not much choice..."

"We stop the buggers killing off MPs, win medals, find new men. But can it wait until," she looked at her wristwatch, "six AM?"

"No, it can't. I mean, you're right, it's bloody early, but we have to strategize. We need groceries."

A MILK RUN

Vic tracks down a faithless friend, Fatima cracks a joke

Victoria, forty minutes on the District line. Once one of the great train stations of the world, now an ungainly amalgamation of buses, tubes, trains, a plane-less air terminal, swept spaces and high ceilings. The two women bypassed the empire façade, gleaming gold in the low-angled dawn outside, and went straight from the tube station to the shopping plaza via the concourse escalators.

They reached Sainsbury's at 6:15AM. The tills were open, the main door's steel shutters rolled up neatly in cylindrical houses, ready for the Gatwick express bus muster. Victoria Place was lightly stirred by a pre-flight mélange of backpackers, early risers, and business flyers on the prowl for anything less than airport prices.

Across from Sainsbury's was an outdoor goods store with comfortable looking camp chairs, neat racks of puffy jackets, and matching space boots. It was all locked behind glass - the store didn't open until eight. They gave up on a stakeout and waded through the checkout rows. Searching for a counter with cardboard coffee cups, they took a slow roll down the aisles. Victoria station might not sleep, but Sainsbury's was, at best, slow to wake up. Most aisles held only drowsy stock clerks unpacking boxes. They reached one end of the brightly lit displays and doubled back.

"You're sure he's coming here? Now?" asked Fatima.

"No, I'm not sure. But he was up and out early, so this is my best first guess. Grab a basket. At least we can stock up."

"It's too early to think about food. That pizza last night, by the way, was awful, and not awful in the way we like."

Fatima nearly dropped her half-full basket when they saw the first customer. Vic put a calming hand on her elbow, "False alarm. This guy's hoody is the wrong colour. Nice to know you think he's coming too, though." They had picked a whimsical aisle leading towards the seafood counter when they saw him, unmistakably, gangly six foot plus with dark blue hood up. He had popped out from the back, trying to look nonchalant by a chiller. His posture screamed 'amateur shoplifter' – single male, lumpy oversized red plastic TK Maxx bag, shopping alone at an odd time, eyes on the stock boys. He hadn't seen them. His attention was stuck on the Sainsbury staffer poised to abandoned his cardboard box flock, Mal's skinny figure, today's interesting yet bothersome jolt out of merchandising catatonia.

Fatima nipped forward, light as a water strider, thrusting her basket between Mal and the stocker. "Oh, there you are! How many times have I told you to stop using that ridiculous bag? Put it in the basket, for god's sake, it's time to pay up and catch the bus."

Framing is a funny thing. Two builders can work side by side on the same job, one is shoveling dirt, the other building a home. Fatima's domestic converted thief to husband faster than hot water on cup noodles. Mal's relief was equally fleeting. Vic came up beside Fatima to form a stockade at the fish counter. "What do you think you're doing?", asked Vic.

Mal was Hugh Grant in his arrest photo. "Running a few errands?"

"At six."

"Love this store. Timings are very convenient." He tugged down his hood. Somewhere along the line he had found some eyeliner and re-applied it. Even on short sleep, he actually looked pretty good. "But I was going to get back in touch."

Both women said, "Right."

Vic had no doubt that Mal was as sincere as Tony Blair, believing every word was true the moment it left his mouth. It was the before and after she was worried about. Fatima waited for her to speak. "I need your help," said Vic.

"Vic, my dear, you know you have my sincere affection. I'm not sure what else I can give. Your dad was the hero. I'm the survivor."

"Mal, I really need you to help me. My mom won't."

"Ah," he said. "I had high hopes for that woman."

"Hopes you could slope off, more like," said Fatima.

Vic shook her head, and continued, "Look, I don't care what happened, or why you decided to cut out. Well, I do, but, damn it, Mal, more than that, we, I, really need your help, something, anything. I can't make you help us. I've got no money, thanks to

Jeremy. We've got little time, not much idea of what to do or how to stop people getting killed. I talked with Fatima last night, this morning, whatever it's been, and she's right, we're the only ones who seem to have a clue. We have to do something. But this is me, Mal, I'm a furniture designer from Bristol. Spy stuff might be OK for Fatima, free-lance journalist of the world's danger zones, but even then it's not England, it's Mali, or Pakistan, or Timbuktu."

"That's also Mali," interrupted Mal.

"Just shut up. I need you, or, rather, I need something more. I thought you had some ideals. You said that elections do matter."

"My ideals might be strong, but like a lot of idealists, I'm personally quite weak. Frankly, I'm not much of a friend. I was never very good at this boyfriend girlfriend thing. Even when it comes to magic, I'm more drifter than powerhouse. All the good ones died off long ago."

Fatima was quietly going apoplectic, nostrils wide. Vic just felt sad. Mal continued, "This isn't my fight, Vic. I'm prone to foolish talk after four whiskeys. People die all the time. I've seen thousands die, people I knew and cared for, people caught up in wars a lot bigger than a little election in a no longer very significant country. One party will win, the others will lose, life will carry on. I'm sorry your father is dead, but even magic can't bring him back. I'm even more sorry your mother has made the choices she did. I'm certainly the wrong man to try and fix that situation. She was always suspicious of me."

"Can't imagine why," said Fatima.

"After we sorted that business out with the wights, I thought to myself, 'I'm done'. If I keep moving and don't screw up too badly, I've got at least a couple of hundred years left. I'm not going to spend them chasing after phantoms and computer hackers."

"You seemed willing to hang around last night," observed Fatima.

"How are you going to spend them?", asked Vic, annoyed by the suggestion of hope in her voice.

Mal leisurely stretched his back against the fish counter, "Well, I was going to start by enjoying some smoked salmon. They have some really lovely salmon here, Superior Gold brand, simply delicious."

"Seriously, Mal, what are you going to do?"

Mal straightened, emphasizing the height difference between him and the two-woman picket fence in front of him. "Suppose I help you. What do I do? We don't know who is behind this. It's not like we can hang around Westminster and hope to catch someone in the act. They're probably not working much magic there anyway. All the mystic business is in some far off constituency, god knows where."

"Fats and I thought we could start by getting on the Internet and contacting Curious George."

Mal snorted. "Look, I don't take someone who models himself after a children's book character very seriously. And the Internet is not safe."

Vic wondered what had to happen for sadness to give way to anger, and vice versa. Was it fatigue, or do you just get bored with a single emotion? She kept her voice even. "Well, that's all we have to go on. Unless you have some other ideas. Look, you can ditch us again, and I can hang out in front of Salim's café and harass you for a few days, but eventually I'll have to go back to what's left of my life, and go to work so I can pay off Jeremy's gift of a credit card bill. I'm broke, Mal, and I'm tired. It's way too early in the morning. Help me. I'm not going to ask you again."

"Darling Vic, OK, fine, granted, this election might matter to many, and I do find your charms delightful. But that was also before I helped to ruin your life, and dragged your mother into all this. What's important to you, Vic? You really want to go through with this?"

"I do. Wasn't sure at first, but now I am. This is important. And I had hoped that you also might be a little important to me and vice versa. At least, I wanted to find out. Seems my horoscope this week should have been 'everything goes wrong', and no one, from Jeremy, to you, to my mother, wants anything to do with me."

"Except me," reminded Fatima.

Mal gave Fatima a nod. "Point to Fatima. Tell you what," he said. "I'll make you a deal."

"No deals, Mal. If you want to help, do it for yourself. I've begged enough. It's not about me, I understand that."

"No, no, hear me out. The deal is, you buy me this..." Mal pulled a sealed plastic packet out of the TK Maxx bag, "...smoked salmon that accidentally fell into this bag, and I'm yours. Besides, I need to unload some clothes on you anyway."

"Don't do me any favours."

"No, no, you're right. Every hundred years or so I should take a stand for something. Something rare and appealing, like your attractive self."

"Damn right, rare. But cut the sarcasm, Mal, we both know I'm an easy lay. Just come and be sincere. Let's settle up at the till. We've got planning to do."

Fatima stopped them. "Vics, I'm perfectly happy for his Highness here to talk himself out of helping us. I know you think he's a good idea but I don't. He's going to take another wad of cash off you, run around pretending to be thirty-five and hitting on anything that moves. I think we go back to our first idea, talk to George, and do the best we can on our own. At least then we don't have to worry about getting done for shoplifting. He might have a story about being a thousand years old but believe me, this Peter Pan will leave us in the lurch again and again. Look at him." Mal listened with a face full of gastric distress.

Vic took the basket handle and nudged them towards the front of the store. "Never mind, Fats, I'll take whatever I can get. Besides, I like the not-too-degraded-Johnny Depp look." Turning to Mal, "Fatima's not the only one with a pretty low opinion of you. Surpass our expectations, Mal."

"In for a penny, in for a packet, my dear."

At the till, of course he had no money. They rang the smoked salmon up last. "Thirteen pounds eighty?" asked Fatima.

"It's a bargain", said Mal, in the buttery tone of a TV spokesman. "Simple math. 400g for thirteen pounds eighty versus the 200 grams at eight ninety. Much cheaper by the gram. Taste it before we split up and you'll thank me. Try this." He opened the packet and held an oily pink flake in his hand. Vic slurped it off his fingers.

"It's really good."

Fatima rolled her eyes. "You two deserve each other. What's this about splitting?"

Mal popped a moist hunk into his own mouth and wiped his hand on the small of his back. "Mmph. Splits. Fatima, we're going to need some funds." He held up a dry hand. "Wait! Funds from me, but I need you to get them. I've promised to give Salim a thousand pounds so he can setup our new bank account. Vic, can you explain to her how to find the bakery? The door's busted, but there should still be about three thousand pounds in the freezer. If the cops are watching, tell them you're a friend of mine and don't know anything. Take the cash and clear out." Fatima looked heavenward but saw only drab acoustic tile. Mal kept explaining. "Slip in, put the cash in a bakery box or something, deliver one thousand to Salim on Edgware road for the bank cards. We'll meet back at your apartment, what do you say?"

"Lots of Salims on Edgware Road. How am I supposed to know which one?" asked Fatima.

"Salim Butt." He spelled it out, "B-U-T-T, like the Pakistani cricketer, but you won't miss him, he'll be the only Salim in Al Baqarah. He might fancy you actually, he's been known to go for the feisty pocket-occidental types."

"Never happen. I'm Eastern Orthodox. My mother would hang herself at the thought of me dating a Muslim, even with my first name. And especially because of my name. Think about it. I've been Fats all my life. Could you imagine me as Mrs. Butt?" While Fatima chuckled, Vic gave quick directions to the bakery and the café. Mal and Vic swapped their Mr. & Mrs. Myron ATM cards for Fatima's shopping bags. Fatima was still laughing softly as she hopped the escalator to the tube station.

Mal lifted his chin at Vic's takeaway cup. "Any chance of a spare sip?"

"No." She softened, "It's already finished, but we've bought coffee powder. You can make some at Fatima's. Reckon it will take Fats a couple of hours to get the cash by tube to Salim and get home. What's our plan in the meantime?"

"We need to think. And get another phone, something that won't be likely to be traced. A proper breakfast is also an idea – how much money did Fats loan you?"

"Fifty pounds."

"Gorgeous! Disposable phone, couple of tube tickets, with money left over for a decent bite. There may even be a cell phone store in this here plaza." The last bit in a Dallas accent. At the centre directory, they found a cell phone store, but learned through a short walk that it didn't open until 9:00AM. "I suggest we breakfast somewhere else. I'm allergic to food courts. In fact, I believe I have a customer nearby – kill two birds with one stone."

"Mal, getting in touch with your customers got us in massive trouble."

"Yes, but not from the authorities. And I think those other fellows are off the case for the nonst."

Mal walked them to a trendy organic café on Wilton Street, with obsequious apologies to the proprietor for the missed weekend delivery that forced them to have a tartless breakfast.

Back at Victoria Plaza, Mal rapped with the phone sales jockeys for twenty endless minutes on the virtues of each model. No place for neglected girlfriends to sit. This must be how husbands feel at frock shops, thought Vic. He finally converted seventeen of Fatima's pounds into a base model NOKIA and SIM. The keys were almost as large as the screen. Mal was ecstatic, Vic was grateful to leave. "Seven pounds for a phone with a web browser, and a data top-up. Twenty-four hours of battery life. Remind me again what inflation means? We're in business." The phone vanished into the kangaroo pocket of his hoody. "Now for the tube."

The office rush had emptied out of the District line by the time they snagged a train. Mal, Vic, and their shopping had the end carriage to themselves. Vic was pleased to note she rode with no ill effects from the horror train journey of the night before. Opportunity to brace Mal a bit. "You know, Mal, I'm surprised by how useless you are."

"Oh?"

"You can do magic! Snap your fingers and tell us who the bad guy is."

"Darling, magic doesn't work that way. Can't see the future, can't read minds. Magic allows you to change the physical world, whip up whatever you can imagine, but you still have to be able to think of and understand what it is that you do. We made dragons because we saw lizards, and wanted them to be big. We made them fly by lifting them up. Somewhat prosaic, I know. And it took an enormous amount of effort. On a good day now I can barely spark a fart."

"Even so, small magic must be good for something. For example, why are you skint? You should be rich."

Mal uncorked a smile. "I am donating several thousand pounds to the cause." He took her hand. "Magic is extremely hard to do, and magical things need constant attention. Well, for everyone except your father. That was his crowning glory, to put magic in a can, but he knew me too well to show me the secret. I'd be tempted to break our agreement and, well, borrow a bit more than my share. Regardless, transmutation doesn't last. You can speed up or slow down natural processes, but you can't make something from nothing and expect it to stick around. You need to keep the power on for the spell to stay. In the old days, this didn't matter. Glamour some copper coins into gold, use them to buy a herd of cattle, ride off, and by the time you sell the cattle for real money, you're in a far country and no one can trace you. It's a decent game as long as you don't mind cheating a cattle trader out of his life savings." Mal looked furtively around the empty compartment. "Now, everything has a trail. CCTV is everywhere. Too many variables to keep track of. Suppose I conjure up a million pounds in notes – what serial numbers do I put on them? Large deposits trigger alerts. When the bank inspects the money and rewinds the camera to me stood at the counter with funny bills, what happens then? Bank computers are too effective. If I do a wire transfer, even with the correct numbers, they'll trace back to the originating bank, ask awkward questions, and my money is frozen. My diminishing store of magic is burned up as well. It's easier to earn it. I'd rather save magic for keeping hide and health intact. I was happily running an unlicensed bakery until you came along. Why do you think I buy fake ID? I could magic one up, but will the name match the government database? I get them like everyone else, from someone with a cousin or aunt on the inside. The magic required to reach into every government office and whistle up a valid ID of about the right sex, age, and appearance is beyond me. Better to find a computer hacker, or a fence, or a handy fellow like Salim. The only really useful magic these days is death magic."

Vic gave a start. "What do you mean?"

"Don't be alarmed. Despite your and Fatima's dim view of my character this is something I seldom resort to."

"Seldom? That's comforting."

Mal ignored her. "All I mean is that even charms and glamours don't really work any more, you know, the whisper in the ear what you want your victim to do? These days, when a person starts acting funny, if bystanders don't think they're just talking on Bluetooth, people either ignore them or send them off to the psychiatrist. The only really useful skill left is killing people. Magic is completely undetectable. A squeeze of the heart here, a slip of the rear tyre there, people can be killed in ways that look natural or accidental. That's the perfect assassination, no one even knows it took place. But besides being immoral, murder has its limitations."

"I'll say."

"Besides the obvious. You typically need more magic than you can siphon out of a corpse to pull it off. And like everything else magical, it's addictive.

Using magic is an incredible kick. Whatever you scrounge up, you'll want to use more. So you start killing more people, and now you're undeniably a bit strange, and running low on the juice. By the time people get suspicious and come for you, you're feeble and used up, unless you happen to practice your dark art in one of the few places of power left. You can't exactly sell yourself as an assassin if your big plan requires them to ride the cog railway up the top of Mount Snowden to have a mysterious heart attack, now can you?"

"Snowden is magical?"

"Of course it's bloody magical, weren't you listening to anything I told you yesterday? Magic exists. Even the most primitive untalented idiots can tell which places have more power than others. At a truly powerful spot, a place which concentrates the energy, you used to not need any talent at all to work some magic, which is why people clustered there, and built dolmens, and damn near burned out all the magic at those places while they were at it. Even you can still feel a bit of it left at Snowden. I like to go there myself, or at least, I used to, before they closed the café. King Arthur's Seat in Edinburgh is a good spot. I'm sure you can think of others. But London, bah, completely dead, too many magicians fancied living here."

"But still, there must be other ways to fetch a coin. You could have bet on the horses, with a little magical influence."

"Oh, I did! Before the covenant, of course. But it's not right. And money you get easy, it flows through the fingers. I was happy to give that up, actually. I don't mind baking. I do miss..."

"What?"

"Creation. Pure joy. I would get an idea, and voila! People look up at the clouds and imagine monsters in their shapes. I was the one drawing them. If I just had a little bit more talent, I probably would have joined your mother in her dream world. I well understand why she can't give it up. And here comes Earl's Court. Do we need to change trains?"

"No, we're fine. Ten more stops."

"So, twenty or thirty minutes to strategize. I have a feeling your friend Fatima will want to hear more from us than what we had for brekky, and why it didn't include deliciously organic Goldeneye pastries. Any great brainwaves?"

"I do have an idea. Cui bono, right? Who benefits? We know from George that all of the constituencies that suffered a tragic loss had a Tory in second place. So it must be someone in the Tory party behind it, maybe even the PM."

"Not necessarily. The industrial complex is firmly behind the Tory party, and they're not on the ballot. Could just be someone who likes the party platform, and wants those policies to continue."

"Possible, but unlikely. This seems to me to be very much an insider's game, polling data, a terminal in Westminster, some very specific candidates, and completely ruthless. The Shadow Finance Minister, for god's sake. We both know that politicians don't like to be told what to do by anyone, even the people writing their cheques."

"And certainly not by the voters," Mal added.

"I don't see it as an outside job. Which means that the chief Tory probably has some idea. You mentioned glamours. Do you have any magic left? I think it's time we took a whisper in the PM's ear."

"Not much." Mal held up Vic's father's ring. "Look at the sheen on this pearl. Took half of what was in there to get you your appointment with the queen of the night."

"So half is left."

"True, but distance is a problem. If we want to do

anything more than give him a slight tickle, we'll have to get close."

"How close?"

"Next to him is best. Perhaps a few blocks away? It's easier if I have line-of-sight."

Did the Underground design its recorded announcements to sound androgynous? A high pitched electronic man, or perhaps a low pitched woman, gave the reminder to change trains for Heathrow and the Piccadilly line at Acton Town. Two passengers boarded at Chiswick Park, interrupting the privacy of the otherwise empty carriage. Vic whispered her cunning plan into Mal's ear as the train moved forward again. When she was through, she leaned back and spoke in a normal tone, "One more thing I wanted to ask you while it was just the two of us. How do you explain that other Mal who appeared with my mother?"

"I don't. Your dream, my dear."

For a split-second, Vic wondered what would be the female equivalent of Oedipus. She decided it didn't exist. Besides. They had arrived at Ealing.

A LITTLE MILD EXTORTION

*In order to forge a deeper understanding, George
cracks a code and Fatima exposes herself*

Mal and Vic slumped like the morning itself into
the grey November noon. Vic let herself into Fatima's
building with the spare key. They tiptoed up the
stairs.

"Why are we doing this? It's midday," asked Mal.

"Shush. Being considerate of others will be a good
habit for you to develop."

The apartment was empty. Mal played detective as
he put the groceries away, opening every cabinet in
the small kitchen. He was assembling vegetables on
the wooden cutting board when the house phone
rang. Vic grabbed it. "Fatima Lapicki's house, whom
shall I say is calling?"

"Vic! You don't have to give out the whole
mouthful. Just say the phone number when you pick
up. It's me."

"Hey, Fats, what's up? Where are you?"

"Salim's. Al Baqarah. I gave him the money, he's asked me to wait an hour to get the cards updated and tested."

"Hey, good stuff. And can you do us one more favour? I need someone to get a few things from my dad's place in Cardiff."

"Can't. No way. I'm done."

"What happened?"

"I'm blown. Got busted by the police at Mal's place. No way I can go to your father's. They were watching the bakery and stopped me when I came out. It's a good thing I stuffed the notes down my shirt instead of taking a breadbox. I think they were curious about the extra 2 inches of bust but were too embarrassed to check. No female squaddie on duty and all that. Two thousand eight hundred and fifty pounds, minus your three hundred and my fifty, plus one thousand for Salim, means your boyfriend has one thousands pounds neat. So now you're rich and I'm a person of interest. Fortunately, they've got nothing on me other than crossing police tape. I told them I was just a friend checking up on him, but still, I'm on file." In typical fashion, Fatima hadn't paused for breath. "Hey, one more thing, did you see the paper today? There should be a Guardian and The Independent for me downstairs. Oxford MP on a ventilator after a massive stroke. Labour, of course. Check it out. I'll be back at the flat by around two, but Cardiff, no can do, Vics."

"No probs, you're still a huge help. We'll figure something out. Let me talk to the bastard. We'll get the paper and call you back on your cell. Be careful. I'll talk to you." She hung up the phone and Mal raised an eyebrow. Vic related developments while he chopped capsicum.

He meditated for a moment and put a pot of rice on the boil. "Fatima is temporarily disqualified, and I don't think it's a good idea to involve anyone who's not already part of this mess. But we need to move quickly, especially if this most recent MP downing isn't natural either. Perhaps we follow through with your pal George. If he can somehow get us on the PM's visitor list, we can beard Daniel in the lion's den, or however that phrase goes. Can you give him a call or send him a twit or whatever it is we need to do to reach him? Lunch will be another fifteen minutes."

Vic cursed continuously as she punched a message into the Internet character by character on their cheap phone's ABC-DEF keypad. When she looked up, Mal had set the table and was serving a simple stir-fry. The mobile rang before she could sit down to eat. Mal read the screen upside down on the table. "I think it's for you. Number blocked."

"Hello?"

"That must be the world's lamest code," said George. Vic smiled and put him on speaker. He read off of his screen, "HonestAbe @CuriousGeorge wants to know which rapper rocks more OT-TripleOne or MC OneUp, call me.' Couldn't you think of anything more subtle?"

"Well, it worked. And 0811162187 isn't out there on the Internet. No one who's not clued in would have figured it out. Glad you called, George, first male who hasn't let me down all week."

"I hear a favour."

"Yes. But it's for the good guys, and you won't personally be involved. All we need is to hack the 10 Downing Street guest list and add two names, so that me and one other idiot can get in to see the Prime Minister."

"Is that all?" George snorted. "Bloody hell, if I could do that, I could steal from the banks. It's a terrorist's dream, get yourself on the visitor's roster and choke him dead with your bare hands. If I was that good, I wouldn't be constantly looking over my shoulder to see if BT knows I'm stealing their Internet, now would I? What else would you like, Swiss account and a chalet?"

"What about the PM's schedule? You're supposedly into a computer in Westminster. Can you access his diary from there?"

"I doubt it. But you don't have to. He's a public figure, lots of events. You can catch him outside the Commons after Question Time, or just attend one of the press meets. Hang on." The line went dead in the same abrupt way as last time. He came back quickly, "'Today, Sunday, 4pm, Prime Minister and Queen inaugurate the newly renovated Commonwealth Heads of Government Secretariat building and reception centre, Marleborough House, Pall Mall.' How's that? Queen's a bonus."

"It's marvelous. You're a genius."

"I'm not bad. And good with computers. Speaking of which, one thing you should know. I've been tracking your dad in the cyberworld. There is insane activity on your dad's accounts, even though he's dead. Not purchases exactly, lots and lots of inquiries. He's clearly a person of interest to somebody."

"Second time I've heard that phrase this afternoon."

"The government's fancy way of saying they think someone's a criminal but can't figure out a charge with which to frame them. Don't take it too hard, probably twenty million files on innocent people out there. You'll be in good company when they find you."

Mal had cleaned his plate. He tapped on it with the pearl ring, which had somehow found a home on his left hand, and mouthed the word 'Cardiff' at her. "George?" she said, "One other thing. Is there any way you can pick up some bits and bobs from my father's house and give them to a friend of mine?"

"No, thanks. I deal with data. I don't meet people. I don't even remember your name. And it's best if we forget all about this. Besides, Cardiff is miles away."

"Where are you now?"

"Nowhere. Do you think I'm crazy? This conversation is feeling extremely dangerous. If anyone links the real me and Curious George, I'm likely to get in serious trouble."

"Trouble like killed? Because that's what we're trying to prevent, remember?"

"I emailed them! My work here is done."

"Did you email the Labour MP for Oxford, who's currently on a ventilator? Check the papers, George."

"Actually, I did. Look, I like to help, but let me stick to the bits and not the bobs. I'm no good with people. I can't get busted. I'll lose my job and a lot of important things that go with it."

"George. My pretty friend Fatima is pretty hopeless with people too. You'll get on fine. Just tell me you'll go to Cardiff, walk into a perfectly safe unlocked house, pick up a couple of brass knickknacks, and hand them off to her. You don't have to do anything more. In fact, you don't even have to meet her, just leave them someplace public. There's a hospital near my father's house, you can put them behind the counter, say they're for a patient who checked out and you're not sure how to get in touch."

"I'll call you back." The line clicked off.

Vic contemplated a cold stir fry with some dissatisfaction. "If not George, who?"

"Not to worry, my dear. He's a computer tech, right? I distinctly heard 'pretty friend Fatima'. George strikes me as the kind of fellow who will work for dates." He took her plate. "I'll heat that up for you."

The cell phone rang. Number blocked was calling

back. "George?"

"Listen, it's a Sunday, I don't have to work and I guess I owe it to your dad. Spire Hospital Cardiff, right? Tell your friend Fatima to look for a white BT van in the parking lot in about two hours. What exactly does she look like?"

"Cute, petite, an even five foot. Pale skin and a motor mouth. You can't miss her." Mal raised his hands from the kitchen and signaled the goal was good. Vic gave him the finger. "She'll be driving a blue Vauxhall hatchback that's a bit of a mess. But give her some time. She's not back yet and then she has to drive from London, ok?"

"Fine. Spire Hospital parking lot, whichever is the furthest from the main building, 5pm. White van. What am I supposed to pick up?"

"Hang on." She passed the handset over to Mal. He spoke briefly and hung up. She held out her hand for the phone. "That's one thing sorted. I'll call Fats, let her know. You and I should change and head back into town."

"Madam, since we have to take our clothes off..."

"No time. Get in the shower already. Lest you forget, we have an afternoon date with the Queen!"

District line again. These dead times were when

233

she missed her father the most. They were moving, but really only by sitting on a thin cushion while tunnels processed past. She sat across from Mal, hands between her legs. "You know Mal, if my dad thought I was really going to meet the Queen, he'd have me wearing something a bit more formal than black jeans and a t-shirt."

"But darling, it's the uniform of the modern era. Best the Queen gets used to it. Fashions change. Time was you couldn't get into a decent restaurant in London without a neck cloth. And now I think very few would turn us away. There are benefits to the decline of civilization."

"Well, we look like an aging rocker and his groupy."

"And those aging rockers can be quite wealthy, so the firms of London have learned to toady to them regardless of how scruffy they appear. Speaking of wealth, we'll get off at Paddington and walk the rest of the way. We should pick up our funds at Salim's."

"And perhaps when this is done, you can buy me a dress."

"When this is done, my dear, you'll be able to go home and get as many dresses as you like. But you seem quite comfortable in trousers. I didn't take you for the dress type."

"I'm not, usually. Which is a point. You barely know me. What do I read? What kind of music do I like? My favorite jokes?"

"That goes both ways. But I'll bite. You had begun to tell me a joke about blowjobs."

"Actually it's about whiskey. Man goes into a bar and orders four whiskeys. The bartender asks 'what's the celebration?' He says he's just had his first blowjob. The bartender gives his congratulations and offers to serve up another on the house, but the guy says, 'No, thanks. If four won't get rid of the taste, nothing will.'"

"That's a terrible joke. I think we're better off with music." Mal stretched out his legs. His feet hugged the outsides of her shoes. "Tell me, my dear, what would be your desert island discs?"

"How do you mean?"

"It's a radio programme. BBC. You must know it - imagine you're a castaway. You can pick eight songs, a book, and some sort of luxury item to have with you on your island. What would you pick?"

"Eight songs? Something by Prince. Be Thankful for What You've Got, Massive Attack. Queen, not sure, either The Show Must Go On or Somebody to

Love. Careless Whispers. Buju Banton, Untold Stories. How many is that?"

"Five."

"OK, Blue Oyster Cult, for my father, probably..." She closed her eyes.

"Yes?"

"Give me a minute. The Red and the Black?"

"That's us, but is it a song?"

"One More Chance, B.I.G., and something Bob, of course. Maybe, Waiting in Vain."

"Biggie, not Tupac?"

"What do you know about that?"

"I love the radio. And I've been known to change the station. If you don't watch television, you have time for diverse interests. And very interesting you are, my dear, all ancient music. I don't think you've named a single song from the current decade. And your book?"

"Bauhaus. Hans Vingler. I'm a designer. What about you?"

"More of a fiction person. I like a good story, tales of travel. Recent era? Perhaps The Painted Veil, Maugham, or Graham Greene. I quite enjoyed The Quiet American. But for the island, you'll want a thick book, something you can read again and again. I think Midnight's Children. Rushdie's stories are always more approachable than people find them. Bayswater, my dear, next stop."

They walked to the café from Paddington. Despite the height difference, she found it easy to walk hand in hand. Salim was waiting.

"Brother, some devil woman you sent me! First, to give me the money, she shows me her breasts. Then, she wouldn't stop talking. Take these things and be gone. Chaley! Jao!"

"Salim-bhaiya, a thousand thank yous. I will make sure she never troubles you again. Unless you want?"

"Shukriya, no. Just go." They walked to Pall Mall with nine hundred pounds in the pockets of Mal's mustard flares. If there was any discrepancy between that sum and what he was expecting, Mal made no comment.

The cordon around Marleborough House kept them at a twenty metre radius. It was a surprisingly small crowd for the Queen, instantly recognisable in a pink pillbox hat. They joined the tourists and amateur photographers who had happened on Pall Mall. Vic overheard a heavyset American turning to his wife. "Honey, what's the Commonwealth?"

"Those are the former British colony countries,

hon," the wife replied.

"Are we in that?"

Vic and Mal moved sideways through the crowd and waited at the barrier for the Prime Minister to appear. The uniformed police behind the barricade looking determined and bored. Others in dark suits and earpieces looked paranoid, scanning the crowd. Vic grabbed Mal's elbow. "Shouldn't we be worried about being picked out by the police?"

"Why? My dear, we've done nothing wrong." Mal put his arm around her and kissed her ear. "Relax. Chances are slim." The PM's limousine approached, between a marked police car and a black Range Rover. "Right. We're done here. Walk away."

"I thought we had to see him."

"No, we're close enough. Thirty yards will do. Hold my hand and walk with me." They turned into St. James square. "And ignore anything further I say. One half of an odd conversation won't hardly make sense."

Inside the limousine, the Prime Minister was gathering his thoughts. 'One does not make the Queen wait' was the main one, followed by 'sod it'. A deep voice disturbed him. "Take out your cell phone, put it against your head." British, but with a slight hint of a foreign origin. Eastern European? Dutch? His secretary and his body-man driving didn't seem to hear anything. "Take out your cell phone, put it against your head. Pretend you've got a call." Quite distinct, but again, the two others in the car acted as if they'd heard nothing. The Queen was walking up the steps towards the ribbon. "I'll be quick. Only you can hear me. Put your phone against your head so you don't look insane when you talk back to me." The PM patted the breast of his light charcoal suit and removed his phone from the inside pocket.

"Hello? Who is this?"

"A friend."

"Go on." The PM's voice was calm.

"Do you know who I am? You don't seem too surprised to be hearing things in the car."

"Look, I don't have much time. The Queen, you know."

"Fine. Tomorrow, you're going to get a real phone call, from your security service."

"Really?"

"Mr. and Mrs. Myron. Remember these names."

"Why?"

"You're going to instruct security to invite them in to see you directly. Myron."

"Why on earth would I do that?"

"Because we're friends. And because we know all about what is happening with the other parties' MPs getting bumped off."

"What rubbish! Who are you?"

"Myron. Tell your security tomorrow. It will be easy. Because, for example, you're going to start to choke in a minute. Your delightful pink tie is going to get very very tight. Can you feel it? Oh, right, you can't respond if you don't have air."

In the backseat, the PM's face filled with blood, his cheeks bright red splotches against a pale canvas. His whooping inhalation startled the driver, "Are you all right sir?"

The Prime Minister loosened his collar.

"Yes. Fine. Fine, just some startling news on the phone."

The disembodied voice rang out one last time, "Myron. Don't forget to tell them," then was gone.

The PM's phone rang. He removed it from his ear and stared at the screen. Press Undersecretary bubbled up from the contact list. His driver turned around again, "Thought you were already on the phone, sir?"

The PM dismissed him with a loose wave. "Smartphone, dual SIM, call waiting, bloody clever, it's the latest thing. Take this and talk to the Undersecretary. I have to get up the stairs." It's salmon, not pink, the PM thought, exiting the limousine and adjusting his tie. By the time the photo-journalists were ready to click, he was smiling and perfectly arranged.

Mal and Vic walked past the equestrian statue towards the London Library. "He took it quite well. Surprisingly well. Like a voice only he could hear was a normal event." His hand in hers was stiff.

"That's not too earth-shattering. To want to be a politician in this day and age, you have to be barmy. And guided by voices."

"No, Vic, like someone else has been pulling my magic trick. And that takes power. Real power. Look." He held out his cupped hand to her. She peeked into it.

"Ash? Dust?"

"The remains of the pearl." He tipped over his hand to expose the empty setting of the ring. Grey dust spilled into the street.

"It doesn't matter. Tomorrow this will all be over."

"For you. There might still be another visit from our friends, the wights. If they come for me again, I'm not sure what I'll have left."

She picked up his hand by the wrist and brushed off some ash residue. "Scared, Mal? Never you mind. I'll look after you." She touched his nose with the tip of one forefinger. "Nothing for us to do until tomorrow morning, and you won't solve the world's problems by worrying."

"True. And the night is young." Mal's baseline cheer seemed to be returning.

"I meant to ask you about that. Fatima won't get back from Cardiff until late. She deserves to sleep in her own bed."

"Well, darling, I'm rich and you're beautiful. Perhaps I can take you to that show you were wanting. Sunday is the new Saturday on the West End, you know, but we might get tickets." Mal borrowed the phone and made reservations on its tiny browser, also with some mild cursing. Vic read their bankcard number out at key intervals.

"No shared toilet, Mal."

"I'm going to put this phone in the toilet. Convent Garden? Bloody spell check." The phone vanished. "But we're done. Dinner, tickets, top secret hotel, had to create a new email account as well, but en-suite and under a hundred pounds. The hotel. Tickets were more. Sixty five pounds each! At least we know the bankcard works."

They dined in Covent Garden, under a glass conservatory. Vic felt like a child exploring the big person's table, duck, crab, scallops, Jerusalem artichokes and truffle oil. They added a bottle of wine to the pre-theatre menu and arrived at the show tipsy. Mal kissed her hard on the lips when they found their seats. They danced out of the theatre, Mal spinning her in the street with an incantation, "Dead yesterday, and unborn tomorrow, why fret about them if today be sweet?"

Vic stopped in the middle of the road. "I know that. I studied that in school."

"I knew him."

"Longfellow?"

"Omar Khayyam."

"Shite."

The hotel turned out to be a reasonably upscale chain, five minute's walk from Covent Garden and four stars as advertised. Mal showed his false bankcard and collected the key to a small, plush room on the seventh floor.

Vic sat down on the bed and gave him the stare of an arranged bride, alone with her husband for the first time. "What the hell are we doing?" she asked. "We haven't even called Fatima. And you really hurt me, you know. This morning. Am I going to wake up alone tomorrow?

"I'm not over it. I'm not happy about it. And if you think you can wine and dine me, take me out for a show, and I'll just bend over, you've got another thing coming."

Mal's face was flat. "I'm here now. I could be a lot of other places, doing lots of other things. I never promised to be a hero. This is me, too. We're both adults. It's not like Samson and Delilah or the world's one true love. I've had some practice. I could tell you fancied me when you first walked in. I didn't take advantage, and I didn't say no."

"And then you gave me a good one and ran out on me. So much for the romance."

"Romance?" Mal's voice rose. "I'm the one who gave up the one thing which defines me. You come along and I break a vow which had held up for forty years, didn't I? And being here certainly isn't all about me. If it were up to me, I'd be in the wind! If you don't see that, maybe I will sneak out in the night. I had a good thing going before your father started poking around. You're easy on the eye, I'll give you that, and a few other things besides, but where is my life? You're happy to spend my money on a night on the town, and then you can go back to sofas and whatnot in Bristol. I'm on the run." He tore off his sweatshirt and top in one motion and threw it on the floor with both hands. Vic saw the big arteries along his shoulders and biceps standing out as he stood, naked from the waist up. He pointed at her on the bed. His hand shook. "Look, you want romance, pick up the room service phone and order yourself some flowers. I've got some business in the bathroom, you do what you like." The bathroom door slammed behind him.

He ran the taps in the bathroom for a long time. When he came out, towel wrapped around his hips, Vic was under the covers. She pulled the sheet up to her chin. "I'm not sorry," she said. "It needed to be said, and I'm not going to apologize for it."

Mal held his hands up, a caught fugitive ready to go quietly. "It's alright. I know I can be a bit hard to be around." His face became suddenly serious. "But there is one thing I need to know." He grinned. "What's the print on your panties tonight?"

"Go look for yourself, cheeky bastard. They're there with the rest of my things at the foot of the bed." She was smiling back at him. "But I'd rather you just turned out the light and slipped into bed." So he did.

ON THE TASKFORCE

Victoria doesn't wake up alone, Mal arranges an unlikely ride, and a minor medical emergency. George holds the fort

The hotel bedside phone rang. Vic fumbled for it in the unfamiliar room. "Hello?" Her tongue was caked with sleep. A recorded voice informed her that this was her 7:30AM wake-up call. She checked the plastic electronic clock and shoved a still-sleeping Mal hard on the shoulder. "7:30? Who on earth did that?"

He rolled languidly onto his back. "I did. There was a phone in the bathroom. Big day today, have to meet the PM." They showered, put on yesterday's clothes, and were back on the train by eight, carriages full with the morning rush. It wasn't until Hammersmith that they had a measure of privacy. This was fine for both of them. After yesterday's events, they were content to surf the anonymizing solitude of a crowd in silence. Despite the crush, it was peaceful until Vic saw their change of train across the Acton Town platform. The sprint to catch the District Line snapped the mood. A more empty compartment reignited Vic's curiousity. "Why do you go on living when all the other magicians are dead?" she asked.

"That's a pretty rude question."

"That's not what I meant. I mean, what keeps you going?"

"Difficult to say. At some level, I wonder why I'm not clinically depressed." He draped his arm around her shoulders. "What would you do if you were no longer able to do the one thing you really loved? Magic is dead. It used to be any fool with a penny farthing of talent could do something, there was so much of magic. Now, you have to be the world's greatest expert just to sniff some out, let alone work with it. If I strain mightily, I can perhaps make a work of magic for a few seconds, and then only if I happen to be in a particularly magic-rich place. My art is dead. And so are all the other magicians. Maybe I should be as well."

"There must be others. You can go someplace where magic is stronger."

"You think we didn't try that? Who wants to live in Antarctica? The world is here, my dear, I love my food, my trade, the storm of souls that is London, all full of energy and art and life. And I'm not sure there would be anyone else left, besides our current villain. My peers, or colleagues, or whatever you want to call them, they got old, they had accidents, they were killed. Some killed themselves."

"My father didn't. You didn't."

"Well, Vic, I'm not entirely sure why. I think your father and I had survived so long we forgot how to stop surviving, until someone forced the issue. Curiousity helps. Your father was always curious about the next thing. He was fascinated with computers, trips to the moon, telephones, indoor plumbing."

"And you?"

"Oh, I hang around for the girls. How poor my life would have been to have ended before I met you?"

"I can flatter myself, thanks. There must be more than that."

"Perhaps. Perhaps it is because your father really was right, that magic shouldn't be lost completely, that he and I should somehow preserve it. Who better to keep the flame alive than mediocre me, the sniffer and seeker, rather than the master? If we get through the next few weeks, you can help me write my memoirs."

"You act flip, Mal, but I'm not sure you're joking."

"Neither am I."

When they reached Fatima's apartment, they were surprised to hear two voices through the door at the top of the stairs. Mal held Vic back from opening it. "Seems like our Fats has a visitor."

"A visitor, or an overnight guest? If my ears don't deceive, I think we get to meet the man behind the monkey."

"George? Then, my dear, open away. I, too, am curious."

Fatima and George were making breakfast. They stood in the kitchen in t-shirts, George's a ribbed vest with cotton boxers, Fatima an oversized number that revealed lithely muscled legs to well above the knee. George seemed decent enough, not much taller than Fats, tousled, thinning curly brown hair and a small swell of a belly. He had an office worker tan, completely pale and almost hairless skin. His face was narrow, wedge-shaped, but his obvious mildness and lack of complication kept him from looking too rat-faced. Mal hailed him loudly, "Comrade George! What an unexpected pleasure! And with my favorite ball-buster no less." George clicked shut his jaw and darted his eyes to Fatima for support. Vic was instantly charmed.

Fatima can never be silenced. "And so nice of you to join us as well. George and I were driving the M4 half the night while you were out gallivanting. So I thought it only proper to give the poor man some rest."

"Rest?" asked Vic.

"Oh, don't go all innocent princess on me. I can't begin to tell you how horny a girl can get listening to their best friend and her gigolo from alone on the couch. I swear, Mal bellows like a bull. So, no more Ms. Prudence Virginal, just introduce yourself to George nicely and tell me what I can fix you for breakfast. And you're welcome, we got those things you asked for."

"Victoria Marrow. And that lanky fellow is Mallory." Vic sat down on the loveseat and took off her shoes. "Yeah, thanks, Fats, how did it go?"

"Well, George did all the hard work. Took me ages to find the hospital in the dark, and there's this white panel van gleaming in the distance like Camelot. Tell them what happened, George."

"Nothing. I parked around the corner, walked up to the house, the door was unlocked, five minutes, I'm back in the van."

Mal raised a mild eyebrow, "No police?"

"Oh, mate, right, the fuzz." George gave a fake slap to his forehead. "They were flipping everywhere. I couldn't park in front because there was the world's most obvious unmarked car bang opposite the house, and still I go in, right, and there are two blokes in police commando kit hanging around inside the door, so they stop me and give me everything short of a how's-your-father. I tell them I'm with BT, as I'm wearing the uniform and carrying the toolbox. I explain that there's been an emergency national security letter authorizing a tap and forward on the residential line of a certain Abraham Marrow and I've been called down from Birmingham on a Sunday to put it in, so could they pull back and let me do my job, yeah? They give my ID card a squiz and then I'm up in Linkoln's office and for a minute I'm a bit stunned. Then I pull out my toolbox and snip a few wires and stuff them into likely looking places, put the antiques in the bottom of my box, and afterwards

I'm downstairs and out the door. Didn't start shaking until I was in the van. If I lose my job over this, I don't know what I'm going to do."

Vic broke out a broad smile, "George, you're a legend."

Mal doffed an invisible cap. "Some quick thinking, Mr. Curious."

"Yeah, I am good. And it's George Lister, so that's Mr. Lister to you. But you don't know me and I don't know you, well, I mean, I'm quite pleased to have met your friend Fatima, but if you could be so kind as to take these brass things from out of my box and off my hands, I think we'll all be better off. It's there next to the sofa. I've called in sick today but I'll need to head out shortly."

"Oh, crap," said Vic. "It's Monday. I told my boss I'd probably be back today. I need to call in."

Fatima held out the house phone from the kitchen but George took it from her and shook it at Vic. "Your dad, he's dead, right, 'bout three days back? No one is phoning any of the likely lines from any phone within a kilometre of me. You ring your boss from the landline here and I expect we'll all be getting a quick visit from the cops. If your dad is so important as to rate a 24 by 7 after death, you can be sure they're tracking the daughter nine ways from Sunday. I say we let your boss figure out you're not coming in and forgive you."

Mal nodded in agreement, "He's right, my dear. It's radio silence until we find our man. Or woman."

"Fair enough. But isn't the next phase of the plan to be arrested?"

George's eyes bugged. "Arrested? Hang on, let me get dressed and out of here, then you can do whatever foolishness you'd like. But count me out."

Fatima put a calming hand on George's shoulder. "Arrested seems a bit radical. Can't you just slip yourself in? I mean, you can do magic. Why not just charm them all into letting us into 10 Downing directly?"

Mal was icy. "Exactly how much have you told our friend Mr. George Lister? This is precisely the problem. Perhaps we could 'slip in'. Through the front door, where there are hundreds of people, tourists, journos with cameras, and I expect a few snipers. Every visitor going in the public way gets recorded. When all this is over, some of us would like to get back to our quiet life in Birmingham, or Bristol, or Ealing, without the threat of someone going through the record and wondering how some unknown odd couple got straight in. In this day and age, everything we do is on file. All it takes is one person to get suspicious. I'd like to get to the bottom of this, but not at the risk of being unable to return to our incognito life after. There are some questions you and I'd rather not answer. Hence the fake ID. Besides, I'm all out of magic. We'll just have to make do with logic. Hence arrested."

"I still don't follow."

"It's the government, Madam Fatima, the leviathan, the behemoth. They have the power to record everything, except those things they intentionally do not record. It was Victoria's idea. We needed a way in that's somewhat clandestine, off the books. She reckoned, and I agree, that the secret police have their own way in and out that doesn't show up on the official registrar of comings and goings. So all we have to do is get them to take us in."

"It has a certain logic," said George, "but I'd still appreciate it if you waited until I was an hour away before putting your kamikaze mission in motion."

"Oh, no, George, you're a key player," replied Mal. "For all we know, it is the PM himself who's behind this. The man behaved extremely oddly yesterday when he and I had a quiet word about things. Your job is to make sure we don't get disappeared until the election."

"And how am I going to manage that?"

"Via the hacked computer. I'd like you to stay here with Fatima, log on to the system Vic's father opened for you, and monitor the Westminster network for anything unusual. We'll try and find out where that system is, and who was likely on it, but if need be, that network could be our only way to call for help. I don't think security will let us take a phone in there. What was the login again?"

"Office double oh eight. But I'm not going to do it."

"George, be reasonable. A wise man once said that one night of love won't make up for six nights alone, but a once-a-week fellow wouldn't have driven down from the North on a whim and a prayer. I'm quite confident that our Miss Fatima will be eternally, demonstratively, grateful if you would grace her with your company for a few more hours, oop!" Mal paused to dodge Vic's kick. He was clearly in his quick phase this morning.

"It's wing-and-a-prayer, not whim-and-a-prayer," said George. "But even if I do stay, I've got no modem, no secure line. And have some respect for the lady."

Fatima broke in, "George, Mal's not taking his throwaway phone, can't you connect through that?"

George could not have gotten any whiter. "Ooh no, love, I don't do wireless links. Wifi, Bluetooth, none of that. It's all a bit, what's the word?" He paused in thought. "Promiscuous."

The word hung in the air for a long second. Laughing, Fatima squeezed George on the bottom, "Oh, George, I'll show you promiscuous, she's me and my best friend. I'm glad you're staying. So, breakfast, anyone?"

"Actually, no thanks, Fats. George has a point. Mal and I should put some distance between you two and us. And there's a key element of our arrest plan."

"Oh, really? What's that?"

"Café brunch!"

Mal insisted on changing trains twice, so they ended up in Clapham. Vic thought that its reputation for smugness might be partly justified – the food was superb. Mal seemed to have an unerring nose for which set of vitrified tiles, distressed wood, and exposed red brick corresponded with gastronomic delight instead of pretentious markup. They had walked past two other chic resto-pubs before settling on the last of a string of three Victorians: an estate agent, a greengrocer, and a narrow but inviting café. As Mal asked for the cheque, Vic reflected that the only bad meal she had with Mal was the takeaway pizza, which was only partially his fault. She pushed in her plate and asked him, "How exactly does eating like a king figure in our arrest warrant plans? I've still got PC Billy Battles card. Do we tell him to drive over from Wandsworth and give us a lift?"

"No, my dear, we simply allow your father to pay. I do hope you've still got his card. When they come, and I'm sure they will, just follow my lead."

They say that in Clapham, you can pick up an Australian in under five minutes. Perhaps they underestimate the weight of the average Australian. Regardless, Mal and Vic heard the sirens faster than you could squeeze out Tie Me Kangaroo Down, Sport. Two squad cars leapt the forecourt curb in stuttering fashion, one after the other, nearly clipped the picnic table out front. Mal calmly signed the bill in Abraham Marrow's name and handed the card and slip back to Vic. He motioned for Vic to get up and called out through the open door, "We're in here. Thanks for coming."

Vic had hardly stood up when she was briskly turned around, bent over the chair back, and zip cuffed with plastic ties. It wasn't exactly brutal, just the speed and ruthless efficiency of a 'ready, fire, aim' mindset. Mal was similarly constricted, but his voice was even. "Hang on, boys, we're on the taskforce."

"What taskforce?"

"THE taskforce. The one we shouldn't be talking about. Look, keep the cuffs on, first let's get in the car, then we'll sort it out. And don't forget her purse."

The lead squaddie murmured into the radio hooked to his high visibility jacket. There were four officers in greenish-yellow fluorescent battle dress. "Just one favour," Mal continued, "put us both in the same car. It will save time later, at 10 Downing Street."

The officer looking through Vic's purse had found the ID in her wallet. "Sergeant, got a driver's license here in the name of Amira Myron."

Mal broke in, "And I'm Gregory Myron. Just call the PM, tell him you're bringing in Mr. and Mrs. Myron."

"Yeah, right, mate. I've got the PM on speed-dial."

"Well I do, on my office phone. Can we have this conversation in the car, please?" Mal started tugging at the officer holding his wrists. "Sergeant?"

They made a clumsy procession out of the

restaurant, their only audience the dumbstruck waiter. One of the officers shot him a 'you-didn't-see-anything' look. The waiter shrugged, picked up the signed receipt, and started clearing the table.

Vic had never been in the back of a police car. The steel mesh and unusually heavy thump of the door closing reminded her she was not going to be getting out of this car on her own. So this is what it used to feel like to be oppressed, she thought. She and Mal had to lean forward awkwardly to keep from crushing their cuffed hands painfully into the seat back. At least the officer had put his hand on her head to keep her from braining herself on the doorsill. Or was he also trying to cop a feel of the hair? And why have all these stressful situations brought out her most inane musings? Mal continued with confidence, "Thank you, Sergeant. Now, if you contact the taskforce, you'll get instructions to usher us to the PM toot sweet."

"Mate, I don't know what taskforce you're talking about."

"MI5 and Counter Terrorism command. The taskforce on the unexplained deaths of the MPs."

"Unfortunate accidents, mate. Read about it in the paper. Convince me that this isn't all a bit of a con job."

"Sergeant. Do you seriously think that when five opposition MPs all pop off three weeks before a knife-edge election that Special Branch wouldn't investigate, accidents or no? Listen, call up the head of Protection Command, ask him to patch us through to the PM. This is about yesterday's threat."

"Now why on earth would I want to do that? If this is all a gas, I'll be on traffic duty for the whole of next year."

"Surely. And if this is as real as I know it is, and you don't make this call, it will be a traffic duty decade. Now, I'm fine either way, Sergeant. Amira and I will sit in your squad car for a short while, and when we're released and back in the taskforce office your partner will be able to corroborate that we told you repeatedly to get through to the PM, but you refused."

The second officer in the car chipped in, "Sergeant, I think we better call it in." The Sergeant's partner couldn't have been much more than twenty.

"Thank you for your genius advice, Constable. I'll get Andy to call from the other car." The Sergeant stormed out of the sedan, abandoning the Constable in the driver's seat. The young fellow took a quick glance at his prisoners and decided to sit eyes front, counting down the return of his Sergeant with thumb percussion on the steering wheel. Mal and Vic shared a moment of strained peace, like when a loud motor is suddenly switched off – you didn't realize the noise had entered your shoulders until it stopped. Vic gave Mal a friendly dig with her shoulder. He shushed her with a jerk of his chin, and she realized his confidence was as real as their IDs.

The back seat door opened. The Sergeant stood with clipper blades out from a folding multi-tool. He reached behind them and snipped off the zip ties. "Just leave the bits on the floor. We've got an appointment at 10 Downing. The back side." The Sergeant took his seat in front and told his partner, "Andy, Whitehall. Trafalgar Square roundabout, then go in through Spring Gardens. We've been told to park under the Admiralty and walk them through to the PM. But I expect we'll be booted off the so-called taskforce the moment you switch off the engine." The Constable grunted. No one else in the car made a sound for the rest of the journey.

It was a beautiful day for a police escort. Andy switched off the flashers at Trafalgar Square. Before Vic could appreciate the familiar-from-school-trips view of Nelson's Column, they had turned down an unobtrusive lane, where a steel barrier lowered into the ground before them. They were waved through a security checkpost and into an underground garage. True to his prediction, once Mal and Vic were extracted from the car, the Sergeant and his partner were dismissed.

Mal's false confidence had turned into genuine cheer. "I could get used to the express chauffeur service. Worth the slight chafing at the wrists, don't you think?" Vic said nothing, eyes on the curved concrete blast walls of the tunnel. The only ornaments on the concrete were bolts and metal cable runs, wholly alien from the baroque columns of the building on the surface. Fluorescent lights made the phalanx of four security guards in dark suits look especially grim. Escorting them through the brutally modern tunnel under the Admiralty, the guards were silent. "Notice that we have yet to sign in on a register."

"I get it, Mal, you're very clever," said Vic, and then, "Oh!" Fear makes you clumsy - she had run into the back of the suddenly stopped guard.

Another dark suit had come running towards them with a hand up. This fellow clearly had a bulletproof vest beneath his coat. He and one of the escorts moved away for a brief conference. The other guards drew pistols from inside their coats and stepped back. Mal and Vic were between three muzzles and a concrete wall.

"Never fear, my dear, the ricochets are just as deadly to them," Mal said.

"That's quite a comfort. These fellows look professional enough to ensure all the bullets end up in you and me. I'm not enjoying being lined up in a free fire zone, you know."

"I do know. But we're only being given the gun treatment because we haven't been frisked." Ignoring the guards, he gave her a hug. Mal had a confounding way of touching her at just the right time. One of the guards tapped his ear in response to a mild electronic bleat and staticky murmur. Pistols vanished into jackets as if they had never been. They resumed walking.

The tunnel terminated in an antechamber furnished in vintage doctor's office waiting room: scuffed white plastic panels, cherry vinyl covered benches built into the walls, and a dropped ceiling of dirty acoustical tiles. The false ceiling's inset black domes were no doubt cameras. The whole thing made a box about twelve feet by seven inside the concrete shell, enclosing a glazed white glass door. The door was translucent. They could see an outline of something behind it, but no detail.

The lead escort leaned close to the grey metal box bolted to the right of the door and murmured into its grille. He turned towards Vic and said, "Take a seat. You've an hour's wait." He took a clear ziplock bag out of his coat pocket. "You can use the time to fill this – phone, watch, USB drives, keys, any other metal items need to be left here with me." He put the baggie on the bench next to her and stood in front of the door, his public speaking over.

Vic didn't wear a watch. They'd left their phones behind. Seated on one bench with Mal, opposite sphinx-ishly silent escorts, she wondered what she would have been doing on a regular winter Monday. No holidays on the horizon – Guy Fawkes had come without any government building blowing up, just the long drag of work until Christmas. She'd probably be checking upholstery seams in the workshop or drafting something like 'a concept for World Toilet Day'. They were always looking to burnish the studio's eco-healthy reputation. Mal hadn't said anything in a while. In fact, he'd hardly moved.

She checked his face. His cheeks were unusually smooth. It looked like the small tendons around his skull had been severed. Eyes half-closed, he asked, "Anyone here have a syringe? I'm all out."

Vic shook his arm and steamed at him in low volume, "What the hell are you on about?" His arm continued shaking after she let go. His whole body shivered.

"Insulin," he said, slumping sideways, head on a loose pivot. "My front pocket." Vic pushed him upright, cracking his head on the plastic panel, and dug into his jeans. She felt a metal lump, roughly circular with projections on opposite ends. Her supple fingers fetched out a small brass bottle. She remembered sketching this tortoise as a child, an intricate city carried on the turtle's back, hammered and chased into the front of the flattened sphere. The stopper was a leaping fish. She held it up to his face. "Yes," he said, and collapsed.

His collapse launched the once impassive guards into a cascade of activity. Pistols reappeared, a grating buzzer sounded. A new figure rushed through the glass door with a disposable hypodermic in a sealed wrapper. The medic took the bottle from Vic and rolled up Mal's left sleeve. An ashen hand shot out and grabbed the medic's wrist. "I'll do it," said Mal. Using the man's arm as a support, he pulled himself upright. Mal stripped the syringe packet with the economical grace of long practice and flipped the hinged top off the bottle, revealing a modern grey rubber membrane over the aperture. Mal shivered once, and then, body still, passed the needle through the membrane.

He smoothly drew into the syringe a clear fluid and injected it into one of the thick veins of his left forearm. As the last drop went in, he slumped back against Victoria, concentration broken. The needle hung in his arm. As if by chance, his lips brushed her ear. "Not a diabetic," he whispered. His ragged breathing evened. He slowly straightened up and removed the needle. "Thanks. The sugar, it can sometimes be unpredictable. Can I keep this?"

The medic laughed. "Not a chance. Just put it down on the bench to your left." The medic carefully picked up the syringe by its barrel, waved it at the ceiling cameras, and retreated back through the glass door at the sound of the buzzer.

Vic couldn't bear to sit. She stood, leaving her purse on the bench. Keys, her phone, her dad's phone, anything she could think of that might link back to her real life, she'd already left behind at Fatima's flat. Her pockets were empty.

Mal tugged down his sleeve, clap-brushed his hands, and stood up beside her. There was a minor sway before he steadied. Vic noticed a familiar crackle around him, a gold film rimming his eyes like some unholy metal cataract. He caught her looking and said briefly, "From your father. The pearl was easier, but the effect is the same. Most potent when injected. Didn't that used to cause some questions, I'll say."

Mal put the small bottle in the baggie, along with the contents of his other pocket, a second brass bottle, longer and thinner like a miniature vase. The pattern on the tall bottle was more abstract, almost Islamic, engraved arches superimposed over etched diamond shapes. In contrast to the ornate pattern, its stopper was a simple wooden plug. Mal added his wallet to the bag. He had no keys. It made a small collection of a life, a thin leather billfold and two old brass containers, one six inches, the other less. "Right," he said. "Frisk away."

The escorts patted them both down, no niceties for gender, just coldly functional. That somehow made it more intrusive, not less. The door buzzed again and the medic, whom Vic had internally christened Laughing Boy, motioned them through. Vic hesitated in front of the door. They were completely off the books, unregistered, invisible to anyone but the security apparatus. Vic wondered if they were indeed going to the slaughter, if there was any way they could make it back out of this tunnel alive.

AN AUDIENCE

*Vic's childhood wish to visit 10 Downing St is
granted, unfortunately*

Behind the glass door was a narrow passage lined
with bands of wires and black plastic. Vic guessed
there must be a dozen different detectors along its
eight feet length. The far door was twin to the first,
glass, with the black sphere of a camera above it. As
they buzzed through the second portal, the world
changed from naked concrete and early-modern anti-
style into a wood-paneled secretariat, complete with
thick green carpet and heavy walnut desks. A bored
looking supervisor put down a phone and pointed to
a steel passenger elevator inset into the left wall.
"He's waiting on the second floor." Retrofitted into
the Georgian mansion, the elevator was not much
more than a closet. They abandoned two of the
security detail and rode up in close quarters, the
display above the door cycling through B, G, 1, and 2.

When elevator doors open, you expect the scene to be familiar, yet there's really no reason why each floor in a building should look the same. The elevator opened directly into a generously sized modern office. The change of scenery was jarring, a pledge betrayed. There was a gas bar on low in a broad, white-mantled fireplace along the left side. A light coloured oriental rug filled the open expanse before a single desk at the far wall. The PM sat behind it, wearing reading glasses, a cardigan, and a contemplative look. The noise of the elevator had clearly snapped his train of thought. He put down a tablet and waved them over with casual command.

Vic gasped when she took in the elegantly curved visitor chairs facing the desk. "Are those Hepplewhites?" she asked, moving ahead of her two escorts. The guards reacted, catching her arms by either side.

"Reproductions." The PM tried to dismiss the guards. "You can leave us. I've been expecting Mr. & Mrs. Myron for some time."

"Sir, these two are unlogged. We're responsible for your safety."

"No, no, it's all right. They're, um, they..."

"We're on the taskforce," Victoria rescued him.

"Yes, that's right. The taskforce. They're one of ours. You can go now."

"Which taskforce, sir?"

"The one investigating the accidental deaths of politicians in the run up to this election." Vic's voice was increasingly confident, although the guards still held her.

"Correct. We're fine." When the guards still didn't move, the PM raised his voice, "Damn it, man, trust my judgment. The people elected me for a reason. And they're going to re-elect me because of that same judgment. You may go."

Vic rubbed her arms and sat in one of the delicate wooden chairs. Mal stood behind her. He waited for the elevator doors to close on the departing security before speaking. "You're awfully sure of that."

"Of what?" The PM took off his reading glasses, looking puzzled.

"Of winning the next election."

"Yes. Why shouldn't I be? We have the best party and the best policies. Now, explain to me why I shouldn't just throw you out right now."

"Because we're going to help you find the other voice. Like the voice that just whispered in your ears alone, to dismiss the security guards. But different.

Probably younger." Mal walked around the second chair and stood in front of the PM's desk.

"I don't know what you're talking about."

"Look," said Vic, "we know what's going on and we know you know about it. We're not going to expose you in the press or anything sly. We just want to make sure the next pol doesn't drop dead. Be honest with us. Is it you, or someone else in your party?"

Mal looked over his shoulder at his Victoria in her chair. "Amira, don't bother. Asking a politician to be honest is like asking a scorpion not to sting. We'll do this the hard way." He rotated his head back towards the PM. His neck kept going, elongating, shifting, the skin of his neck tightening, mottled grey scales erupting on its surface. His hair spread sideways in a corona that hardened into a cowl. The enormous trunk of a snake sprouted from the collar of his sweatshirt, neck draped heavily over the documents on the desk and head curled up in front of the PM's face. Massive jaws opened wide enough to swallow the PM's head whole. A drop fell from a tooth the size of a dagger, burning a smoking hole in the wool of the PM's trouser leg.

"NOT ME," the PM screamed, hands held up. As quickly as it had appeared, the snake head vanished, retracting into Mal's normal shape with a wet slither.

"You have been playing with something about which you know nothing," said Mal, normal but for a gold sheen over his eyes. "Tell us when it first started."

"What if I don't?"

Mal sneered his lips, showing hooked snake teeth. "I stop your heart."

"You'll never get away with this."

"Of course we will. Because as far as anyone can tell, we've done nothing. And you're going to help us as well."

"I am the Prime Minister of England. In thirty seconds this room can be flooded with lethal force."

"Indeed. It's unfortunate that by then, you'll also be dead. Care to try me?"

The PM stood up and eased away from his desk, and Mal. "Fine. Doesn't matter. You'll prove nothing. It was about one month ago," he said. "I was returning from the City airport with the Chancellor. I heard a man's voice talking, except strangely, it wasn't the Chancellor or the driver. Took me a moment to work out the voice was talking at me. It said that only I could hear it, so of course I asked the Chancellor if he heard anything, and then suddenly the voice in my ear screamed so loudly it was painful. There was no reaction from the driver or the Chancellor, except to ask what had made me wince. I made some excuse. Then this voice asked me something very similar to your question. I believe he said 'The election is four weeks away. How confident are you of winning?' Of course I told him I was very confident of winning the next election, which brought a somewhat depressing response from the Chancellor, as I had unwittingly said this out loud in the car. And then we had a bizarre conversation, where the Chancellor thought I was talking to him, and this strange voice was quoting me polls. I remember mentioning that we had a slight lead in several swing constituencies, and that with a bit of hard campaigning we would continue in power. This put the Chancellor at ease, I mean he must have thought it a bit odd that I would be bringing this up out the blue, but he tucked back into his iPad and shut up. And then the voice mentioned four polls all showing Labour likely to form a government with a majority of ten to fifteen seats. Fifteen seats, can you imagine?

"That was when I was given an unlikely offer. What if this voice could change the candidates in ten tightly contested constituencies, or make the fellows drop out so Tories ran unopposed? Why, then we'd squeak through with a majority of five seats to Conservatives."

"And what did the voice want in return?" Mal sat down. He crossed his legs American-style, ankle resting on knee and leaned forward, elbows propped on thighs, fingers bridged under his nose, a relaxed and thoughtful interrogator.

"Precisely my thought, which the voice kindly completed. Money, of course, one hundred million pounds as a contribution to some NGO, no links back to the Tory party at all, simply some concerned private individuals making donations to a worthy cause. To be revealed and given after we won the election, of course. And then it asked for a small bit of help, on a couple of votes in the new government. 'You'll know it when I need it,' it said, some support for the voice's view on a measure or two so that they pass. Nothing that is not already part of the business of government, but the voice went on to say that 'if I can count on you, then you can count on me to deliver the election.'"

"So what did you say?"

"I thought I was going mad. A man who hears

voices is not likely to be trusted to run one of the most powerful countries on Earth. I didn't say anything."

"And?"

"A week later, when I was in this office, I heard the voice again. This time we could have a private conversation. I decided to humour the voice, as certainly no one would be able to show that it wasn't just me talking to myself. This room is swept for bugs daily."

"This voice is killing people! Haven't you been following the news about candidates in marginal seats?" Vic blurted.

"Stuff and nonsense," thundered the PM. "There have been a series of unfortunate accidents, none of which are related. Separate tragedies, unfortunate, but nothing more. Besides, this voice is most likely a delusion, like the hypnosis that you have obviously used on me to get in here. A trick of the mind. Campaigning is a stressful business. It will all be gone in three weeks."

Mal stood up, eyes reptilian. "Hypnosis won't kill you, but I will unless you help us find the person behind this." Vic heard a credible savagery in Mal's level statement. She felt cold.

The PM remained calm. Perhaps he was growing used to insane events. "Threaten me as much as you like. Even if I wanted to help you, I just have a voice. It could be anyone. Or a hallucination."

Vic broke in again, "That's where you're wrong. In order for this plan to work, they'll have to be a Tory MP, someone who can bring up a floor vote. And they're probably under forty."

"I know all of the Tory MPs in the House. I am very sure I'd never heard that voice before that day in the car."

"So it's a candidate," replied Vic. "Who are the young turks running for open seats?"

"This is getting very far-fetched. I think all this is just too much stress, and that I've wasted enough time with a certain Mr. and Mrs. Myron." The PM picked up his desk phone. "Anthony?" Then nothing more.

Mal's eyes were glowing, and the PM's face was turning red. She could hear faint tinny hellos from the receiver. The PM didn't make a sound.

Mal took the receiver from the PM's hand and put it back on the cradle. The PM's breath came back with a tremendous whoop. He looked grey, panting and clutching his neck.

"When you've caught your breath, I'd suggest you call Anthony back and ask him to email a list of first-time Tory candidates in the upcoming election, under the age of 40. Have him send it from the computer with the sign-in of Office008." Mal sat back down, his tone mild. The PM did as he was told.

As they waited for the gentle bong of a new email message, the PM glared at Mallory, but said nothing. The list arrived with four names, and photographs. Mal asked, "Is there anyone there that looks like my wife?"

Vic was startled. "What do you mean, black?"

"I mean, that looks like you. I'll explain later."

The PM turned his tablet around. "Phillip M. Lightfoot. But this is all highly irregular. Even if this is the fellow, it's been a series of natural calamities. There can be nothing deliberate about any of this."

Vic grabbed the edge of the tablet and addressed the PM. "Grow up. This is your fault, and now you're going to help us fix it. Start by squaring things with the gate guards. Tell them Mr. and Mrs. Myron are finished with their audience and are ready to go."

"That's it? I let you run off and take care of things?" The PM sneered, "This is the dynamic duo that's going to save England, the election, and everything just and fair in the world - an aging hippie hypnotist in yellow flares and his young darkie lover?"

Vic fired to their defense, "It's not what you think. Although it's clear that the Conservative party is still the racist sexist party."

Mal looked up at PM. "She's right," he said. "It's not what you think." His head expanded again into the giant snake, its fangs dripping acid onto the floor. Drops sizzled as they touched the carpet. In a voice from a prehistoric age, he finished, "It's much worse."

A QUICK EXIT

*Her Majesty's government deals with terrorists, Vic
rediscovers the best way to lose a tail: go shopping*

"This government does not negotiate with
terrorists and extortionists." The PM rubbed at the
burnt spot on his trousers, but his voice was
unwavering.

"That's rubbish and you know it. Just tell security
to let us retrace our steps to Trafalgar Square. It will
be like we've never existed." His normal face stared
meaningfully at the PM. "So pick up the phone, no?"

The PM put his hand on the handset, "What's to
keep me from having security arrest you on a
detainment order for the next several weeks?"

"Nothing. Your impending mortality. Luck. I'm
personally not that fussed about the election, or
whether it's you or some other MP who dies next.
Phillip Lightfoot will answer to me for other matters.
But do what you like. You are the most powerful man

in England, after all. Pick up the phone, call security, tell them what you wish." Vic was again astonished by Mal's confidence, and secretly pleased that a measure of it seemed to have rubbed off on her. She had never expected to be in 10 Downing Street, telling off the PM. Too bad she'd never be able to tell anyone.

As the elevator doors opened behind them, the feeling of impending doom came rushing back. If she had thought she was completely wrung out of adrenaline, some rogue pump within ratcheted up again. She jumped out of the seat and took an involuntary step backwards. The elevator opened on Laughing Boy, the medic.

"Mr. and Mrs. Myron. You're to come with me." They boarded the elevator and watched as it counted backward, 2, 1, G, B. When the doors opened into the green baize suite, Vic couldn't quite believe it was real. They repeated the routine with the buzzers, collected their belongings, and retraced their steps through the tunnel, this time with just the one escort. The metal car barriers recessed into the pavement seemed ridiculous when they passed them on foot. Laughing Boy handed them through a steel wicket door inset into the larger garage door. This must have been open when Constable Andy drove them in.

The medic left them in the quiet cul-de-sac of Spring Gardens, sun shining peacefully on a splendid late Autumn afternoon.

Warm sunshine on her face was both welcome and bizarre, a sharp contrast to the feeling of hopelessness inside the tunnel. At each step, she had thought the game would be up. Masked figures in dark suits would appear and whisk them away into a secret cell, their futures unknowably cloaked by black files and black prisons. She stopped to soak in a brief dose of joy with the sunlight, but Mal strode off exuberantly towards the square. Never a dull moment, she thought, hurrying after him.

She caught him as he stopped for the traffic along the Strand. "'And we're off' and that's it? They just let us go? It all seemed too easy, Mal. What else have you been doing that I don't know about? What ARE you?"

He looked side to side like a sinner in the choir. "My dear, we should thank God that's it. I'm completely done. Knackered. Absolutely nothing left but my long legs. Now, come on, we have to make them lose our trail."

"For what, Mal? They know where we're going to be going. I'll call Fats and we'll get the address of this

Phillip Lightfoot. They can certainly do that as well."

"That's precisely what I'm trying to avoid."

"What?"

"Not the address. Involving Fatima. Or rather, drawing a link between us and her. We should avoid that."

"Yes, fine, sure. But we don't have a phone or anything right now."

"Correct, which is why we're going to go into Charing Cross, and you're going to purchase us two day passes, and we're going to change trains like maniacs until we reach a place where we can catch a taxi that won't bankrupt us in getting close to where we want to be. Bus routes are predictable. At least they haven't started putting government video cameras in the cabs. Yet. Most of all, get us somewhere crowded."

An hour later, Mal was munching falafel and idly shopping for a new jacket at Shepherd's Bush Market while Vic gave Fatima an update and got the Lightfoot address from a pay phone. He was just putting on a new-to-him navy toggle coat when she found him.

"7 Gayfere St, London W2," she told him. "That's just around the corner from Big Ben."

"Westminster, why am I not surprised?" His tone was laconic.

"And Fats said that she's coming with us. George looked up the details on all four the moment it flashed on the network, and he's matched Phillip Lightfoot's travel schedule to at least two of the accidents. Incidents. Whatever they were."

"It's too dangerous."

"For her, or for me, Mal?" She dragged him out of the market alley and onto Uxbridge Road. "This whole thing is sick." She set off away from Shepherd's Bush Common. It was he who had to keep up.

"Dangerous for all of us. But I'm thinking of her. What are you trying to imply?"

"Imply? You tell me, Mal. What exactly are you? You took a needle like a professional addict in the Admiralty. I don't know where you've been or what all you've done. For all I know, you were getting high and I've got HIV. I think you would really have killed him, too."

"Don't be hysterical. Of course I would have killed him. How else do you make it a credible threat?"

"See, that's just it, Mal. You're cold, like an alien. I can't trust you to do the right thing."

"What is trust, my darling? It's belief. It can only

come from within, can't be given, bought or sold. So, I can't make you trust me, and yes, I thought a death threat was an appropriate way to let him know how serious you feel this situation is. But that stunt I did in the PM's office, it was just a glamour. It wasn't real. Even his trousers will be fine. All I can manage these days are convincing illusions."

"That's just it, Mal. When I'm around you, how can I know what's real or not? Maybe the Mal I saw in that dream with my mum is actually the truth. After all, the only thing I have to go on is your word. How do I know I've even met my mother?"

"You're hung up on this idea of trust. I thought we settled terms last night at the hotel. I'm with you on this little adventure, whether I like it or not."

"Well, you unsettled it in the PM's office. I heard you sounding like truth when you said you didn't care about the election. I also believe that you'll help me find this Phillip Lightfoot anyway. But how did you know that he'd look like me?"

"The same way you knew he'd be under forty."

"That was a guess, based on your covenant nonsense. You're avoiding my question."

"Come, my dear, you had an idea as well. Why would a mother not help her daughter? Why does this all seem to revolve around your father? And why did a couple who had been together for more than a lifetime suddenly call it quits?"

"You told me why. You said that my mother wouldn't give up magic, and that when I was born they fought over whether or not to break the agreement and teach me."

"There is another possibility, one that you're not admitting to. Think about children. Until about age two, even if you want to, there is not much you can teach them. You can barely get them to keep their pants dry. That they would split at the moment of your birth seems unlikely."

"So you mean..."

"That's exactly what I mean. Phillip Lightfoot is your older brother."

THE KABULI SETUP

Fatima issues a warning, hard-earned. Victoria's friends are picked off one by one. She meets her brother at last

"Bullshit."

"You saw the photograph."

"Yes, I did. In fact, I've asked Fats to fetch a printout. But you and I both know that black people look alike to the majority."

"My dear, I'm a minority of one, and you certainly can differentiate your people's facial features. He looks like you, and like your father." Mal affected a Jamaican accent, "Da fadda's blud is strong."

"Stop it, Mal. This is all a bit hard to take."

"Yes. I can see how it would be." It was irritating, exasperating, she thought, how he suddenly turned sympathetic. But damn if she couldn't use a bit of it.

Vic flagged down the white van driving towards them on Uxbridge Road. "Ah, George," said Mal.

"You've stayed on. Good, good." As they squeezed four into the front bench seat, Vic once again marveled at Mal's ability to accept each situation with unruffled grace. Fatima ended up half on Vic's lap, the two women in the middle.

"Lucky this one has an automatic transmission. Mostly they're manual. And with me extremely sick too, can't you tell? Pity I've left the key to the van at my mum's, and she's out, so no one from work can nip round to pick it up. Unfortunate. But I expect to get suddenly, remarkably better this evening, and be back at work tomorrow, regardless of what happens."

"I'd surely not stop you, George. But that you're here implies some sort of plan. Do tell."

"Actually, Fatima should explain." George swung back out into traffic, heading towards the City.

Fatima could hardly move without hitting the rear view mirror. She spoke out the side of her mouth like a gangster, "When Vic told me you both got out so easily, I was suspicious. A similar thing happened to me in Kabul. If it wasn't for the fact that I'm small enough to fit into the tyre well of a four-by-four truck, I'd be rotting there now. As it was, when I heard them open the boot and poke around in the rug they'd put on the floor panel, I nearly died. It was probably only a few seconds, but I felt I'd never held my breath so long."

"Please explain, madam," asked Mal.

"Right. I'd been in Afghanistan for almost six months at that point, enough time for a few free-lance articles to make their way by Internet trickle even to Kabul. One of the ruling gangsters decided that he didn't like what I had written about him. So I guess I should be grateful that he didn't put a contract on me straight away. He sent word through one of the locals in the Swedish embassy that he wanted to see me. At that time, the British embassy staff were essentially living in a bunker, with no locals allowed. How they expected to get anything useful done, I don't know, but the Swedish weren't there with guns and such, so they had a bit more of a free run. It turned out that one of our people assigned there was married to a Swedish diplomat also in Kabul, so he became the official unofficial channel to track down any Brit. It was all a bit of a joke. They would let him off the leash for a few hours to catch up with his wife, conjugal visit I guess. I went to their Swedish apartment, a big suite in the downtown expat hotel, quite posh really, and they had a maid..."

"Fats, focus." Vic tried to find a more comfortable

position. The front seat of a BT van wasn't meant for four passengers.

"Right, right. So I get the summons and of course you're shit scared. We started a debate, do you go and get disappeared or do you not go and possibly get blown up or gunned down on the street. Ultimately, I decided to go."

"And you obviously made it out again."

"That's precisely my point. The audience was a big nothing, really, all grave courtesy and veiled menace. I was told in an elliptical way that if I knew what was good for me I'd be on the next flight home, and so of course I cut straight to the chase and told him that if he'd read my articles then he should be able to tell that I didn't know what was good for me, but I sweetened it by asking if he could guide me. And he became all avuncular and did I know my name was the daughter of the prophet and the wife of the Imam, because he was Shia, and he personally escorted me to the door with pleasantries, so I thought I was safe, right?"

"I told my driver and he was uneasy. Apparently Qasim Mohammed is curt and ungracious to his friends. He saves his honey for the people he hates. But it was hard to argue with the evidence. I'd been summoned, and then in and out in fifteen minutes, with tea and even a compliment. The smooth exit was the setup."

"The next evening, we were going to one of those typically Kabuli restaurants, the kind that look like an abandoned house from the outside. It was night, absolutely pitch black, the black you only get in places with unreliable electricity and no street lamps. You get out in front of the door in the dark and knock and inside it's all bright plus a full security detail with a metal detector, another bomb-proof door, and only then you get through that and it's total party, fancy electric lights, fantastic biryanis and kebabs, as much liquor as you can hold. Where they hide the generator I don't know, but their blackout curtains must be the best in the world. And their intelligence is top notch, because all of the white people partying with me didn't have a clue that a hit was about to go down but two of the waiters came over to me with a large duffel bag, one of those navy sailor kit bags that are like a long tube open at one end, and he told me to stand up. I was half in the bag already so of course I went along with it, and then his partner put the duffel over my head and now I'm a walking canvas popsicle stick. That didn't last more than a second. The two fellows bundled me up and carried me out the back faster than my dining companions could react. Several of them told me later in London that they'd tried to stop them, but I don't believe it and worse or better, that they didn't stop them saved my life. They throw this duffel under the lift-up floor in the boot of a giant truck where the spare tyre should be and voila, I lived to tell the tale, although there are some nights when I can feel the steel straps which are supposed to keep the tyre attached to the bottom of the truck in my shoulders. Which is the point. We can't just forget about this. I think there's going to be some kind of government hit on you this evening and George and I are here to stop it."

Mal cut in, "Madam Fatima, the government could have detained us in the Admiralty tunnels, in absolute secrecy. What the government chooses not to retain, it rejects."

"You're not thinking like a warlord. Or a bureaucrat. If they pick you up in the Admiralty, after getting you in off-the-books, at some point you're going to have to go on the books somewhere, especially when you're been so close to the Prime Minister. Someone is going to ask questions about how you got in, what you did, or something else awkward. Much better to have some completely unrelated and officially plausible security event happen far far away from any politicians. Give it a bit of distance, make it as boring as possible, perhaps a house break-in or a bit of arson, put you away for a few weeks and then bury it. That's how I'd do it."

"As Irrfan Khan once said, your story sounds 'strangely plausible'. So what, dear Fatima, do you recommend?"

"I recommend that we stake out Phillip Lightfoot's house with a video camera while you go inside, and that we broadcast whatever happens on the Internet and to anybody I can reach in the mainstream media if things go funny."

"Quis custodiet, ipsos custodes?" quoted Mal.

George accidentally poked Fatima with his elbow as he took the van through a sharp turn at the Shepherd's Bush roundabout. "Sorry. Yeah, it's who guards the guardians, innit? I reckon we've got about thirty minutes of inching traffic until we see Big Ben. Vicky, can you pull out the A to Z? It's in the glove box."

"Sure. And it's Vic or Victoria, please, George. But I'm grateful for the lift. George, we'll be going well within the Congestion Zone, which means your employer and the government will have a record of this van's license plate on photographic file."

"Under control, Vic-toria," he said, stretching out the last half of her name. "My little BD61PPN is currently BD61BRN. Took me a minute this morning with a Stanley knife and black tape. The font's a real bugger, but it's possible if you trace over templates from the web. Fatima found a Halfords nearby and we were home and housed. I always prefer a van with a P in its plate, just on the off chance. Attention to detail, mate."

"That's thin cover, George," said Vic.

"Not much time. It will have to do. Besides, we know he's home. I routed a VOIP call through a TOR server on a maintenance number, and he picked up immediately. Sounded quite cool and calm on the phone." There was a grit to George that Vic hadn't noticed before. "Speaking of cover, Fatima put your change of clothes in the back."

They crawled past Hyde Park and the Serpentine. George turned before Buckingham Palace, the trees in the palace grounds a vegetable crown on the brick wall to their left. It made a pleasant contrast to the dull sandstone of the Empire office blocks lining the right.

Lower Grosvenor Street was completely packed. With some swearing, George maneuvered the large van across painted lanes to make progress towards the clock tower. He turned off the main road before Westminster Abbey. They were in rich territory, between palace and abbey, the price of an address a minimum million pounds. He drove past Gayfere Street, a short, bone-quiet residential lane of terrace houses amongst the corporate and church headquarters. The pavement was so neat it gleamed in the late afternoon sun. The next lane was one-way the wrong direction so George took a loop around the Abbey proper. Twenty minutes of traffic buggery later, they were on Tufton, parallel to Gayfere. That's where they saw the black Range Rover.

It was ahead and pointed away from them on the narrow street. Two separate fins of gelled hair crested above the leather headrests. George parked three cars behind it, as unobtrusively as a large white van could.

"George, I have to get out," said Mal. "My left knee is frozen solid from the air conditioning duct, and I think Vic dislocated my right shoulder during the last few maneuvers." He fumbled for the door lever.

"Mal, don't try anything cute," said Vic. "I have a feeling we have one shot at this." The fear Vic had felt in the tunnel was creeping back.

"Never you mind, my dear. I'm an old man who couldn't manage cute with a year of puppy dog calendars. I'm just going to strange and check out in the back." Mal popped the door and limped down the side of the van. They heard the back door panel open.

"I think he meant change and stretch out. You go too, Vixen. George and I will get set up here." Fatima gave her a brave smile and a nudge in the ribs. Vic traced Mal's route to the back of the van. She caught him with his sleeve rolled up, gearing up to inject another shot.

"What are you doing?"

"The sensible and rational thing, my dear. We're about to walk into the nest of thieves. I figured I should be a bit powered up." He smoothly compressed the plunger, and gave a wolfish smile of satisfaction.

"But with whose needle?"

He shook his head to clear it. "My own, the same one, from the medic at the PM's office. A bit suspect, but not too bad."

"I didn't see you pocket that."

"Ah, my dear, fast hands. I also managed to get in and out of the PM's office with this." Mal waggled his fingers. The needle vanished, replaced by the wicked black folding knife from the thug on Saturday night. Its serrated edge locked into place with a dry-firing click. "Here, unlock this for me," he said, handing it to her handle first. "I can't do it with one hand, I've got the needle in the other and I'd rather not prick myself again. Dramatic gesture, ruined at the finale."

She took the knife and fiddled with the recessed lever. "How exactly did you get this into his office? Didn't we go through a dozen detectors?"

"Of course. But the people behind the screens were only looking at us. Why should they comment on a knife tucked into a security guard's belt? They were authorized for guns, a little blade gets lost in the shuffle. Come, my dear, undress for me again." He turned and passed Fatima's rainbow knit bag to her by its wooden handles. "Your other things are in there. Then we'll take a walk around the block."

They emerged almost matching. Mal wore his Shepherd's Bush toggle coat, just a shade lighter than Vic's navy duffle, black jeans barely peeping out below. They left the sweatshirts and loud clothes behind in the truck, with Vic's purse and everything but the fake ID. Fatima had thoughtfully thrown in two wool hats, a bit warm before dusk but anonymous. Vic whispered an "all set?" through the grille to the front seat and got an affirmative noise in return. They bailed out of the back of the van and walked towards the low fenced park at the end of the street.

Mal took her arm and dragged her into a deli on the corner of Dean Bradley Street. "Mal, now's not the time to be eating."

"Indeed, my dear, tell that to the man loitering on the opposite corner. Time to shake up our profile." Mal suddenly burst forth in a full-throated but flat American accent. "Hey buddy? Is this the café by the circle? I'm supposed ta' meet my guide there."

The counterman looked up with an angry start, and wiped his hands on the front of his apron. He saw the innocent grin on Mal's face and took a deep breath. "Out of towner? You'll be wanting St. John's Smith Square Café. But you better move quickly, they close at five."

"St. John's Smith's Square?" asked Mal, with naïve helplessness. "Where's that?"

The counterman lifted up the counter flap and walked Mal to the door. "I'll show you. It's the big roundabout, there," he said, pointing up the street. Vic watched the suit on the opposite corner pivot to observe Mal and the deli man.

Mal's prairie vowels boomed through the deli window. "See, you give a square two names, and it isn't even a square. No wonder I get lost in this town." Mal drew the deli man halfway down the block by force of personality. Vic watched the suited watchman dismiss Mal's lone tourist and return to scanning the main road. She waited a moment and made a solitary way up the quiet street towards the circle, wool cap firmly pulled down over her ears. The circle was capped by a grand hall, almost a cathedral itself, three huge doors separated by tall stone columns at the head of a broad stone stair. Mal was reading the board posted on the first landing of the staircase. She instinctively walked past him and inside the building. There was a small foyer with a staircase to the basement and open doors leading deeper into a large open concert hall. Both foyer and hall were empty.

She was about to go down the steps when Mal joined her in the foyer. He pulled her behind one of the columns and spoke urgently, "There's a car with two friends in it parked halfway around the square, about eight o'clock on the dial if we've come from six.

I expect they'll also be a team on Gayfere Street itself, and at the exits. I think our Lady Fatima was right. It's a set up."

"So we pick up our ball and go home?"

"Of course not, my dear. Sometimes when you hit an immovable obstacle, you have to find ways to go around it. It just means we can't work as a pair. They're surely expecting the two of us. Now, the moment someone knocks on the door to number seven, all hell will break loose. So I'm going to give you this package for delivery, and you're going to try and serve it to the house next door." Mal pulled a folded brown paper bag from his jacket. It had the logo of the deli where he'd stopped for directions. Mal shook it open and gave her the tall brass bottle from her father's house to put in it.

"And what will you be doing while I'm delivering a bottle of god-knows-what to some random house?"

"I'll be knocking on door number seven. You see, we've got one other problem. Phillip has been a very bad boy. He's clearly using magic. In fact, he's used up every last scrap nearby. This whole neighborhood is an amazingly dead zone, a desert. Now, for a guy like me, I need something, some trickle of background radiation, or else I can't keep my youthful good looks going. Once I venture into that house, I'll have about thirty minutes before the dose I took in the van wears off. If I'm not out of this area by then, I'm dead. So, my dear, I think the better part of valour is for me to get arrested and taken safely away from here."

"I'm on my own?"

"Yes," he said bluntly. "Here." He handed her the lock blade. "Keep this in your pocket. You've been questioning me about trust for three days. Shoes on your foot, now. Can I trust you to do what needs to be done?"

"He's my brother!"

"He's a brother to you like I'm a brother to a chimpanzee. The only thing you have in common is genetic material. Feelings? Forget they exist."

"Damn it, Mal, you're always running out when I need you."

"You don't need me for this. Besides, I knew it was a suicide mission when we saw that first Range Rover. There is no way we can get in and out of a narrow one-way street, with watchers at both exits, without someone being sacrificed. Experience should make way for youth, my dear."

"Mal, I don't like it."

"You think I do? Unless you've got a better idea, go first and linger at the door with the fake deli delivery. Don't be alarmed if they tense up as you get near number seven. Just keep cool. Pretend you're on a mission of cuisine mercy." Despite his stern expression, Mal had a twinkle in his eye. "We'll never get a chance to do something like this again. At least, hopefully never. Enjoy it. Now go."

Vic left the concert hall, paper bag in hand. The weight of the bottle made it swing awkwardly on its string handles. It was almost jaunty. She passed the men in the dark coloured sedan. There were no police lights, but it had a steel mesh divider between the front and back seats and was parked where Mal had described. A shivery finger went up her spine, but she kept walking. Hard to believe only three days ago she was searching for a different address, on Middlesex Lane.

Another man, with a Bluetooth headset in his ear, was polishing a large motorcycle with a chamois at the entrance to Gayfere Street. His military-style haircut was unremarkable, but he was rubbing struts that were already sparkling. She kept an even pace and walked by him. Numbers nine and eight Gayfere Street looked residential, and deserted, their inhabitants not yet home from a busy day buying and selling things in units of hundred thousand. She saw the door of the sedan in front of her budge slightly as she slowed to check number seven, and then subside as she went into the alcove of the building at number six. It seemed to be a law firm, dark wood panels and a CCTV call box inset into the entranceway arch. She pressed the button and heard a faint buzz from the interior. A single track of sweat dripped down her neck.

Tuned for Mal's footsteps, she didn't hear the speaker box at first. On the second hail, she held the deli bag up to the camera lens. "Delivery. Gourmet olive oil, for, uh, Peter Marshall." The reply was lost in a sudden commotion. Mal had knocked on number seven's blue door. The doors of the sedan on the corner burst open. Two men in regulation dark suits rammed Mal into the closed door. The motorcycle polisher had come up in stance, snub-nosed pistol pointed in Vic's direction by a steady hand. She put her hands up, dropping the bag. It landed with a hollow clunk. Mal was cleaning the upper part of the door with his face, one arm twisted behind his back.

As the pistol swung away from her, she bent to pick up the bag. She watched from a half-squat as the number seven door swung open and all four men vanished inside. She straightened, looking up and down the short street. The driver and passenger doors of the sedan were propped wide, held in place by some internal hinge. She wondered, hesitating, how soon they would come back to lock the car, then took three quick steps from the shelter of the law firm alcove, up the paving slab step, and through the open door of number seven.

Inside was a white painted foyer. Walnut risers led up the wall on the right. To the left was an open arch into a small sitting room. She heard a series of heavy thumps from the ceiling above her head, stomping footsteps, or someone being thrown around. She poked her head through the arch. The sitting room was empty. There was a white leather sofa under the window facing the street, a small cotton rug with a mass-produced abstract pattern, and a round glass dining room table with metal chairs leading off to what must be a kitchen in the back. Little sign that anyone actually lived here, other than stacks of printouts and a legal pad on the table, neatly arranged to an invisible grid. There was something about the furniture and stillness that said 'executive money'. It was a far cry from the bargain bin chaos of her apartment, or her father's comfortably threadbare home in Wales. More distant thumps from the ceiling, then quiet voices. She put a foot as gently as she could on the stairs and looked up.

Above the archway into the sitting room, the stairs jogged left along a banister. Through the banister rails she saw a landing and a corridor running towards the front of the house. There was a small door at the first turning, and another door, slightly ajar, halfway along the landing. Both doors had old-fashioned black iron hinges and handles. The voices were coming from further above. Taking the weight off each step, she padded to the top of the stairs and tried the smaller door. It swung smoothly open, lock and hinge well maintained. She heard retreating footsteps and closed the door soundlessly behind her. She was alone in a small bathroom, radiator, small clothes rack, and toilet on the right, tub and sink on the left. She turned and looked through the antique keyhole in time to see three flashes of dark cloth, matched by heavy treads descending the stairs. They closed the front door firmly behind them. She was in, seemingly undetected.

"Vic? That you? I think Phillip's upstairs." A familiar voice came through the keyhole. Vic opened the bathroom door and went onto the landing. She pushed the second door open wider. Fatima was sitting on the wooden floorboards of a neat bedroom, in the open space between the bed and a chesterfield wing chair. She waved one hand weakly. The other was connected by a metal cuff to the radiator.

"How did you get here?" Vic whispered.

"Bad luck. After you two left out the back, I thought I would do a forward recce. When I stopped in front of the downstairs door, all of a sudden I'm handcuffed and bundled up the stairs."

"Are you all right?"

"Completely fine. And I saw him. He does look like you."

"Phillip? Where is he?"

"He's gone upstairs, with Mal."

"What happened?"

"Not sure. Phillip was talking to me, trying to figure out who I was, when the front door banged again. He went out on the landing in a hurry, left me a sliver of a view. I saw them frog-march Mal past. They all seemed to head up. Then I got a glimpse of the heavies going back to their posts. I haven't been here long, but from what I can tell, it's just Phillip and Mal upstairs. Don't suppose you have a key to these cuffs?"

"I'm going up. Are you going to be all right?"

"I'm fine, Vics, but you're supposed to say that in reverse order. Go sort him out, nothing you can do for me right now. I just hope George hasn't been picked up. Nice bag by the way. You going to offer him a sandwich?"

"Something like that. Don't go anywhere."

"Hardly." Fatima winked after Vic, but she was already out the door. The landing wrapped around into another flight of stairs. She walked briskly up the stairs, no longer trying to conceal her steps. At the top was a smaller landing with two white doors. She opened the first and stared blankly at linens and towels for a moment. She closed it and tried the second. It opened into a long hall running the depth of the house, with polished wood floors and clerestory windows over open rafters. The effect was light and air, like a hangar for an urban glider. Only a few scattered pieces of furniture broke up the huge space. Vic spotted two Van Der Rohe style chairs, and a desk at an angle that hinted it had recently been moved. Mal was positioned like Fatima had been on the floor below, against the radiator by the back window. His head was slumped. He seemed unconscious.

At the far end, she saw a slim male figure watching a large TV bolted to the brick wall. The sound was off, but it looked like the news broadcast. Phillip turned off the TV, put the remote on the desk, and faced towards Vic. He was about her height, but with a slim athletic figure. He dressed as if he knew it, a well-fitted button down that accentuated his shoulders and tapered trousers capped with some kind of designer belt, small metal bosses with the head of a dragon or a medusa. Disconcerting, Vic thought, to encounter a stylish, trim, male version of yourself dressed as the evil elf who's coming to dinner. And then he came towards her.

LIGHTFOOT AT REST

Vic and Phillip bond over family, Mal loses his head, or at least part of it; Fatima refuses to toe the line

Phillip walked slowly over the bare floorboards, a slight smile on his face. "You're not the police. I was expecting the police. Or the secret service. You must be with him."

"I'm your sister."

Phillip clapped with delight. "So you are! Haven't looked for you in ages. Well met, sis! What are you doing here?"

"I've come to stop you."

"Stop me from what? Subduing a house-breaker?"

Vic was temporarily nonplussed. For a split-second, she wondered if this whole thing really could have been a string of horribly unlucky accidents. Mal let out a soft moan.

"Stealing an election," she replied.

"Unfair, sis. I'm trying to win an election. In

Oxford, actually. Oxford West and Abingdon constituency."

"Perhaps I should ask you, then, what are you doing here? Oxford is bloody miles." Vic shook her head. "You're up to something wrong. Something magical. I've met our mother."

Phillip spread his hands wide and dropped his head, in resignation, or acceptance. Or awaiting applause. "Yes, I know," he said, when it didn't come. "She told me. Said you paid her a visit, accompanied by the old man at the window." Phillip's expression grew wistful. "I'm glad you know the truth. Mom and I watched you grow up from a distance for a while, but it was hard. Father obscured the house. We could only watch you in public places. I hadn't thought about you in years. Seem to have turned out all right. A little, shall we say, unambitious, but all right. Have you gotten rid of that boyfriend? Mum said he was a real turd."

"And what about you? How are you turning out?"

Phillip spun around. "How do I look?" He laughed. "I reckon I've come out well, considering. You must admit, this place is nice. Quite central. Rented, but I plan to buy after the election. I mean, I've done about as well as one might expect given my broken childhood home. Did you never wonder about me?"

"No." The syllable sounded harsh, even to her ears. "I didn't even know you existed."

"Oh, but I knew you-hoo."

"Vic, he's dangerous. Don't forget he's killing people." Mal's voice was a cracked whisper. He lifted his head from where he sat by the window. There were deep lines in his face, a spider's web of wrinkles, the canals of Mars.

"Oh, ignore him," said Phillip. "I've done nothing wrong. That I happened to be near the scene of some tragic deaths is coincidence."

"Really? I'm your sister. You can come clean to me."

"Sister? So close, so loving! I'm surprised you can even let the word cross your tongue. I lost my father because of you. Dear mum told me that she and father were just fine until the second child. She hadn't agreed to his silly covenant, but even so, happily together until you came along. Then pure Abraham, Honest Abe, decided that if she was set on teaching the next generation magic, it would stop with me. And so he left, taking only you."

"How can you be so sure that's what happened? How can you blame me? I never knew my, our mother."

"Because I talked to dear old dad myself. He summoned me about a year ago. Wrote me an e-mail. Isn't that now how parents assert themselves out of the blue, email? Said I had to come to Cardiff to 'discuss the use of finite resources'. And like a good son, I went."

"He didn't tell me about this."

"Oh?" Phillip closed the distance between them, and ran an aristocratic finger down her cheek. "There was lots he didn't tell you, now, isn't that so, sister?" He turned and walked back towards the black leather and steel chairs. "Take a seat, I'll tell you all about it."

"I'd rather stand."

"Suit yourself. If only our father was as broad-minded as I. This all started because he wouldn't share. He had the world's greatest source of power at his fingertips for hundreds of years. Once it was almost used up, he decided that only he and his friends could play with it."

"Well, there were these kind of vampire magic creatures that would otherwise be killing people."

"I know. That's what got me back in the game! You see, mother and I went away. I grew up like any other English bastard, during the day. By night, she taught me, almost from when I learned to speak. In a way, I was literally raised in a dream world. Dear Mum taught me a lot. There is strong magic in dreams. But when I would wake up in the real world, it felt dead. I was weak. Defenseless. Fortunately, I was quite a bright little chap. After all, I was in school morning and night. But there was still something about the 'real' world that didn't satisfy. And of course, we didn't have much money. Mother wasn't very concerned about things like that. When necessary, she'd give someone an omen in a dream, and we'd have a sudden windfall. That was the way I got into Westminster school. I think there was something about a premonition among the faculty that I should come in on a scholarship. Hard to say, really. After that I was pretty much on my own. Except when I went to sleep, of course. I don't think our mother has left the dream world in twenty years."

"What does this have to do with the wights?"

"Yes, the wights. Quite delicious, they are. I was in 10th form, almost 16, and we were just discovering which clubs in London would let in the underage. Wouldn't you know one night some sweet older woman took a fancy to my chocolate looks? She pulled me aside to teach a young man the facts of life.

Or death. She gave me a kiss like you wouldn't believe."

"I think I would. I've had one of them."

"Ah, but you've got no nose for magic. If you did, you would have seen what they were doing. I did. After that, I was off to the races. Imagine being able to work magic in the real world. I began to take a year or two from girls and boys at the dance clubs. They'd think that they just had a heavy session, perhaps drank one too many. And I got the ride of my life. It didn't take long before my activities came to the attention of the London pack."

"Who?"

"The wights, the London pack. They're quite organized. And afraid of nothing and no one except for my old man. And your older man. So I guess now it's just one. Although they're afraid of me too."

"You know, Phillip, this is all a bit of a moral cop out. You've just gone from killing people slowly to killing them quickly. I'm not impressed. And a troubled childhood is no excuse. I had the same thing, without the magic, and I'm not planning to kill anyone."

"Not even me?"

Vic felt the weight of the knife in her coat pocket.

315

"Not you, not anybody. Our father taught me that killing people is wrong. If you had talked to him, you would have heard it too. He was against the death penalty as well."

"That's just it. He didn't want anyone to die, and, he didn't want me working magic. Well, sis, you can't have it both ways!" Phillip gave a little giggle.

"What did he really say?"

"Oh, some nonsense about how what I planned to do was wrong, that he would intervene to stop me, and that while he wouldn't kill his only son, he wouldn't stop working against me and my magic until he was dead. There was some tearful talk about what he and our mother had worked for, and that we needed to let old things stay buried. Sentimental crap, frankly."

"So you killed him."

"Ooh, sis! You are a firebrand. Patricide? Tempting, but you can't hang that one on me."

"Then who did?"

"The London pack. The same nice chaps I sent after Mal. We're quite friendly nowadays. And can you blame them? Because in trying to stop me, he was trying to stop them too. They told me all about it. Seems he'd gotten so careful and cautious with his hoard of magics that when they broke into his house one evening he had only one medallion on him. So they did an interesting thing, let him fry up a few young ones until he ran out of puff, and then they just sucked the life out of him. That's why there were only four left to send after you. Quite brutal really, but these fellows play a long game. Centuries. What's one or two when the survival of the species is at stake?"

"But what could you promise them that they don't already have? If anything, your working magic is making their lives harder."

"Power, darling sister, power. If magic is mostly gone from this world, then we'll need a more sordid sort. Politics and administration. The wights are starting to get trapped by the mundane. Do you realize you need ID for even the most basic transactions? The older ones have never had a passport. But a friendly minister can get you passports, permits, whatever is required. Besides, banking is too boring, and the real money is with the government – our economy is a hundred times larger than any bank. Hell, didn't we nationalize one or two the other day? And I'll be in charge of it!"

"I'm not impressed. And it's not likely they'll put

you in charge. I just met the PM this morning and he doesn't seem too keen to hand over the reins."

"Indeed. But he and I have come to an understanding. He knows who I am now. It was easy to convince him to give me a roll of the dice. Nothing has been exposed and he'll be very much in charge after we win this coming election, which a few accidental deaths has made much more likely. I'll just need the occasional favour. Like a kind telephone call that you were on your way, with your pal, and the use of a private detail. Which was supposed to keep you from getting in here unannounced, but no matter."

"Vic." A weak voice. "I don't have much time." She ran to Mal on the floor. "My pocket. Carefully." For the second time, she gingerly dug inside the front pocket of his jeans. She felt the cool shape of the round brass jar, and the barrel of a syringe. "You'll have to do it." He'd folded a wad of paper over the needle, but it stuck on the lip of the pocket. She overbalanced from her crouch, the needle gleaming as Phillip wandered over to inspect.

"Woah, sister, you are a more dangerous person than I thought."

"It's for him." She opened the cap of the jar and

poked the needle through the now familiar grey rubber top.

"Ah, I smell something in there. Is that one of our father's delightful supplies?"

"Back off, Phillip." She drew out the plunger and watched the barrel fill with clear liquid. She tapped the needle and squeezed out a few drops like she had seen on the medical TV shows and pushed up the sleeve of his uncuffed hand.

"Oh, but I want a taste."

She pushed the needle into a vein as best she could, without delicacy, and squeezed the plunger in. She must have hit a good enough spot. The effect on Mal was immediate. The sagging folds of skin on his face tightened up. His chin lifted. He looked up at Phillip and barked, "She said, back off."

"Or else what, she'll stab me with her needle?"

Vic stood and pulled out the lock knife. She flicked it open. "Maybe I'll stab you with this. You're crazy, and I'm not going to let you get away with it. Besides, there's not enough magic in this house to harm anyone."

Phillip stepped back, hands in the air. "A mad woman with a knife is calling me the crazy one. It's a topsy turvy world. What is one to do?" Phillip snapped his fingers. Mal's bottle and syringe flew into his hands. "Don't be so shocked, sis. It's like magic. Oh wait, it IS magic. I also know how to save up a bit. And about that knife." The knife suddenly became immensely heavy. She struggled against its weight. It fell from her straining fingers and buried its point in the wood floor. "Naughty thing that." Phillip focused on the bottle. He poked the emptied needle through the rubber seal and drew a centimeter of liquid.

Mal nudged her with his knee. He whispered, "He'll be mostly used up now. That trick with the knife is probably his limit. Tackle him."

As she gathered herself, Phillip held the needle point in front of his mouth. He pressed the plunger with his thumb, squirting a spray of liquid into his mouth. "Delicious! And in the nick of time. Now to try it out." He took a deep breath, then blew out. Vic was hurled against Mal by a hurricane gust of wind. The window panes above the radiator shattered, raining glass on the two of them. A shard of glass opened a long cut on Mal's scalp. Mal was stunned, semi-conscious.

Vic gently brushed glass off his head and rounded on Phillip, her hand slick with Mal's blood. "Stop it, you're killing him."

"What else would you have me do?"

"Stop all of this. Live your life without magic. Let us go. Stop killing people."

"You make it sound simple. But we've come so far, and I have promises to keep. And one day you'll come after me again, when I've done something else you disapprove of. Only you'll have more firepower than a small brass bottle and the talkative pixie downstairs." Phillip shrugged, as if 'what to do?'. "At first I thought you and your friends could just share Her Majesty's hospitality for a few weeks, after which we have a tearful family rapprochement. I see now that you're going to have to disappear a bit more permanently. I should have known better than to try to talk sense to any woman other than my mother. A severe miscalculation."

"Don't do this, Phillip. I'm your only family on this Earth."

"Yes, and you came after me with a knife. I'm handsome. I date. I'll make more family easily enough."

"And how are you going to explain our dead bodies to the police outside, especially since they were the ones who brought us in alive and locked Mal and Fatima to the grillwork?"

"That is a minor hiccough, one that I think I can overcome with another dose of this stuff. But let's not be too morbid and awkward. Your old fellow will definitely have to go, but you are family after all. If you're willing, I can put you in trance and help you forget this every happened. It's like hypnosis, as long as you're a little bit disposed to it. With enough power I can make you sleep through anything. But power is so fleeting."

The cut on Mal's head was welling blood. Vic pressed her hand against the cut. She begged her brother, "Do you have a towel, a handkerchief, anything? He's going to die."

Vic saw real anger for the first time in Phillip's eyes. "Leave him. He's going to die anyway. You should worry about yourself, and your little friend downstairs." He shook the small bottle and listened to the liquid shake inside. "Not much of this stuff left. Are you willing to miss a few short days, and live, or will it have to get messy?"

Phillip fished a handcuff key from his pocket. "I'll give you an easy choice. Fetch your friend. Come back here and submit to a small spell. When you wake up, I'll let you both go free. Or you can try to fight your way through the police on your own. If anyone besides me exits the house, their orders are to arrest and remand until after the election. By which time, it won't matter what two crazy females claim. What do you say?" He held up the key.

She looked at Mal. Thin blood was squeezing out from under her palm. His eyes flickered. She thought she heard him say 'go', but she wasn't sure. She nodded at Phillip, and held up her other hand. He tossed her the key. She caught it one-handed and left Mal alone with Phillip.

She wiped her bloody hand on the wool of her coat as she ran down the stairs. Fatima was still locked to the radiator. "I heard everything. The floorboards of these old houses have gaps, it's like being in the same room. He's nuts, you know."

"I know," Vic said, unlocking the handcuffs, "and he's also incredibly dangerous. He could just kill us. Listen, follow my lead. We're going back upstairs."

"Not out? I'm not going along with this. He can try and put his dirty fingers in your head, but I'd rather take my chances with the Old Bill."

"Trust me. If we're to have a chance of stopping anything, we have to go along with Phillip now."

"Jesus, Vic, I thought you had more balls than

323

this. What about Mal?"

"Mal is my problem. Let me worry about him."

"You mean, let him die."

"Shut it, Fats. You've been friends with me for a long time. I'm not about to change now. Let's go." Vic helped Fatima stand, her legs stiff from sitting chained on the floor. They scrambled up the stairs, half-limping, half-running. So this is what 'dread' really means, thought Vic.

ABRACADABRA

Fatima has to choose between Mal's life and her own, Phillip robs them of all they've brought, the election proceeds

Phillip had repositioned his desk to the centre of the room. He sat on its wide surface, facing the door and Mal simultaneously. "Ah, you've come back. I knew you'd make the right decision. Be good girls and sit on the floor next to your friend. Toss me the key, please."

Vic threw the handcuff key intentionally short. It slid on the floor in front of where Phillip was perched on the desk. Fatima saw Vic look at Mal with a grim face. "Scalp wounds always look worse than they are," said Fatima. She reached behind her back, made an awkward movement with her shoulders, and pulled her bra out through the neck of her shirt. "Here, I don't really need this, it's padded, and about the right shape. Press it to his head." Vic did as she was told,

325

cradling Mal's face with her other hand.

Phillip picked up the key and put it into his trouser pocket. He snapped his fingers to get their attention. "Ladies! I want you to imagine what you've been doing for the last week, instead of meeting me. Get a clear idea in your head, and relax." His eyes silvered slightly, and Vic suddenly felt bone tired, as if she had stayed up for two days straight. Fatima's athletic posture slumped slightly. The silver glow of Phillip's eyes filled her vision. She couldn't concentrate on anything but falling asleep, until Phillip shouted, "Stop! You're ruining it!" The spell was broken.

Fatima smiled wanly at Vic. "I couldn't not resist. Not in my nature to put up with this kind of nonsense, even if it means getting killed."

Phillip was standing now, furious. "Empty!" He flung the brass bottle at Fatima, clipping her over her left eye. She clutched her face and sprawled on the floor with a moan. "The brown bag, give it. I can feel the heat from here. Show me what's inside."

The deli bag was where she had left it at Mal's feet. She reached inside, removed the second brass bottle and held it up in front of her. Phillip smiled. "Another storehouse. Open it."

Vic crossed to him, shielding the bottle behind her back. She stopped uncomfortably close to him, and touched his forehead with a bloodstained thumb. "What happened to you and me? Our lives could have been so different, if we had just known about each other before."

He shoved her shoulder with an impatient hand. "Our lives will be different," he said. "But I've got an election to win first. Open and give."

She put the bottle in his hand, wooden stopper intact. "Open it yourself. Mal's lived a long long time enough, and I'll go along with your scheme, but some things, you'll just have to do yourself." She turned her back and walked to where Fatima was lying on the floor. "Come on, Fats, get up. Let's get this over with." They knelt together, facing Phillip, who was trying to remove the stopper. For a moment it looked stuck, and then it gave slightly. He looked up to confirm the women weren't moving, then gave all his attention to working the stopper back and forth, keeping the bottle upright.

The stopper came loose with a wet sucking sound and a puff of smoke. The bottle clanged to the floor, wooden stopper rolling in a small circle nearby. Phillip was gone. Fatima leapt up in shock. "What the hell just happened?" she asked.

Mal's clear deep voice startled them, "To get a genie into the bottle, you need two things. A special bottle, and a genie dumb enough to open it. Your father was only lucky enough to have the first. Nicely done, Victoria." He chuckled.

Fatima turned to him. "Are you ok? You sound ok. What the hell is going on?"

Mal folded the bloody bra into a neat half-moon and stuffed it into his coat pocket with a sour expression. His head wound had healed as if it never was, a slight ruddiness along the scalp the only evidence of a pint of blood spilled. "It was Vic's idea. We talked about it over dinner on Sunday. She wanted to know why Ali had been so against teaching her magic. The problem has always been that once the genie gets out of the bottle, you have a hell of a time getting it back in. Ali never taught Vic a thing. Even a hint would have been enough to set her on a lifetime of searching. Once you get your first taste, you just want more and more. Needles are nothing! For a bit more magic, you'd suck from the tit of the devil himself. Which reminded me that Ali had more than one type of contraption at his house. So I set George to get them. And to answer your question, I am definitely not ok. I've been faking a bit of the aging, and the head is nothing, but I'll be in serious trouble unless we can get out of here soon. And I fear that Phillip has gone into the bottle with our only handcuff key, unless you count the gents outside."

Vic got up from her crouch, and maneuvered gingerly to where Mal was locked to the radiator. She held up the handcuff key in triumph. "Am I not my father's daughter? The great Emir Ali! I lifted the key when I gave him the bottle." She unlocked Mal and helped him up.

"Fatima, can you fetch the bottle and put the stopper in tightly?" asked Mal. "We don't want to leave that thing lying around." The diamond pattern flashed silver in the twilight as the bottle rocked on the floor. Fatima quickly retrieved it and hammered the stopper in firmly with the heel of her palm. She joined Vic and Mal by the broken window.

Vic gave her friend a playful slap. "You really thought I would have gone along with his stupid scheme? My father taught me half the work of a good magic trick is selling the bait. I knew I could count on you being obstinate."

Fatima was a long time in responding. "I don't know, Vic. Do we really know anyone as well as we think?" Fatima went to the knife handle sticking out of the floor. She bent over to tug at it, overbalancing when it suddenly came free. "For example, would you really have used this on your brother?"

Vic was helping Mal to the door. "I'm not sure. I think I would. What if his charm would have worked? I'd definitely rather have had a couple of uneventful days. Does that make me a bad person?"

Fatima made a dismissive noise. "I think we should be more worried about what we're going to tell the cops. We can't afford for Mal to hang around here for too long. And I don't fancy getting arrested. Frankly, I'd rather be reading tomorrow about the guilty plea of a rogue Tory candidate who admitted to murder, but that's not going to happen either. And the bastards still might win. Think of the PM. We've got nothing on him."

"Don't be so sure," said Mal. "I think we can turn the tables on the security detail. What will they do when they discover that Phillip has slipped out of their cordon?"

"They'll start looking for him, and they'll detain us as well," growled Fatima.

"On what grounds?"

"Do you need grounds in today's England?"

"A fair point. But let's think about the instructions of our friendly police force. Phillip said the private detail was supposed to keep us from getting in unannounced. They knew we were coming for a little light repartee. After that, then what? If we come out and Phillip is gone, to whom will they go for orders? Are they authorized to make a scene in public?"

"Mal, you're being awfully optimistic."

"And why not? We just stared down a raving lunatic. We're carrying the boldest magician in forty years out of his own house in a bottle. Besides, there aren't that many of them. Budget is the bane of the bureaucrat. I count the Range Rover in the other lane, the watcher on the corner, the three blokes on our street, that's six and probably it. Fatima, can you see if there's a house phone? Let's call your boyfriend, have him drive the van around in, oh, say, four minutes?"

They reached the landing on the first floor. Fatima ran ahead to the sitting room. Mal and Vic ducked into Phillip's bedroom to check from the window whether the motorcycle cop was still on station. He was. The sedan on the corner was also occupied, same as when Vic had first walked up Gayfere Street. Fatima hung up the receiver of an old-fashioned wall phone in the kitchen as Vic and Mal reached the front vestibule. "He's on his way," she said, joining them behind the front door.

"Right," said Mal, "time to get to work." He opened the door and stepped smartly out, angling towards the polisher by his motorcycle. "Hey, Phillip's done a runner," he called. "He bashed me on the head and ran out. Is there a backdoor in this place?"

"There's a lane," replied the startled security man. "But we've got a car posted opposite it. Hang on." He put down the cloth, pulled a handset from under the bike and started talking into it. Mal had already turned and was walking towards the sedan. The sedan's driver was out and standing on the pavement, one hand on the open door.

"Mate, he's gone," said Mal, his hands innocently open wide. The passenger side door opened as well. The second cop leveled a gun at Mal's chest, propping both arms on the top of his open door. "No need for that," said Mal, still relaxed. "We're not going anywhere. But search the house. He's run off." The driver ran past Mal to the front door. Fatima and Vic pointed up the stairs and joined Mal on the street, a chaste group covered easily by a single pistol. The motorcyclist was still on the radio. They saw a large white BT van turn the corner into Gayfere Street, and stop at the point where the open passenger door of the sedan made the road too narrow for the van to fit. George punched the horn.

The cop looked over his shoulder from his shooting position and smoothly hid the gun inside his jacket. He closed his door and went around the front of the car to where Mal was standing. "Wait here. More police are on the way. Don't try to wander off." He took up a position just inside the vestibule of the house.

The van drew past the sedan and stopped. Its unlatched back door flapped lightly with the change of momentum. Fatima pushed the rear door open properly. All three scampered into the back of the van, Mal's long arm reaching behind them to snag the inside handle and pull the door to. George rolled in a steady crawl down the narrow street. The third cop was engrossed in his radio as the van made the left into Saint John Smith Square.

They were on Lambeth Bridge, heading for the A2, before the guards made the connection between their fugitives and the telephone van. George stopped for fuel at an exit off of the M25, having circled halfway around London. Fatima raced out of the back and gave George a full-bodied hug. "George, you were brilliant."

The journey back to Ealing was uneventful. Mal and Vic sat on the metal floor in the back, his arms around her as they had been in Rob Roy's basement on Saturday night. Fatima was in the cab with George, chattering away.

Mal and Vic listened to the election results on the radio from the bed of her apartment in Bristol. Fatima had gone up to Birmingham to watch with George. It was past midnight when the Prime Minister came on the broadcast to announce he had accepted the gracious congratulations of an opposition that had conceded the election. The Tory party had won, including every marginal seat except Oxford West and Abingdon, where the Green candidate claimed an uncertified victory in the turmoil following the sudden disappearance of Tory candidate Phillip Lightfoot. "I guess that's it, then," said Mal. "The bad guys won."

Vic shushed him. "I've figured out the luxury item I'd want on my desert island: a man who doesn't interrupt."

The PM continued through loud cheers and clapping. "The Conservative Party will once again form the government. I'd like to thank the great people of the entire United Kingdom for honouring us with their trust, that we may continue the progress begun during my last term. I would also like to honour the memory of my former colleagues in Parliament who died tragically in the run up to this election. While I am confident it did not affect the outcome of the election as a whole, these deaths are a tragedy for both the candidate's family and our democracy. My prayers and best wishes are with them during these most difficult of times.

"In fact, it is these deaths that have prompted me to recommend to Her Majesty that she appoint an alternative candidate to the post of Prime Minister in the new government. While the Conservative Party will govern, the tragic events of the past several weeks have been a wakeup call. I would like to announce my retirement to the backbenches, so that I might spend more time with my family. I'd also like to thank the London Special Branch for their service in the past several months. I have instructed them that it is the government's wish not to pursue any investigation against the free-lance journalist Fatima Lapicki regarding her sensational and at times defamatory reporting on missing person Phillip Lightfoot until his whereabouts can be determined and his side of the story brought into account. Thank you, and, God bless the United Kingdom."

Mal switched off the radio. "You should talk to your mother."

Vic poked him under the covers. "What nonsense! I wanted a lover, not a husband."

"I've never been married," said Mal. "It could be a first marriage for both of us."

"Speak for yourself. Jeremy wasn't the first mistake I've made. Speaking of mistakes, if we're going to be serious, I should know what your arrest warrant is about, no?"

Mal smiled briefly and looked into her eyes. "Oh," he said, "nothing in particular."

ACKNOWLEDGEMENTS

Thank you for reading. This book would not have been possible without the forbearance and support of my wife, Malathi Velamuri, whose smile conjures more happiness than magic ever could. I'd also like to thank Dhayaa Anbajagane for encouraging me to publish, Sathya Ganapathi for her creative cover designs and layout, and of course, my parents, for whom writing is more requirement than pastime or career.

ABOUT THE AUTHOR

Matthew Wennersten is based in Washington, DC. Find out more at http://wennersten.org.

Continue the adventure on Amazon.

Book 2	Book 3
14 Curzon Street	12 Harrows Close
Available Now	Pre-order on Amazon